EVIL *never* DIES

CORA HUDSON

 SIGNALMAN PUBLISHING

Evil Never Dies

by Cora Hudson

Signalman Publishing   2012
www.signalmanpublishing.com
email: info@signalmanpublishing.com
Kissimmee, Florida

ISBN: 978-1-935991-62-5 (paperback)
978-1-935991-63-2 (ebook)

Typeset in Adobe Garamond Pro
Cover and Interior Design by Joel Ramnaraine

SIGNALMAN
PUBLISHING

I

Cally stared into the mirror with her baby blue eyes as she made the final touches to her long blond hair and glided her favorite cherry lip gloss onto her perfectly shaped lips. Although Cally wanted her hair and makeup to look good, that was not the part she was worried about. The thing that worried Cally was the huge bruise on her neck, which Ryan had put there by choking her after she had said a quick hello to her best friend, Kyle Davis. Cally had known Kyle since kindergarten, and he had always been there for her no matter what, and Ryan hated that more than anything. Ryan was insanely jealous over their friendship; he did not want Cally to have any friends, let alone a guy friend. Cally did not like it, but she had to distance herself from Kyle, just so that Ryan would not hurt him over some jealous rage. Kyle meant the world to Cally; she often wondered what her life would have been like if she would have gone out with Kyle instead of Ryan. With that in mind, Cally patted her neck down with concealer so that she could hide the huge bruise from her parents. The last thing that Cally wanted was for her parents to see the bruise and start freaking out. Cally had enough to deal with. Tonight was the night she was going to put an end to her relationship with Ryan; she just could not handle his abuse any longer. Cally had to put a stop to Ryan and his cruel ways, and breaking up with him would be the only way to do it.

"Cally, are you almost ready, or do you need for me to help you with anything?" Kate called from the bottom of the stairway, interrupting Cally's thoughts.

"No, Mom, I don't need any help. I'll be down in just a few minutes," Cally replied, hoping that her mom would stay downstairs while she added more concealer to her bruised neck.

"Okay, sweetheart, but if you change your mind, just let me know and I'll be on my way," Kate said with the hopes that Cally would ask for her help.

"Tonight is the night; it is time to put an end to this horrible nightmare before something bad happens to me. I know that I can do this, I just have to be strong and stick to my plan. No matter how much Ryan threatens me, I cannot let anything stop my decision," Cally whispered softly to herself, as she took one more last look in the mirror, making sure that her bruise was not bleeding through her concealer.

Downstairs Kate was pacing back and forth anxiously; she could not wait to see Cally in her prom gown, the gown she had helped Cally pick out a month before. Kate felt a little unwanted—she could not understand why Cally did not want her help. Kate and Cally had always been close to each other, sure, they were mother and daughter, but they were also like the best of friends. Kate knew that Cally was nervous about prom, and she hoped that was the reason for Cally's strange, distant behavior. Kate just prayed that if something were bothering Cally, she would open up and tell her about it. After all, Kate had always told Cally that she could come to her with anything, it did not matter what it was. Kate just hoped that Cally would trust her enough to do that.

"Oh Cally, you look absolutely beautiful! You will be the most gorgeous girl there, you are positively breathtaking," Kate softly said, as she caught her breath and watched in awe as Cally descended the staircase. Her lavender gown draped from her hips in a perfect flow, as her crisp satin gloves glided down the railing. Although Kate had helped Cally pick out the gown, she had no idea how perfect the dress was for her little girl.

"I agree with your mother, sweetheart, you look like an angel straight from heaven. You positively glow," Bill said, as he also watched his only child grow up and slowly slip away.

"Thanks, but you guys are just saying that because you are my parents, and you're obligated to say something nice," Cally jokingly said.

Cally stared at the clock nervously, wishing that the night were already over. Part of Cally was terrified of breaking up with Ryan, but another part of her was ready to get it finished so that she could move on with her life, a life without Ryan Jones. Ryan had been so mean and abusive toward Cally, and he always tried to put the blame on her by saying that it was all her fault. He tried to make Cally believe that she had provoked him in some way, and the bad thing was, Cally was starting to believe him. She was starting to be sucked into his twisted little game, and that was something that she did not want to do. Cally knew that Ryan would never change, he was too far gone, and there was no helping him. That is why she had to break up with him, so that she could help herself.

"So, Cally, when did Ryan say he was picking you up?" Bill asked, snapping Cally out of her thoughts as he sat down in his old, worn-out but broken-in recliner.

"He should be here any minute now; he really did not give a specific time. I'm sure that he will be here soon, though," Cally answered as she walked into the kitchen, so that she could have a few minutes to clear her cluttered mind before Ryan arrived.

"Cally, is everything alright? You seem a little distracted. I just want you to know that I'm here if you need to talk about anything," Kate said, as she followed Cally into the kitchen, hoping to get in a little mother-daughter time before Cally left for the prom.

Kate had been waiting for the right time to have a talk with Cally, and when she saw her walking into the kitchen, she decided that it was then or never. Kate could tell that something was bothering Cally, she just did not know what it was. Kate hoped that Cally would open up to her or at least give her some indication as to what was bothering her. Kate could not stand to see Cally in a sad mood, especially on her prom night. Prom night was supposed to be fun and exciting, but Cally did not look like she was having any fun, and she did not look excited at all. Cally looked as if she had just lost her best friend. It was a look Kate had never seen before, and it worried her that Cally might be hiding something.

"Cally, I'm going to ask one last time, are you sure that everything is alright, because if something is bothering you, you know that you can tell me, right?" Kate asked as she patiently waited for Cally to answer her.

"Everything is fine, Mom, I'm just a little nervous. This is my first prom, you know, and I can't help but feel a little on edge," Cally snapped, feeling that her mom was asking too many questions.

"Well, don't be nervous, dear, you'll be just fine, I promise. You should be concentrating on having a wonderful time tonight, instead of worrying. I'm sure that you will relax after you get there," Kate explained, trying to reassure Cally that everything would be okay as she wrapped her arms around her and gave her a comforting hug.

"I hope that you're right, Mom," Cally said, swallowing hard as she stared down at the floor.

Cally knew for a fact that things were not going to be fine, nor was she going to have a good time. Cally had a long night ahead of her, and it was not going to be an easy one. In fact, it was going to be the hardest one she would ever face. Cally was on a mission to put an end to her relationship with Ryan. It was long overdue, and Cally knew that it would be the only way for her to get any kind of peace in her life. Ryan had to go, and that was all there was to it.

"Oh my god, Cally, what has happened to your neck, how did you get that bruise?" Kate asked, as she pushed Cally's hair over to the side, so that she could have a better look at Cally's neck and the huge bruise that was there.

"Oh that, it's nothing. I cannot believe that it is still there. I figured that it would have gone away by now," Cally replied, jerking away from her mother's grasp, as she tried to pretend that the bruise was no big deal.

"That is not what I asked you, Cally, now tell me what exactly happened to your neck, and it had better be the truth. Do not lie to me; I want you to be honest with me," Kate demanded, crossing her arms as she waited for Cally to start talking.

Before saying a word, Cally just stood there and looked into her mother's strict but caring eyes. Cally knew that her mother could see the hurt and pain in her eyes; she also knew that her mother could see the truth. Cally tried to think of a good excuse, one that her mother would believe and not question, but there was no excuse that good. Kate was like a detective, she always found the underlying cause of things no matter what they were, and Cally knew she could not keep the abuse a secret much longer. Eventually Kate would figure everything out, and when she did, Cally knew she would have a lot of explaining to do.

"Look, Mom, Ryan and I were wrestling around the other day, and he put me in a headlock. I probably just bruised my neck when I tried to get loose. I guess that we were playing a little rough, honestly, though, it was really my fault. I should not have pulled away from him so forcefully," Cally said, taking the blame for something that Ryan had done out of jealousy.

"Yeah, I would say that you were playing too damn rough. It looks like he tried to choke you or something, not just hold you in a headlock. Cally, you would tell me if Ryan was abusing you, wouldn't you?" Kate asked, very open and honest, hoping that Cally would trust her enough to tell her the truth.

"Of course I would, Mom, and you know that! I would never keep anything from you, I promise," Cally said, as a feeling of guilt spread all over her body and she looked down at the floor in shame.

Cally hated lying to her mother more than anything, but she did not want to upset her with the truth. It would break her heart, and Cally did not want to hurt her mother. She had done enough damage with her lies alone. Cally figured that after she broke up with Ryan, things would go back to normal, and she would not have to tell her mother anything. After all, Cally was almost a grown woman; it was time that she started taking responsibility for herself and her actions. Cally knew that she could not run to her parents with every little thing; it was time for her to step up and handle her own problems.

"Okay, Cally, I'll believe you for now, but if I see another bruise on you, I promise you I'll not stop until I get to the bottom of this. Have I made myself clear?" Kate asked with anger and disappointment in her voice.

"Yes, Mom, you have made your point, but I promise you that nothing is going on. Ryan and I get along with each other very well, and he would never do anything to hurt me. He loves me too much to do anything like that. So, would you please stop worrying about things that are not happening?" Cally said, lying to her mother for the second time, trying to smooth things over so that her mom would not worry.

"Well, I hope that you are telling me the truth, because if I find out that you have lied to me, I promise you that there will be some serious consequences, and I'll never trust you again," Kate said in a stern voice as she walked away from Cally.

Kate could not help but feel that something was not right with Cally. Cally had never lied to her before, and it killed her to think that Cally would start now. It was as if Cally were hiding a secret, a deep, dark secret, and it frustrated Kate to think that Cally would keep something like that from her. Kate knew that the truth would come out eventually; it would only be a matter of time before Cally let something slip, and when she did, the truth would come out. The only thing Kate could do now was wait patiently for that moment to come.

Cally sat down at the kitchen table and watched in sadness as her mother walked away from her. Cally could not believe what she had just done; she had deliberately lied to her mother and pushed her away. Cally knew that she should have told her mother the truth and asked for her help, but Cally needed to do this on her own. There was no way that Cally was going to drag her mother in on her problems. Even Cally did not know what Ryan was capable of, and she did not want to put her parents in harm's way; she would rather take the heat from her own mistakes.

As Cally sat at the kitchen table gathering her thoughts, the dreaded ring came from the doorbell. Cally felt her heart speed up to a fast and steady beat, so fast that it almost took her breath away. She knew that Ryan was at the door, and there was no turning back now. Cally had to end her misery tonight. Cally took a deep breath as she got up from the table and rubbed her trembling hands down her gown to straighten the wrinkles out. Although Cally was nervous and scared, she could not let it show. Cally had to pull herself together long enough to get away from her parents. Cally could hear her dad and Ryan talking as she made her way to the living room. Just hearing Ryan's voice and laughter made her sick to her stomach, but she knew that this would be the last time that she ever had to feel that way. After tonight, Cally would be rid of Ryan for good, and then she could stop lying to her mother and get on with her life.

"There you are. I was just about to call you. Ryan is here to pick you up," Bill said.

"Oh, wow, Cally, you look absolutely gorgeous. I'll be the luckiest man at prom tonight," Ryan complimented Cally as she walked into the room, as if he were trying to score points with her parents, so that he would appear to be the perfect boyfriend.

"Thank you, you look really good, too, but I think that you exaggerated a bit when you said that you would be the luckiest man at prom tonight," Cally said, letting Ryan know that she was not going to buy in to his fake compliment.

"Oh, don't pay her any attention, Ryan, she is just being modest. She knows that she looks beautiful," Bill said with a smile on his face.

While Ryan was saying what a lucky man he was, Kate was still thinking about the handprint bruise on Cally's neck. Kate did not want to be one of those nosy and meddling mothers who always butted into her child's life, but she also did not want to be a mother who would let something happen to her child just because she was too scared to ask questions. Kate had to make a decision, and it did not take her long to decide when she saw how slowly Cally approached Ryan. It was as if Cally were afraid of him. Kate had never seen Cally act that way around him before. Kate knew right then that she had to say something to Ryan.

"Ryan, we need to have a little talk about something, just you and me," Kate said as she walked over to Ryan, with a firm and serious look on her face, trying not to lose her temper.

"Sure, Mrs. Smart, what's on your mind?" Ryan asked with a confused look on his face.

"Well, I'm usually not a prying person, but I saw a bruise on Cally's neck earlier, and as her mother, well, I need to know what happened to her," Kate asked, catching Ryan completely off guard. This was exactly what she wanted to do, so that she could compare his story to that of Cally's.

"Well, to tell you the truth, I really do not remember, but I can assure you that I would never do anything to hurt Cally. Cally is the love of my life, and I would never even dream of hurting her," Ryan lied, with a deer-caught-in-the-headlights look on his face.

Cally could not believe her ears. How could Ryan lie, and yet sound so honest? He had forced tears to roll down his innocent-looking face, and it shocked her to see that her parents were buying his made-up story. Cally was not buying in to it, though; she knew that Ryan was nothing more than a fake. He might have fooled her parents with his lies, but he was not going to fool Cally. The only time that Cally had ever seen true tears come out of Ryan's cold green eyes was right before he went into a mad, crazed rage. Cally knew at that moment, she would have to face that rage just as soon as they got out of her parents' sight. That much was obvious by the way he was glaring at her.

"Oh Ryan, please don't cry. I'm so sorry that I questioned you, can you ever forgive me?" Kate asked, as she gave Ryan a peace offering hug, letting him know that she was truly sorry for accusing him.

"Of course I forgive you, and there is no need for you to apologize. You were just being a good mother. If I were in your shoes, I would have done the same thing," Ryan said, trying to suck up to Kate, so he could make himself look good once more.

"I never doubted you for a second, buddy. I can see just how much you care for Cally. It shows in everything that you do for her, and to me a picture is worth a thousand words," Bill said, letting Ryan know that he had nothing to do with his wife's suspicions.

Cally had heard Ryan talk his way out of many things before, but this time was different. This time he was much more convincing than he had ever been before. It was if he were playing a role in a movie. Ryan's act was flawless, and her parents believed every single word that came out of his lying mouth. Bottom line, Ryan had Cally's parents eating out of the palm of his hand. It frightened Cally to think that Ryan could be that convincing. It was as if he had practiced that speech for days. Ryan was becoming a professional at making people believe his lies, but Cally was not going to believe them anymore. Cally was going to stick with her plan and end the abusive relationship, come hell or high water; she was going to put an end to this nightmare.

"Well, I guess we should be going now, we don't want to be late," Ryan said, forcing a smile onto his face as he took Cally by her trembling hand, squeezing it so hard that Cally could feel her knuckles starting to pop.

"Okay, I'll let you two lovebirds go right after I get some pictures. Let's go outside so the lighting will be better. I do not want anything to ruin these pictures," Kate said, grabbing her camera off the table.

"Come on, Mom, do we really have to do this now? We are already running behind schedule," Cally argued, hoping that her mother would just let them go without having to take the unwanted pictures.

"Don't worry, Cally; we will have plenty of time. Besides, it would be rude to leave before your mom got some pictures," Ryan said, giving Cally a devilish grin.

"Thank you very much for agreeing with me, Ryan. Now you two go stand over by the flowers and I'll take a few pictures. Do not worry, Cally. I promise that I'll not keep you long," Kate said, assuring Cally that she would not be late for prom.

Cally was standing beside Ryan in the front yard when she slipped into a trance of thoughts. Cally wondered what was going to happen to her after Ryan got her out of her parents' sight; she wondered if she would ever see them again. Ryan was acting so odd; she could not help but wonder what he was going to do to her. Cally hated guessing games, and that was exactly what this was, one big guessing game. Cally was so deep into her thoughts that she did not hear her mother calling her name.

"Cally, earth to Cally, hello, can you hear me?" Kate asked, snapping her fingers in front of Cally's face, trying to get her attention.

"Oh, I'm sorry, Mom. What did you say? I didn't hear you," Cally said, feeling a bit embarrassed by her confusion.

"Are you sure that you are feeling okay? You look a little pale," Kate said, placing the back of her hand on Cally's forehead to see if she felt feverish.

"Yeah, I'm fine, Mom, just a little tired, and I have a headache, but don't worry. I'll be alright, I promise," Cally said.

"Well, do not worry. All of that will go away after Ryan pushes you around on the dance floor a few times. Now, you two should get going. Time is of the essence, you know," Bill said, giving Cally a hug good-bye.

Cally felt so terrible. She had just lied to her mother again. It was starting to feel like second nature to her, and it was all Ryan's fault. Cally could not wait to break up with Ryan, at this point; she absolutely hated the very sight of him. Just to look at Ryan made Cally feel like throwing up. If she did not know any better, she would swear up and down that he was the devil. Cally never thought in a million years that she could dislike someone so much, but Ryan had brought this on himself. He'd had chance after chance to change his abusive ways, but he did not. Instead of treating her better, he started to treat her worse, and Cally knew that she could not go on living her life this way. Everything had to stop, and it had to stop tonight, no matter what.

"Hey, I just want you both to know that Cally is in good hands. I promise that I'll have her home safe and sound by eleven, so do not worry about a thing," Ryan said, reassuring Cally's parents with his heartless lies once again.

"Oh, before I forget, they are calling for heavy rains tonight, so please drive safe and wear your seat belts. I don't want anything bad happening to either one of you," Kate called out to Cally and Ryan as they walked toward his sports car.

"Don't worry about a thing. I'll take good care of her," Ryan answered as he opened Cally's car door, putting on one last show before they left.

Cally stared out of the dark-tinted windows of Ryan's car and watched as her mother walked back into the house. Cally could feel her heart starting to break; she absolutely hated the person Ryan had turned her into. She knew that she should have told her mother the truth when she had the chance, and now it was too late. Now there was no turning back. Cally had made her bed, now she would have to lie in it, no matter how bad things got. Cally knew there was only one person to blame, and that was herself. Cally had gotten herself into this hellish nightmare, now she had to get herself out of it.

2

Ryan sat down in the car and started digging around in the console, looking for his car keys. Cally could tell that he was pissed off by the way he was throwing stuff around the car. Cally wanted to say something to break the ice-cold silence between them, but she was afraid to. She was afraid that it would only make things worse, and by the way he had squeezed her hand earlier, she knew that she was already in over her head for the night. Ryan was already like a ticking time bomb, just waiting to explode, and it was only a matter of time before he did.

Ryan put the keys into the ignition and started the car. He revved the engine as if he were a race car driver ready to participate in a race that involved only him. Suddenly Cally felt the urge to get out of the car, run back into her house, and lock the door, but she knew that would not solve anything; she had to confront Ryan, not run away from him. For the first time, Cally had to stand up for herself, not back down. Cally knew that the task would not be easy, but it would all be worth it in the end.

Ryan put the car in DRIVE and slowly moved up the street, still not saying a word or even looking in Cally's direction. Cally did not want Ryan to hit her, but she knew that it was coming, and the anticipation was worse than the actual strike. She had no idea what Ryan was going to do to her, let alone where. Cally had so many things running through her mind that it made her sick on her stomach. She could not begin to imagine the rage she was going to face. All Cally could do was pray that Ryan would not lose it completely and end up hurting her worse than he already had. Cally did not know how much more abuse she could take.

Okay, we are coming up to the stop sign, and nothing has happened yet. Maybe he is not as mad as I thought he was, maybe he really is trying to change, Cally thought as they neared the stop sign, but just when Cally thought that she was in the clear, Ryan hauled off with all of his might and backhanded her right in the mouth. Ryan hit her so hard that her bottom lip burst open and started bleeding. Cally could not see the damage, but judging by the impact of Ryan's hand, she knew that it was bad.

"Bitch, do not ever put me on the spot like that again or I'll kill you. Do you understand me?" Ryan screamed as he grabbed Cally by her hair.

"I did not mean to put you on the spot. My mother saw the bruise on my neck and asked me how it happened. I had to tell her something, so I told her that we were just wrestling around," Cally cried as she tried to make Ryan understand before he decided to hit her again.

"You know, Cally, you bring all of this on yourself. If you were not so pathetic and useless, I would not have to punish you. Trust me, all of this is for your own good. You have to know your place in this relationship. It is no one's fault but yours, Cally!" Ryan yelled in Cally's ear as if she were a military recruit and he were her drill sergeant.

"Why are you doing this to me? What have I ever done but be good to you? How can you hate me so much, Ryan?" Cally pleaded as tears fell onto her lavender gown, causing a wet stain to appear.

"Are you really that deaf, bitch? I have already told you that you are pathetic and you bring it all on yourself, only you, Cally, no one but you," Ryan repeated as he stared at Cally with his devilish green eyes.

All of a sudden, things got quiet, so quiet that you could hear a pin drop. All Cally could do was wonder if, in fact, everything *was* her fault. Cally could not help but conclude that maybe she did deserve all of the beatings and punishment that Ryan delivered. Could this terrible nightmare really be Cally's destiny? Was she meant to be with Ryan and his abusive ways, or was there more out there that she had not seen yet? Was the grass going to be greener on the other side, or would it just appear to be that way?

"Clean yourself up. The last thing I need is for one of your nosy friends asking a lot of questions about business that doesn't concern them," Ryan ordered in a cold, heartless voice, throwing an old stained napkin from inside the console onto her lap.

"How can you do this to me? Am I really that bad? Please explain it to me because I do not understand how you can hate me so much. I have always been good to you, and this is the thanks I get," Cally said with tears streaming down her blood-splattered face.

Ryan just sat there in silence as Cally waited on a response that she was not going to get. She could feel her heart breaking into a million little pieces, as she pulled the sun visor down with her shaking hand and slowly opened the mirror. Cally was afraid to look in the mirror and see the damage that Ryan had done to her lip. When Cally's tear-filled blue eyes met with the mirror, all she could do was stare at the huge gash, still bleeding on her lip. Cally wondered how she would explain her busted lip to her parents; it had even crossed her mind that she might never see her parents again. Cally had never felt this distraught before, and it was the worst feeling in the world.

As Cally cleaned her face with the dried-out, rough napkin, she could not help but feel trapped. She felt as if she had locked herself into a life sentence in prison, and she feared that there was no way out of this abusive, heart-breaking relationship. It was obvious to her that she would never be able to rid herself from Ryan completely. Cally knew that Ryan would always find a way to be near her, he would never let her go, and that is what scared Cally the most. It absolutely chilled her to the bone.

"Damn, Cally, could you possibly be any slower? You know that if we're late, your dumbass friends will call your parents to find out where you are. I do not feel like seeing your stupid, nosy parents again, they can go straight to hell for all I care. I never liked them anyway," Ryan said as he constantly checked his rearview mirror, as if he were expecting someone.

"Look, I'm going as fast as I can! It is not easy getting this blood off my face with a dried napkin, you know," Cally snapped, letting Ryan know not to rush her over something that he had done himself.

"Do not get smart with me unless you want a black eye to go along with your busted lip, because I'm just in the mood to do it. Do you understand me?" Ryan asked in an intimidating voice, trying to scare Cally and put her back in her place.

Cally wanted to go home so badly she could not stand it, but she knew what would happen. If she even mentioned going back home to Ryan, he would go ballistic and end up hitting her again, and Cally knew that the next time she might not be so lucky. Next time, Ryan could end up hurting her badly or, even worse, killing her, so to save a lot of drama, Cally just kept her mouth shut. Cally knew that she had to finish out the rest of the night with Ryan. She also knew not to anger or provoke him in any way, because that would only cause more arguing and punishment.

"Okay, Ryan, I'm ready to go now," Cally said in a soft, but clear voice, as she folded the bloodstained napkin, trying not to make any kind of eye contact with him.

"Well, it is about damn time. Do you think that you took long enough? I swear, if I did not know any better, I would say that you are trying to stall just so we will be late," Ryan said in a pissed-off voice as he glared Cally's way with his evil green eyes.

"Whatever you want to think, Ryan. You are going to believe what you want to anyway. It doesn't matter what I say," Cally said, feeling agitated at Ryan and his stupid accusations.

Without saying a word, Ryan stomped down on the gas pedal, causing his hotrod Mustang to slide sideways in the middle of the highway. Although Cally was caught off guard by Ryan's actions, she did not budge a bit, special thanks to her seat belt. Cally tried not to show any fear, not anymore, even when Ryan hit speeds of 120 mph on a curvy, winding road. She knew if Ryan sensed that she was scared, it would only encourage him that much more.

Finally, after almost losing control of his prize car, Ryan slowed back down to the speed limit. Cally wanted to let out a sigh of relief, but she did not want to give Ryan the satisfaction of knowing that he had frightened her. Cally was actually proud of herself; for the very first time, she did not give in to Ryan's stupidity. She held her own, and when he saw that he could not upset her, he gave up. Cally knew that she could do this now; she only had a little while longer. The night would be over with before she knew it, and she could not wait.

While Cally was concentrating on getting through the night, her cell phone started to ring. Cally dug through her purse to find her phone, and noticed that Ryan was giving her one of his usual pissed-off, go-to-hell looks. Although it was only Cally's mom calling, Ryan would swear up and down that it was Kyle, or another guy for that matter, just so he could pick another fight with her. Ryan was good at making liars out of people, and he was even better at starting arguments; he had done it for so long, it was like second nature to him. Ryan just looked for a reason, any reason, big or small, it did not matter to him just as long as it was enough to start an argument.

"Hello?" Cally answered the phone, trying to sound like everything was okay so her mother would not notice any tension and start to worry.

"Hi, sweetie, how is everything going? Are you okay?" Kate asked in a concerned voice when she did not hear any people or music in the background.

"Oh, hi, Mom. We just stopped by the store to get some gas and a soda. Do not worry, though; we are almost at the prom," Cally lied to her mother once again.

"Well, that is good; I just got a little worried when Kyle called. He told me that you had not arrived yet, but now that I know everything is alright, I'll let you go so you can enjoy the rest of your night," Kate said, not wanting to sound too nosy to Cally or Ryan.

"Okay, Mom, thanks for checking on me. I'll call you before we leave prom tonight to let you know when we are on our way back, and, Mom, before I forget, I just want to say that I love you," Cally said with a slightly different tone in her voice.

"Oh, sweetheart, I love you, too, and I hope that you have a wonderful time tonight. I'll see you soon," Kate replied in a choked-up voice as she hung up the phone.

"Who was that on the phone? Is everything okay? You look as if you got some bad news," Bill said, walking into the kitchen, noticing Kate's tear-filled eyes.

"Well, I was just on the phone with Cally, checking in, and she said that everything was alright, but I have just got one of those gut feelings that tells something is not. I know something is wrong, I just cannot pinpoint it yet," Kate said, pacing back and forth with a worried look on her face.

"Oh, I'm sure that everything is okay. It's her first prom, and she's probably nervous. Remember your first prom; you were the same way, so I wouldn't worry too much if I were you," Bill said, hoping his advice would help Kate relax.

"Clever girl, telling your mother that you would call her before you left, but just what makes you so sure that you will even make it to prom?" Ryan asked in a cold tone, with a devilish grin on his face.

Cally sat there in silence. Although she was concerned about Ryan's threat, she could not help but think about Kyle. It was so sweet of him to check up on her. Just the thought of it made her smile from ear to ear. To know that he cared enough to do that for her made Cally's night, and she did not care if Ryan saw her smiling or not. This one special moment was Cally's, and she was not going to let Ryan take it away from her. He could control many things, but he could not control her thoughts, nor could he control her heart. Cally had known Kyle long before she had ever known Ryan, and she was not about to give up Kyle for Ryan. There was no chance in hell that she would ever do that.

"What in the hell are you smiling about, and what did your nosy-ass mom want? Or was that even your mom on the phone?" Ryan asked, snatching the phone out of Cally's hand so he could check the number for himself.

"Go ahead, Ryan. I do not have anything to hide. You can look through my phone all you want; you are not going to find anything. I can promise you that," Cally said with confidence, knowing that the only number Ryan would find was her mother's.

"Oh, do not worry. That is exactly what I'm going to do, and I do not remember asking for your permission," Ryan smarted off, flipping Cally's cell phone open.

Ryan scrolled through Cally's phone, checking all of her calls and texts, just looking for a reason to start another argument. Cally could not believe how controlling Ryan was. He had always been jealous, but this time he was taking things too far. It was as if he had completely lost his mind. He was acting like a total basket case, and Cally could not help but feel a little scared and nervous. Cally thought that she would be able to handle Ryan's reactions, but now she was rethinking her judgment.

"What do you take me for, Cally, a complete fool? I know that that you have erased some of the numbers off your phone, so do not sit over there and act so innocent," Ryan demanded after accusing Cally of something she did not do.

"Look, Ryan, believe what you want to. I know that I'm telling you the truth. I have not erased anything out of my phone, because I have no reason to," Cally said, defending herself as if it would help any.

"Well, since you are not being honest with me, I'll just hang on to your phone for the rest of the night, and don't even think about asking me to give it back, because if you do, I'll bust it into a million little pieces," Ryan warned as he shoved the phone into his pocket, just waiting for Cally to object.

"Okay, that will work out better. I didn't want to keep up with my purse tonight anyway. The less I have to carry, the better off I'll be," Cally said sarcastically, staring down at the floorboard, pretending that it did not bother her at all.

Cally was growing wise to Ryan's petty childish games. She knew that he was just itching for a reason to hit her again, and she was not about to give him one. Cally could see Ryan gritting his teeth in anger. His whole face was blood-red, with beads of sweat popping out all over his forehead. Ryan's evil green eyes glared as they filled with anger and fury. Cally knew right then that she had gotten under Ryan's skin, the look on his face told her that. Cally expected some kind of harsh punishment for the remark she had made, but she was not going to let it concern her. Cally was fed up with all the worrying. Ryan was going to hit her whether she worried or not.

"Real cute, Cally. Just keep pissing me off tonight, and see what happens. I promise you that you will not like the outcome," Ryan said bitterly as he focused more on Cally than he did the road.

"Look, Ryan, I'm not trying to piss you off. I'm just merely trying to avoid an argument, and so would you please stop assuming things," Cally said politely, hoping that Ryan would stop trying to start an argument.

"Look, Cally, I swear to God, if you do not shut up, I swear that I'll beat you till you cannot move, so if you know what is good for you, you had better shut your mouth. Do you understand me, or do I have to make a believer out of you?" Ryan asked, grabbing hold of Cally's arm and squeezing it until it started to go numb.

Cally could feel the front tire starting to go off the shoulder of the road, and Ryan was not in any hurry to pull it back onto the highway. Cally could see a row of mailboxes getting closer and closer as Ryan kept speeding down the road, with no intention of stopping. Seeing that Ryan was not going to do anything, Cally closed her eyes tightly and braced herself for the worst. Cally waited nervously for the impact of the mailboxes, and just as she started to pray, she felt Ryan jerk the car back onto the road. Cally opened her eyes and let out a sigh of relief when she saw that they were back on the road completely.

"Look, bitch, I'm the one in charge, and do not ever forget that," Ryan said, staring Cally down, making sure he got his point across.

"Okay, Ryan, you win, and you have made your point. I understand. Please, just keep your eyes on the road before you kill us both," Cally cried in fear after looking into Ryan's cold, emotionless eyes.

"I thought you would see things my way, and do not ever forget your place again, or next time I'll wreck and kill us," Ryan warned with an evil laugh.

Cally sat quietly and tried to think of a way she could call her parents or the police. The more she thought though, the more confused she became. Cally knew that her thinking was hopeless; Ryan would never let her out of his sight to do anything, let alone make a phone call. Bottom line, Cally had to do something herself, and she had to do it quickly, before prom ended.

Ryan pulled into the school parking lot and cursed with every breath. Every parking place was full in the front, so Ryan cursed some more and blamed Cally because she had taken so long cleaning her lip. As Ryan circled the parking lot for the second time, Cally could not help but notice Kyle. He was standing beside his truck in his tuxedo, with his dark brown hair swept to one side making his light brown eyes sparkle under the streetlight. Cally was so consumed with staring at Kyle that she did not even notice that Ryan was staring at her. He was looking at her with his cold and heartless eyes, like he could kill her dead right where she sat.

"Do you mind telling me just what in the hell you are staring at, or should I say *who* in the hell you are staring at?" Ryan asked, full of fury, as he slammed on the brakes so hard, they made a screeching sound, drawing everyone's attention toward them.

"What are you talking about? I was only trying to help you look for a parking place," Cally answered quickly after being caught off guard by Ryan's question.

"You do not expect me to believe that shit, do you? I'm not stupid, Cally! I saw the way you were looking at Kyle. It is as if you are in love with him," Ryan said menacingly.

"Honestly, Ryan, I was looking for a place to park. It is not my fault that Kyle was standing there. Besides, Kyle and I are just friends, nothing more," Cally explained, trying to defend herself, as if it was going to help her any.

After Cally had finished what she was saying, she could not help but wonder if she was, in fact, in love with Kyle. Could she ever be more than just a friend to Kyle? Why did life have to be so complicated? Why could she not figure anything out? It was as if she were a kid standing in a gigantic toy store surrounded by millions of toys, and could only choose one. While Cally was gathering her thoughts, she did not notice that Ryan had parked right next to Kyle. She knew that he had done it on purpose, though, just hoping that he might catch her glancing once again in Kyle's direction.

"Now, Cally, if you were really looking for a parking space like you said you were, then why did you not see this one? Oh, that is right. You were too busy looking at your new love, Kyle," Ryan said hatefully, letting Cally know that he knew her excuse was nothing more than a lie.

"Can we just drop this, please? I don't want to spend my prom night arguing and fighting with you. I just want tonight to be special for the both of us," Cally said, hoping that Ryan would just let everything go instead of causing a scene in front of Kyle and everyone else.

Although Cally was hoping for a miracle, she knew it was only a dream on her part. The look in Ryan's spiteful, devious eyes told her that he would definitely not be letting anything slide by him tonight. When Ryan got something stuck in his head, he would not let it go, no matter how much Cally begged and pleaded with him. It was as if Ryan did not want to be happy with her. He would look for a reason to get mad at her, and then he would hold a grudge until he found another reason. No matter how hard Cally tried, she could not understand him, it was impossible.

As Kyle stood by his truck, he could not help but notice the depressed look on Cally's face. He did not want to stare too much because he knew that Ryan would get pissed off and try to start a fight with him or, worse, take it out on Cally. Kyle was not afraid of Ryan. He just kept his distance, for Cally's sake. He knew that Ryan was the jealous type. Cally had never really told Kyle much about her relationship with Ryan, and he never made it any of his business to ask. Kyle had known Cally all his life, and he could tell when something was wrong with her. Judging by the look on her face, Kyle knew that something was going on with her. Not wanting to cause any trouble for Cally, Kyle took one last glance and started to walk back inside.

"Oh look, there goes your new lover. How sweet of him to wait out here for you," Ryan said, forcing Cally's head to turn in Kyle's direction.

"Would you please just stop with all this stupid nonsense? Like I told you before, Kyle and I are just friends, nothing more," Cally cried out as Ryan dug his hand into her hair.

"You are a lying bitch, and you make me sick every time I look at you. I swear, Cally, I wish that you were dead right now," Ryan said with an evil, but serious look on his face.

Cally felt so embarrassed by Ryan's behavior. He had never acted out this much in public before; usually he would wait until they got behind closed doors before he acted out. This time Ryan had taken it too far and Cally had reached the end of her rope. It was time for Cally to take a stand and stop being so powerless against Ryan. Feeling herself starting to crack, Cally pulled Ryan's hand away from her hair and took some control over the situation, just to let Ryan know that she was not going to put up with his abuse anymore.

"You're getting a little too brave, bitch. You should not try to piss me off more than I already am. Trust me; it is not a good idea, Cally!" Ryan warned, trying to scare Cally as he always did.

"I don't care anymore, Ryan! I'm sick and tired of bowing down to you, and I'm tired of being trapped by you. You don't treat me as if I'm your girl-friend; you treat me as if I'm your property, and I'm tired of it! I just hate that it took me this long to see how bad of a person you truly are. Leave me the hell alone," Cally screamed as all of her sadness and frustration turned into anger and hatred for Ryan.

"What in the hell are you talking about, Cally? Get your ass back in this car, before I kill you!" Ryan demanded as Cally slammed the car door in his face and proceeded to walk away.

As Ryan sat in the car watching Cally walk away, he could hear laughter coming from a group of people in the parking lot. It made Ryan furious that Cally had made a fool out of him in front of everyone. Ryan knew at that moment that he would make Cally pay dearly for the stupid stunt she had just pulled. No one made a fool out of Ryan Jones, no one! Still fuming with anger, Ryan blocked out all of the noise and laughter and started plotting out a plan for his dear, sweet Cally. Ryan knew that he would have to put on a good act, a perfect act, in order for Cally to trust him enough to get back into the car with him. This act had to be the performance of a lifetime. Knowing the challenge ahead of him, Ryan got out of his car, gritting his teeth so hard that the muscles in his jaws were flexing.

"What the hell is everybody laughing about? Come on now, stop being a bunch of chicken shits and tell me!" Ryan yelled out to the staring crowd as if he could kill all of them.

After snapping at the group of people standing outside, Ryan walked inside and looked around for Cally. Something told him that Cally would be sitting with Kyle, but that feeling changed when he saw Kyle sitting alone at a table. After seeing that his suspicions were wrong, Ryan could not help but wonder where Cally was. *Maybe she is in the bathroom, sobbing like a little crybaby,*

Ryan thought as he scanned the room for a second time. Finally, Ryan spotted Cally sitting at a corner table by herself. Preparing for his speech, Ryan took a deep breath and started walking toward her quickly before anyone else had a chance to sit down with her.

"Cally, can we talk? There is something that I need to tell you. Look, I know that I have not been the best boyfriend to you the past few months, but I can explain all of my actions if you will please just hear me out," Ryan pleaded in a low, sweet, caring voice as he pulled out a chair beside Cally.

"I don't have anything left to say to you, Ryan, therefore we do not have anything to talk about. I know that you do not love me, and if the truth was known, you probably never did, so if you don't mind, I just want to be left alone. I have to clear my head and think about some things. I suggest you do the same," Cally said, turning her back to Ryan so she would not have to look at him.

Cally could feel Ryan's eyes piercing through her, and she waited for him to go into his next crazed rage, but to her surprise, nothing happened. At this point, Cally was getting confused. It was not like Ryan to let her talk to him like that without some sort of punishment. There was always a severe consequence for backtalking Ryan. Cally was so curious about Ryan's facial expressions, she wanted to turn around and look at him, but on the other hand, she really did not want to make any kind of eye contact because sometimes Ryan's devilish eyes could be very paralyzing.

"Come on, Cally; please give me a chance to explain. I'm sorry that I have been such an asshole toward you. It is just that I'm so afraid of losing you, and I thought that if I took control of you it would make you stay with me forever. The truth is, Cally, I want to spend the rest of my life with you. I love you with all my heart, and I can't stand the thought of losing you to someone else. That would absolutely kill me! Please, Cally, give me another chance to make things right, I promise that you will not be disappointed," Ryan begged as he took Cally by her hand and gently kissed it, hoping that he could get her in his grasp one last time.

Cally was speechless—she had not heard Ryan talk that sweet in months. It was as if he had changed back to the old Ryan, the one she fell in love with a year ago. Cally wanted to believe Ryan, but she was afraid that if she did, he would change back into the same mean, abusive, cold, and heartless person he had been for the past three months, and Cally did not want anything to do with that person ever again. Finally, after a lot of consideration, Cally took a deep breath, slowly turned around, and raised her head up to look at Ryan, only to see him holding her cell phone in front of her face.

"I'm sorry, Cally; I should have never taken your cell phone. It's just that sometimes I let my jealousy get the best of me. Can you ever find it in your heart to forgive me?" Ryan asked in a very sweet, low-sounding voice as he took Cally by her hand and gave her cell phone back.

Cally was glad that Ryan was opening up to her, but she was not about to let her guard down that quickly. There had to be a reason behind Ryan's change, she just had to find out what it was. Cally wondered if Ryan was just putting on one of his famous acts to lure her in so he could continue with the same abuse, but then she wondered if he was really trying to change to save their relationship. Whatever the reason, Cally planned to be cautious of everything; she did not intend to give Ryan the upper hand ever again.

"Well, Cally, what do you say? Can you find it in your heart to forgive me and give me one last chance to prove my love for you?" Ryan asked for the second time as he started to grow more impatient by the second.

"I don't know, Ryan; I still think that we should spend some time apart. I think you have some serious problems that you need to work on before we can continue our relationship," Cally replied, still standing her ground with Ryan, letting him know that she was taking all of the abuse very seriously.

"No, Cally, you can't do this to me, to us! I'll go crazy and kill myself if I cannot have you. I'll admit that I have made some mistakes, but doesn't everyone? You cannot just throw our relationship away like a piece of garbage. Please, just say that you love me, and that you will give us another chance," Ryan begged desperately as his blood started to boil with anger.

Ryan could not take it anymore. He could not fight back the demons and urges inside of him any longer. Not only had Cally made a fool out of him, but now she was making him beg, beg like a stray dog that had not eaten in days. It was almost as if Cally was having a good time humiliating him, and just when Ryan started to lose his temper and grab hold of Cally, he heard the words he had been waiting and begging to hear.

"I forgive you, Ryan, and I love you very much, but if you want this relationship to last, you need to work on your temper and your anger problems. I cannot take this abuse anymore, it is driving me insane and it is tearing me apart from the inside out," Cally said, hoping that she would not regret giving Ryan another chance.

"Thank God. I thought I had lost you forever! I promise that I'll treat you like the princess you are. Trust me, you won't regret this. I'll be the boyfriend you deserve to have," Ryan lied as he faked another smile and pretended to be excited and happy about Cally's decision to give him another chance.

"I hope that you're right, because if you mess up one more time, I swear to you that I'll leave and you will never see me again," Cally firmly stated as she gazed into Ryan's eyes, making sure that she did not see a hint of the old Ryan.

While Cally was busy looking into Ryan's hard-to-read eyes, Kyle was watching her from across the room. Kyle knew that he needed to talk to Cally and make sure she was alright, but he knew that he could not get her away from Ryan long enough to do anything. Keeping a steady watch on Cally, he could tell that something was going on; he just had the feeling that something was not right. Wanting to find out more, Kyle got up from his table and started walking toward Cally and Ryan's table, pretending to mingle along the way with other people so Ryan would not get suspicious. The last thing Kyle wanted was for Ryan to drag Cally away before he got a chance to talk to her.

"Hey, you two, I'm glad to see that you made it. How's everything going?" Kyle asked as he walked up on Cally and Ryan.

"Oh, hey, man, I meant to speak to you earlier, but I got a little distracted. You understand, right?" Ryan replied in a very nice, but scary manner as he gave Kyle a forced smile.

"That's okay. I had to get back inside anyway," Kyle said, trying to make small talk.

"Cally, are you not going to speak to Kyle?" Ryan asked politely, as he kept the forced smile on his face for show.

Cally could not believe her ears; Ryan was actually being nice to Kyle. Cally had not heard Ryan be nice to anyone in quite some time. It was almost as if Ryan was a different person. Although Cally was pleased with Ryan's actions, she still could not help but have her doubts. She found it hard to believe that Ryan could change that quickly. Everything just seemed too good to be true, and something told her that it probably was.

"Well, Cally, are you going to speak or not?" Ryan asked for the second time, interrupting Cally's thoughts.

"Oh, I'm sorry, my head was somewhere else. How are you doing, Kyle?"

Cally asked, looking up at Kyle, forgetting all about her bruised neck and busted lip.

"Oh my God, Cally, what happened to your lip and your neck?" Kyle asked first thing, as he moved a little closer so he could have a better look at Cally's wounds.

"Oh that. I cannot believe that it is still noticeable. I thought it would have been gone by now. I guess that Ryan and I need to stop wrestling around so much," Cally lied, trying to cover everything up so that Kyle would stop asking so many questions, before he pissed Ryan off.

"That is odd, Cally, because judging by the fresh blood on your lip, it looks as if it just happened. Are you sure that it happened a while back?" Kyle asked, glaring toward Ryan.

Kyle wanted to ask Cally straight-out if Ryan had hit her, but he knew that she would not tell him the truth with Ryan standing beside them. Kyle had to ask when Ryan was not around, that way Cally would feel more comfortable and maybe tell him the truth. Kyle took his eyes off Ryan, and put his focus on Cally, hoping that she would just say something, but he only created an awkward silence. Knowing that his plan had worked, and he had Cally right where he wanted her, Ryan looked at Kyle and gave him a little smirk. Kyle knew right then, without a doubt in his mind, that Ryan had complete control over Cally. There was no way that he would ever get Cally alone long enough to ask her anything.

"Well, I guess I'll leave you two alone, so that you can enjoy the rest of your night," Kyle said in a disappointed voice, after seeing that Cally was not going to talk.

"Okay, Kyle, we'll probably see you later on, and by the way, thanks for checking up on us," Ryan replied in a sarcastic way, letting Kyle know that he knew the real reason for his coming over.

As Kyle walked away, he wondered if he should call Cally's parents, just to inform them that something was going on between Ryan and Cally. He felt like they needed to know, but at the same time he did not want Cally to get mad at him. Kyle had never been more confused in his life. He was stuck in a difficult situation. If he did call Cally's parents, she could get mad at him for prying and never talk to him again, but on the other hand, if he did not call and something bad happened to her, he would never be able to forgive himself. Kyle felt so torn and confused, as he looked over and saw Cally wrapped in Ryan's arms.

"Maybe I should go over and talk to Kyle. I think that he is mad at me, and I don't want our friendship to end over something so stupid," Cally said, lifting her head off Ryan's chest.

"Trust me, Cally; Kyle is going to be just fine. He is a big boy, and he will get over it in due time. Just do not worry yourself about him. Everything will be alright, I promise," Ryan said, pushing Cally's head back down on his chest.

Things were going smoothly for Ryan, and he intended on keeping it that way. Once again, he had lied his way back into Cally's heart. Ryan was feeling so good about his accomplishments, but Cally was not. She felt terrible, and it showed. Cally wanted to go over and talk to Kyle so badly, but she knew that Ryan was not going to let that happen. Cally could not believe that she had fallen for Ryan's lies again. It was evident he was not going to change. Ryan was still the same abusive, controlling boyfriend that he had been for the past three months.

"What is wrong with you, Cally, why are you acting like this? I thought that everything was okay between us," Ryan asked nervously, hoping that Cally had not caught on to his lies.

"Look, Ryan, I have to go and talk to Kyle. I just can't ignore him like this. I at least owe him that much," Cally said, pulling her hand away from Ryan's firm grip.

Cally knew that she had to break away long enough to explain things to Kyle, whether Ryan liked it or not. Cally felt as if Kyle needed to know the truth. She could not just keep him guessing all night. It was time for Cally to speak out while she still could.

Ryan knew at that moment that Cally was not buying his lies anymore, and now there was only one thing left to do. Get Cally the hell out of there, before she started telling people the truth about her neck and lip. Ryan watched in anger as Cally started talking to Kyle, but he knew that he had to keep up his act for just a little while longer, so that she would get back in the car with him. Cally would pay for all of the humiliation that she had caused him. Ryan could see that Cally was in love with Kyle, and that made him regret not killing her when he had the chance. The longer Ryan stared at Cally and Kyle, the madder he got, and then it happened. Ryan finally snapped. While he looked the same on the outside, everything in him began to fall apart on the inside. The demons had overpowered him and taken control over his actions.

"Hey, Kyle, can I talk to you for a few minutes? It is really important and it cannot wait," Cally said as she touched Kyle softly on his arm.

"Yeah, sure, what's on your mind?" Kyle asked curiously, hoping that Cally had come to tell him the truth, although he already knew what the truth was.

As Kyle was talking to Cally, he could see Ryan staring him down from across the room, but Kyle was not going to let that bother him. Kyle did not care how mad Ryan got, he was not about to walk away from Cally again, knowing that she might need his help. Kyle just prayed that Cally would tell him something quickly before Ryan made his way over. That way he would know what to tell her parents when he called.

Cally took a deep breath as she stared into Kyle's gorgeous brown eyes; she wanted to let him know exactly what was going on, so he would be aware just in case something bad happened to her. Cally knew that she could trust Kyle with anything, even her life, but just as Cally opened her mouth to speak, Ryan quickly interrupted and grabbed her by the arm, giving her a tight squeeze, a squeeze that Cally knew all too well. Cally could literally feel the anger in Ryan's squeeze.

"Come on, Cally, it is time to go. I want to get you home on time so your parents don't get worried," Ryan said, finding it harder and harder to control his raging temper.

"I'll be ready to go in just a second. Right now I'm talking to Kyle about something," Cally replied, feeling angry with herself for believing Ryan's lies.

"Excuse me, but could you give Cally and me a little privacy? I really need to get her advice on something. I promise it won't take long," Kyle said politely, hoping to get rid of Ryan long enough for Cally to say what she had to say.

"Here's an idea. Why don't you just give her a call later and get the advice? I'm sure that you two talk all the time anyways," Ryan snapped back sarcastically as he moved closer to Kyle, trying to intimidate him.

"Look, everything is alright. Just give me a call later and we can talk then," Cally said, putting herself in between Ryan and Kyle before they started fighting.

Cally looked at Kyle, and gave him a quick smile and wink, letting him know that everything would be all right, when, in fact, not everything was going to be all right. Cally knew that it was only a matter of time before the real Ryan showed himself, and she wanted to get him away from everyone else before he exploded. Kyle knew that he could not let Cally leave with Ryan; there was no telling what would happen to her if he did. He felt as if he would never see Cally again, and that scared the hell out of him.

"Look, Cally, why don't you just ride home with me? I need to talk to your dad anyways, and it really can't wait," Kyle said casually, hoping that he could keep Cally from leaving with Ryan.

Ryan could feel his heart pounding as his temper flared. His rage was like a speeding train, completely unstoppable. Then before anyone knew it, Ryan had grabbed Kyle by his throat and slammed his head into the brick wall with more power than any man should have. Kyle saw his life flash right before his very eyes; he knew for sure that Ryan was going to kill him. Kyle could feel Ryan's grip getting tighter. As his nostrils flared like a raging bull, even his appearance changed. Cally watched in horror as Kyle's face started to turn blue from lack of oxygen. She did not know how much more Kyle could take, and Ryan did not look as if he was in any hurry to let him go. Something had to be done, and it had to be done quickly, before Ryan ended up killing Kyle.

"Maybe you didn't hear me the first time, so I'll say it again. Cally is leaving with me, and that is final. She is my girlfriend, not yours. So whatever you are thinking, just forget about it. Have I made myself clear?" Ryan asked as he finally pulled his hand off Kyle's throat.

"Ryan, please stop, he has never done anything to you, so just leave him alone, before you end up killing him," Cally begged as she started to help a lifeless-looking Kyle.

"Let's go, Cally, before I get really pissed off. Just leave the little crybaby bitch alone, or I swear to god, you will be sorry that you did not listen to me," Ryan demanded before a teacher came over and saw what was going on.

Ryan grabbed Cally by her arm and started dragging her across the dance floor, before someone noticed what was going and called the cops. Kyle watched in horror as Ryan forced Cally across the crowded dance floor. He wanted to do something to help Cally, but he could not even catch his breath. It felt as if Ryan had crushed his airway completely. Gasping for air, Kyle watched as Cally slowly disappeared through the crowd. Kyle knew that Cally was in grave danger, and there was not a damn thing he could do about it. Ryan had the strength of ten men, and he knew that he could not fight him alone; Ryan was just too strong for him. The only other thing that he could do was call the police and her parents.

"Leave me alone, Ryan, or I swear, I'll scream at the top of my lungs and expose you for the monster you really are," Cally warned Ryan as he continued to drag her across the dance floor as if she were a rag doll.

"Go ahead and scream, bitch, and I'll kill you right here on the spot! If you do not believe what I'm saying, just try it and see what happens to you. You will be dead before you know it," Ryan said in anger and hate as he pulled on Cally's small, weak arm, as if he were trying to pull her apart.

This is it; I'll never see my parents or Kyle ever again. I'll be dead within the hour, Cally thought as she looked back one last time, hoping to see Kyle or someone else behind her, trying to help. All she saw, though, was Kyle lying on the floor with people gathered around him. Cally was so upset with Ryan; she did not see how he could just go off on Kyle for no reason. Ryan was completely out of control, and Cally had no idea how to stop him. At this point, it could be impossible to put a stop to his reign of terror.

"No, you killed him, you killed Kyle!" Cally cried after seeing a lifeless-looking Kyle still lying on the floor.

"Good, I hope that the bastard is dead. It serves him right; he should not have stuck his nose in where it did not belong. Our relationship is none of his business. You are mine, and that is all he needs to know," Ryan said, showing no concern or remorse for Kyle.

Ryan had become a different person. He had only one thing on his mind, and that was to get Cally alone so he could follow through with his evil plan. Cally knew that she was in way over her head; she was so scared that she could not stop shaking. She had never seen Ryan this angry before. It was as if he were demon-possessed. He had never acted out this much in public before; this time he did not care who saw or heard him. Ryan was like a rabid dog taking out anyone and everything that stood in his way. Cally knew that her only way out was to beg and not do anything drastic. She had to keep her head clear so that she could come up with some kind of plan that would save her life.

"Please, Ryan, just let me go. I promise that I'll not say anything to anyone. Just give me a chance to prove that to you," Cally begged and pleaded as Ryan continued to drag her through the parking lot.

"How does it feel, Cally? How does it feel to have to beg for something that is never going to happen? You did not honestly think that I would just let this shit slide by, did you? You have done some bad things, Cally, and now it is time for your punishment," Ryan said as he shook Cally violently, causing people to stop what they were doing and stare.

Everyone knew that something was going on, but none of them had the courage to say anything to Ryan. He was acting like a crazed lunatic, and they did not want any part of that. Cally looked back one last time, praying to see someone coming to help her, but all she saw were cowardly people standing by watching Ryan drag her across the parking lot. Cally could not understand why everyone was just standing there; it made no sense to her. Cally knew right then that she was on her own. There was no sign of Kyle, and there was no sign of anyone coming to her rescue.

"Help me, please, someone help me! He is going to kill me! Someone, please call the police and let them know that I need help!" Cally screamed across the parking lot, hoping someone would hear her desperate cries for help, as Ryan forced her into his car, almost slamming the door on her leg.

Cally watched in fear as Ryan walked around the car in a fast steady pace. She knew that she did not stand a chance against Ryan. Cally wondered how she could have been so stupid and naïve. Now, because of her screw-up, she was going to pay with her life. Cally had never been more disappointed in herself. She was so mad that all she could do was clench her fists together tightly. Upon clenching her fists, though, she realized that she still had her cell phone in her hand. Watching Ryan get closer to the door, she quickly tucked the phone under her leg, so that Ryan would not see it. Ryan got into the car and slammed his door so hard that it made the car shake. He stared over at Cally in disgust as he started the car and revved it up.

"I cannot wait until you see what I have in store for you, bitch, and trust me, you deserve everything that you are going to get. You should have never gone against me, Cally. That was a huge mistake on your part," Ryan said with an evil laugh as his eyes turned a darker green.

"I have already apologized for disobeying you, Ryan. What more do you want from me? Please just tell me what I can do to fix this, and I'll do it, no matter what it is," Cally cried as tears streamed down her face.

"Oh no, Cally, it is a little too late for apologies. You have already over-stepped your boundaries and that cannot be forgiven. Now it is time for you to face the consequences, so just shut the hell up before I make you shut up," Ryan said, giving Cally her first and final warning.

3

Still giving Cally a cold, heartless look, Ryan put the car in DRIVE and sped recklessly out of the dampened parking lot. Cally knew that it was going to take a miracle to save her, and that was something that she did not have. Ryan had a determined look on his face, and Cally knew then that there was no talking her way out of this mess. Scared for her life, Cally looked over at the speed odometer and suddenly noticed the rain was getting heavier. Ryan was running 80 mph on not only a curvy and winding road, but also a wet one at that. Cally could feel the car slide as Ryan went into the sharp curves, but it did not seem to faze him. He looked as if he were enjoying himself.

"Please do not do this, Ryan. Just pull over so we can talk this out, before you do something that you are going to regret," Cally begged, trying to convince Ryan to do the right thing before he followed through with his deadly plan.

"No, Cally, this has to be done. I cannot trust you anymore, and you have proved that to me tonight. You are a self-centered little whore who doesn't care about anyone but herself, and I think that it is best that I put an end to your screwed-up life. But before I do, I need you to put this ring on your finger. It is a symbol of my undying love for you." Ryan handed Cally a small red velvet box for her to open.

"No, Ryan, I do not want your stupid ring! I hate you so damn much, and I do not want anything whatsoever from you, so take your stupid little ring and go to hell," Cally screamed, knocking the ring box out of Ryan's hand, causing the heart-shaped ring to go flying out of the box and land on the floorboard.

Cally was so frustrated that she had reached her own breaking point. She knew that nothing she said would make a difference, and she was sick and tired of begging for her life. After all, that was what Ryan wanted her to do. He enjoyed making Cally beg and suffer, and she was not going to give him the satisfaction this time. Cally's feet were planted firmly and she was not about to budge, even if it meant paying with her life. Ryan was going to do what he wanted to, not what someone else wanted him to do, no matter who they were.

Ryan was so busy fighting with Cally that he did not notice his car was going off the highway until it was too late. Ryan quickly lifted his head and saw that his car was heading straight for a huge tree. Panicked, Ryan tried to pull the car back onto the road, but it was no use, Ryan's car struck the tree, causing it to spiral out of control and flip several times before coming to a stop off an embankment. Upon impact, Cally's head smacked into the dashboard and split open as if it were a ripe melon, knocking her out cold. After Cally came to, she started to become more coherent. That is when she noticed the strong smell of gasoline. Cally knew that she had to get out of the car before it caught on fire and exploded, but her door was jammed up so badly that she could not get it to open. Cally could hear Ryan moaning in the distance, but she could not see him. Even after everything that Ryan had done to Cally, she knew that she had to help him; there was no way that she could just leave him there to die. Cally could never be that cold and heartless to anyone, no matter what they had done to her.

"Stay calm, Ryan, I'll be there in a minute to help you," Cally called out as she kicked the window glass out with her feet.

"Please, Cally, hurry up. I don't know how much more pain I can take," Ryan yelled to Cally, hoping that she could follow the sound of his voice and find him.

"Just hang in there. I'm on my way to help you. I'll be there in a second," Cally replied as she crawled out of the broken window, cutting herself along the way.

After crawling out of the jagged window, Cally began to drag herself across the cold, wet ground, with a broken arm and busted head. With every move that Cally made, blood gushed down her face, causing her to fade in and out of consciousness. Cally could hear Ryan moaning helplessly on the other side of the car, and she knew that she had to speed up in order to get to him

quicker, but the more she moved, the weaker she got. Finally, after the pouring rain slacked up, she could see Ryan lying beside the driver's side door. Not
knowing how badly he was hurt, Cally braced herself for the worst and pulled
her body closer to his.

"Ryan, can you hear me? Please, just answer me, say something. I need to
know that you are alright," Cally said as she checked for a pulse on Ryan's
neck.

"Cally, please help me, my legs are pinned under the car and I cannot
move at all. Please, I'm begging you; do not let me die like this," Ryan cried
desperately as Cally started to pull on him with her good arm.

"This is hopeless, Ryan. I'll never get you out by myself. I'm just not strong
enough. I'm so sorry, please forgive me," Cally said, panicking as tears rolled
down her cut-up, bloody face.

"No, Cally, you cannot do this to me. You have to help me. My life de-
pends on you, and only you, so please try to pull a little harder," Ryan said
hoping that Cally would not give up.

After pulling on Ryan one last time, Cally had almost given up hope, when
she saw her cell phone lying on the ground a couple feet ahead of her. Cally
let go of Ryan's hand and pulled herself across the soaking wet ground as fast
as she could with one arm, praying the whole time that her phone would
work well enough to call for help. Cally picked her cell phone up and flipped
it open to see if it was working, when she noticed some large flames coming
from the car. Cally's heart started to steadily pound, as the flames grew bigger
by the second. Thinking of Ryan's safety, Cally dropped her phone and hur-
ried back to him, grabbing Ryan by his hand. Cally pulled with all her might,
hoping for some kind of inner strength that would help her free Ryan before
it was too late.

"Come on, Ryan, you need to work with me on this, so we can get away
before the car explodes and kills us both!" Cally cried out hysterically, hoping
it would motivate Ryan into helping her more.

"It is no use, Cally; I cannot move my legs at all. You see, I really did not
plan for us to die like this, but it looks as if we have no other choice. It is time
for us to accept our destiny together," Ryan said in an evil voice, as he gripped
Cally's hand tighter so that she could not pull away from him.

"What in the hell are you talking about, Ryan? I do not want to die, I
want to live! Please let go of my hand! I do not want to burn to death, and

you should not want to, either," Cally begged as she tried to free herself from Ryan's determined grip.

"This is the only way, Cally. We have to die together. I could not rest in peace, knowing that you are still alive. As I told you before, if I cannot have you, then no one can. Just think, Cally, in a few minutes the car will explode, killing us both, and then we can be together forever," Ryan replied, still holding on to Cally's hand so tightly that she could not break loose.

"Ryan, please, do not do this to me. It is not right and you know it, so please, just let me go," Cally pleaded as she frantically scrambled, trying to get away before it was too late.

As Cally fought to escape Ryan's death grip, she saw a stick lying on the ground just within her reach. Knowing that it was her only hope, Cally picked up the stick and swung it, hitting Ryan in his already blood-drenched head, causing him to loosen his grip enough for her to pull away from him. Noticing that she was not far enough away, Cally pushed herself back with her legs, distancing herself further from Ryan before he had a chance to grab her again.

"Cally, you bitch, get back here and help me!" Ryan demanded as the flames started to burn his pinned-down legs.

Cally wanted to help Ryan, but she was scared to get near him again. She knew that Ryan was determined for her to die with him, and that was something that Cally did not want to do. Cally watched as Ryan's legs engulfed in flames. She tried to cover her ears so that she could not hear his screams, but it was no use. Ryan's painful screams, along with the smell of burning flesh, filled the dark woods around her. Cally hated the fact that she could not save Ryan; she had never felt so bad in her life. Not wanting to see Ryan's suffering, Cally closed her eyes tightly and tried to picture something else besides Ryan burning to death, but it was no use. The only thing Cally could see was a poor, helpless Ryan dying from his own stupidity. If Ryan had never gone into his jealous, stupid rage, they would both still be at prom, enjoying their night, but thanks to Ryan, they were both fighting for their lives.

"Cally, please help me! I'm sorry for hurting you. I swear that I'll never do it again, please just help me, I do not want to burn alive!" Ryan screamed, hoping that Cally would have pity on him, so he could get her in his grasp one last time and finish his deadly plan.

"Okay, Ryan, I'll try to help you one last time, but please do not play any more games with me. If you want to live, then you have to work with me," Cally said, agreeing to risk her life one last time to save Ryan's.

Ryan knew that he was going to die, and yet the only thing that bothered him was to know that Cally would still be alive. Ryan watched and waited eagerly for Cally to come to his aid, but before Cally could move a muscle, the car exploded, causing her to fall back onto the cold wet ground. Cally could hear Ryan's painful screams echo through the dark and lonely woods as the flames spread all over his pinned-down body. Not knowing what to expect, Cally slowly sat up and watched in horror as Ryan's skin started to bubble clean off his bones and turn black. Petrified of what she was seeing, the only thing Cally could do was sit there and cry.

"I'll get you for this, Cally! I swear, I'll come back for you. This is not over yet!" Ryan threatened as he stared at Cally with his cold, empty green eyes, letting her know that she would get what was coming to her for letting him die alone.

"This is not my fault, Ryan. You have done this to yourself! You just could not leave well enough alone," Cally screamed out, reminding Ryan that everything was, in fact, his own fault.

While Cally watched Ryan struggle for his last breath, she could feel herself fading in and out of consciousness again. Cally tried to fight it off, but it was a losing battle. She could not fight it any longer. Cally's body was too weak to do anything but fall back on the soaking wet ground, while the heavy rains washed the blood off her cut-up face. As Cally lay helplessly on the muddy wet ground, she could hear a car coming down the highway. Cally listened and prayed to God that the car would see the flames and stop to help her, but just as Cally's luck would have it, the car kept going. Knowing that she was going to die, Cally gave up all hope and braced herself for the worst, before blacking out completely.

"Cally, can you hear me? Are you all right? It's me, Kyle; I have an ambulance and your parents on the way," Kyle said, holding Cally's cold, wet body close to his, as he stared in complete horror at Ryan's badly burned body.

"Kyle, is that really you? Are you really here? I thought that you were dead; I thought Ryan had killed you," Cally whispered in disbelief, praying that Kyle was not a hallucination.

"Yes, Cally, it's really me. Just hang in there. Help is on the way. Everything is going to be okay, I promise," Kyle explained, trying to keep Cally calm and comforted until the ambulance got there.

"It's about damn time they got here!" Kyle said, flashing his flashlight on and off so that the paramedics would know where to find them. "We're down here, please hurry, she's hurt really badly!" Kyle yelled out to the paramedics as they rushed down the steep embankment with a backboard.

"How many people were involved? Is there anyone else down here?" the paramedic asked as he took a quick look around the woods.

"Actually there's one other person, but I don't think he will need your help," Kyle answered, pointing toward Ryan's crisply burned body.

After seeing that they could not help Ryan, the paramedics started working on Cally. Kyle did not want to leave Cally's side, but he had to so that the medics could check her condition. Kyle could not help but feel that everything was his fault. If only he had called the police for Cally when he had the chance, none of this would have ever happened. Kyle did not think that Ryan would have ever taken things as far as he did, but he was wrong, and he just hoped Cally could find it in her heart to forgive him. Feeling a tremendous amount of guilt, Kyle followed the medics as they carried Cally back up the embankment, praying the whole way that she would be all right.

"Cally, baby, are you alright? Please, someone tell me if my baby is going to be okay," Kate cried in a frantic voice as she rushed to be by Cally's side.

"Mom, is that you? Where are you?" Cally asked, reaching out her hand for her mother to hold.

"I'm right here, Cally. Do not worry about a thing. I promise I'll not leave your side. I'll be with you every step of the way," Kate said, holding on to Cally's cold, trembling hand as she stared sadly into Cally's bloodstained face.

"Mom, where is Dad? Didn't he come with you?" Cally asked softly as she tried to turn her strapped-down head.

"Yes, baby, he's here, too, and he is going to follow us to the hospital, so don't worry about a thing," Kate answered, trying not to upset Cally more than she already was.

Kyle watched in guilt as the ambulance drove away with Cally. Kyle felt so bad for Cally, but he could not have cared less about seeing Ryan's badly burned body lying on the ground. In a way, he was glad that Ryan was dead; at least now, Cally would not have to put up with his abuse anymore. Now that Ryan was gone, Cally could live her life in peace and Kyle could not have been happier.

"So long, Ryan. I hope that you enjoy hell, because that is exactly where you are going," Kyle whispered as he caught a glimpse of the other medics putting Ryan's crisply burned body into a body bag.

4

Kyle pulled into the hospital parking lot with nothing but Cally and her condition on his mind. He was still so upset with himself, and he still could not help but feel one hundred percent guilty. If only he had stood up to Ryan sooner and called the police, none of this would have ever happened. Cally would be okay, instead of lying in some cold hospital room, having God knows what done to her. Even as Kyle walked through the hospital parking lot, he could not shake the image of Cally and her blood-covered face from his mind. It was the most horrific thing Kyle had ever seen, and he had seen his fair share of accidents, thanks to a year spent in the fire department. Actually knowing the person, though, made everything hit a little closer to home—too close.

Upon entering the hospital, Kyle did not know what to expect. He knew that Cally was hurt badly in the accident; he just hoped and prayed that she was strong enough to pull through despite the odds. Kyle cared very deeply for Cally and if anything happened to her, he would never be able to forgive himself. As Kyle approached the front desk, he could see Cally's parents sitting in the waiting room with looks of fear and confusion on their faces. As he started walking toward them, he could feel his stomach tying up in knots. The last thing Kyle wanted to do was bother them in their moment of despair, but he had to. He had to find out how Cally was doing. Kyle just prayed that he would get good news, instead of bad. Kyle knew that there was no way in hell his heart could handle any more bad news.

"How is she? Is she going to be okay?" Kyle asked nervously, hoping that their response would be a good one.

"Well, as of right now, they have her in surgery, and we won't know anything until the doctor comes out to talk to us," Kate answered with tears rolling down her tired, worried face. Bill sat quietly in the chair beside her with a lost expression.

"This is ridiculous, why doesn't someone come out here and tell us how our little girl is doing? This just doesn't make any sense, and speaking of things not making sense, Kyle, do you know what in the hell happened tonight? Can you please tell me why Cally is in this damn place?" Bill asked with hostility in his voice, as he stared Kyle down and waited for an answer.

Kate watched in fear as Bill got up close and personal with Kyle, treating him as if the whole ordeal was his fault. She knew that Bill was not taking the accident lightly. That much was obvious, and she was afraid of what Bill might do to Kyle if he did not start explaining things and telling the truth. Bill was usually a calm person, but when it came to his family, that was a different story. Cally meant the world to Bill. She was his whole life and his only child, so finding out the truth about her accident was something he was going to do. No matter what, Bill would not stop until he found the underlying cause of this tragic accident.

"Bill, could you please lower your voice and sit back down? You are causing a scene, and I don't want to be kicked out of here, so would you please pull yourself together for our daughter's sake?" Kate asked, trying to make Bill come to his senses before the hospital staff said something to them.

"You know something, Kate, that is easier said than done. I want to know what happened to Cally tonight, and as her mother, you should too, so would you please stop acting as if you don't care!" Bill snapped with his hurtful remark, causing Kate to burst out in tears.

"How dare you talk to me that way? I care about Cally more than life itself, so stop making me out to be a bad parent, because I'm not and you know that," Kate replied, letting Bill know that he had overstepped his boundaries.

"You're right, Kate. I'm sorry for talking to you that way. I know that you are a good mother. It's just that I'm so worried about Cally, and not knowing how she is doing makes me worry that much more," Bill said, explaining his behavior to Kate the best way he knew how.

"It's alright, Bill. I just want you to know that I'm deeply concerned about

Cally, but I know that I have to keep myself together, for Cally's sake and for her well-being," Kate said as she wrapped her arms around Bill to comfort him in his time of need.

Kyle watched as Bill and Kate held each other close. There was so much love and affection between the two, and after seeing how loving and caring they were, Kyle knew that he had to tell them what he knew. It was imperative that he tell them the truth about everything, so they would have a better idea of the whole situation. It was not fair to keep them guessing about Cally's accident. Kyle had to tell them about Ryan and the way that he had treated Cally, even if it meant Cally hating him forever. It was time for Kyle to start doing the right thing, for Cally's sake and for her parents.

"Look, I don't know a whole lot, but I'll tell you what I know and what I witnessed. I have to warn you, though, the details are a bit disturbing," Kyle said, warning Bill and Kate so they would be prepared for what he was about to say.

"It is okay, Kyle. Just please tell us what you know. I promise that I'll not be upset with you. I just want to know what happened to my little girl," Bill explained, letting Kyle know that he was not upset anymore.

"Well, I sensed that something was wrong, as soon as they pulled into the school parking lot. The look on Cally's face made it obvious, but it was not till later on that I knew for a fact that something was wrong. I had approached both Cally and Ryan, and when I noticed that Cally had a busted lip, she tried to play it off like it had happened yesterday. But there was no way possible because the blood was still fresh. When I asked her if she was sure it happened yesterday, she got really quiet, which let me know that it had just happened and she was afraid to say anything in front of Ryan. Not wanting to start an argument, I walked away and went back to my table. Within a few minutes, Cally came up to me and told me that she had something to talk to me about, but before she could tell me anything, Ryan came over and got an attitude with both of us. After I saw how angry Ryan was, I asked Cally if I could take her home, and the next thing I knew, Ryan had me by the throat, choking me until I passed out. When I came to, it was too late. Ryan had already taken Cally. Knowing that Cally was in serious trouble, I left and tried to find her. I'm so sorry for all of this. Everything is my fault, if only I had called you or the police sooner," Kyle said, as his eyes filled with tears and his hands started to shake.

"Oh Kyle, this is not your fault, so stop blaming yourself. There was no way that you could have known what was going to happen. You did every-thing that you could do, and for that, I thank you sincerely. I'm the one who should have known better than to believe Ryan. I should have gone with my gut feeling and made Cally tell me the truth, but instead, like some idiot, I let my baby leave with that monster. What kind of mother am I?" Kate asked herself aloud, placing the blame on herself.

"It is not your fault, either, Kate. There is only one person to blame for this, and that is Ryan. I swear if he was not already dead, I would kill him myself," Bill said as all the anger came rushing back to him.

Suddenly it dawned on Kate that Ryan was dead. Although Ryan had done wrong, she still did not think he deserved to die. She could not, nor did she want to imagine Cally dying. Just the thought of it chilled her to the bone. As a mother, Kate's heart went out to Ryan's mother; she knew that Mrs. Jones would be devastated by the news. Hearing that her only child had died in a horrific car accident would absolutely kill her. Kate could not help but feel sorry for her and the heartache she was going to go through, but no matter how sorry she felt, it still would not bring back her son. Ryan was gone, gone forever. Kate knew that it was selfish, but she prayed to God that her little girl would live to see another day.

"I cannot take this anymore; the wait is driving me crazy. I have to find out something about Cally, and that is all there is to it. Someone in here has to know something, and they are going to talk to me, whether they like it or not," Bill said, quickly getting up from his seat and walking toward the front desk.

"Bill, sweetheart, why don't you just relax for a few more minutes? I'm sure that someone will be out shortly to fill us in on her condition," Kate suggested, hoping that Bill would take her advice and sit back down.

"I'm sorry, Kate, but I have to find out something now. I cannot wait any longer. There could be something bad wrong with Cally," Bill said as he still proceeded to the front desk.

Kate knew that Bill was hurting; she just hoped that he would not cause a scene, because she knew that she could not handle any more stress. She was already on the verge of a nervous breakdown, and it would not take much to send her spiraling out of control. Although Kate wanted to be strong for Cally and Bill's sake, she did not know how much longer she could put on a brave face, because deep down, she was going crazy. Kate had always been the strong one in the family, but this time, she herself needed someone to lean on.

Kyle hated to see Bill and Kate going through so much pain. He wished that there was something that he could do to help them out, but there was nothing he or anyone else could do. The only thing that would help Bill and Kate would be to know that Cally was going to be okay. Even Kyle himself could not wait to get word on Cally's condition. Kyle could not wait to wrap his arms around Cally and tell her how much he truly cared about her. Kyle had never realized how much he cared about Cally until tonight, and if Cally could just pull through this ordeal, Kyle swore that he would never let anything happen to her again. He would treat her as if she were a fragile piece of glass that he wanted to keep safe forever.

"Well, did you find out anything new, or did they give you the runaround?" Kate asked, interrupting Kyle's thoughts as Bill came walking back from the front desk with a disappointed look on his face.

"No, I couldn't find one person in this place that knew anything. I swear these people are really beginning to piss me off," Bill said, sitting back down in his chair.

As a man, Bill had never felt more helpless. All he wanted to do was find out how Cally was and he could not even do that. Bill had never been one to handle anything remotely bad, especially when it involved Cally. From the time Bill held Cally in his arms after she was born, he promised himself and her, that he would never let anything bad happen to her. He promised that he would always be there to protect her from anything that would harm her. Bill hated himself for breaking his promise to Cally, and he hated himself even more for believing Ryan's lies. Bill knew that he would never be able to forgive himself for what had happened. As long as he lived, this one huge mistake would haunt him forever.

As Bill and Kate sat in their seats, not saying a word, Kyle could not help but feel out of place. He wanted to stay and see Cally, but he did not want to irritate Bill and Kate with his presence. Kyle felt as if he was wearing his welcome out, and that was something that he did not want to do. Kyle had the utmost respect for Cally and her parents; he just wished that he could do more for them, but the bitter truth was he could not do anything to help them or Cally. All Kyle could do, along with everyone else, was pray, pray to God that He would keep Cally safe and help her get through the problems that lay ahead.

"Can I get the two of you something from the vending machine while we are waiting? A cup of coffee or a soda, just name it," Kyle asked considerately, as he threw in a few choices for them.

"I could not possibly tolerate anything on my stomach right now, but maybe Bill would like to have a cup of coffee, or some water," Kate replied as she concentrated more on Bill than Kyle.

Kate hoped that Bill would take Kyle up on his offer, but all he did was stare at the floor with a blank look on his face, as if he did not even hear them talking to him. Kyle looked at Kate in a state of confusion. He did not know if he should get Bill anything or not. The moment was already awkward enough and Kyle did not want to add fuel to the fire, so during the silence, Kyle took the opportunity to sit back down in his chair and drop his head to the floor.

"Mr. and Mrs. Smart, I'm Doctor Caine and I would like to take a moment of your time, so that I can discuss your daughter's condition," Dr. Caine said, interrupting the dead silence that filled the waiting room.

"Oh God, please tell us that our little girl is going to be okay!" Kate said, as she and Bill both jumped up from their seats, bracing themselves for the news they had waited so long to hear.

"Well, as you may already know, your daughter has been through a horrific ordeal tonight, but as of now, she is in serious but stable condition. We will continue to monitor her throughout the night and hopefully by tomorrow, she will be doing a little better," Dr. Caine explained with a positive attitude, putting both Bill and Kate's mind at ease.

"Thank God! Do you know when we will be able to see her?" Bill asked with anticipation, as tears of joy rolled down his face.

"Well, she will be moved to recovery soon, so just as soon as she gets there, you can go back to see her. I'll send a nurse out here to get you when it is time. You know, your daughter is very lucky to be alive. I saw the body of the person she was with, and it was the most horrifying thing I have ever seen in my life. The only way to identify that body will be by dental records. My heart goes out to his family and yours," Dr. Caine said, giving his condolences before walking away.

As Kyle sat there quietly, he could not help but overhear the good news. Cally was going to be okay, she was going to pull through this catastrophe after all. This was truly a miracle, and Kyle could not be happier. He could actually feel the weight lift off his shoulders and he was thrilled for both Bill and Kate. They were both in such a good mood, and the smiles on their faces lit up the whole room. It was evident how much Bill and Kate loved Cally; even a blind man could see the love that they held for their daughter.

"Did you hear the news, Kyle? Cally is going to be all right, and it is all thanks to you. If it had not been for your courageous, quick thinking, Cally might have died. Thank you so much for saving my little girl," Kate said, praising Kyle as she wrapped her arms around him and showed her appreciation.

"Kate is right, Kyle. You were the one who saved Cally, and for that, I owe you my life. I would also like to apologize for the way I acted earlier. It is just that I had a lot on my mind and I was looking for someone to take my anger out on. Can you ever forgive me for the way that I acted?" Bill asked as he reached out to shake Kyle's hand, hoping that he would accept his apology.

"There is no need to apologize; I would have done the same thing if I were in your shoes. I'm just glad that Cally is okay," Kyle said, letting Bill know that there were no hard feelings.

Kyle wanted to see Cally so badly, he could not stand it, but like at any other hospital, Kyle knew that only so many people could go back into the recovery room. Knowing that, Kyle was not about to impose by asking if he could be one of those people. He would never try to put himself before Cally's parents, no matter how badly he wanted to see her, even if it meant having to come back the next day. Kyle knew that in due time, he would get to see Cally; he just had to be patient and wait.

"Oh no, I'm such an idiot, I did not even ask Doctor Caine if you could come back to the recovery room with us. Do not worry, though, I'll ask the nurse as soon as she comes out to get us," Kate said, totally reading Kyle's mind, as if she were psychic.

"Thank you so much. That would mean a lot to me if you did. At least then I could rest better tonight, knowing that I got to talk to her before I left," Kyle said, showing his gratitude.

Even if Kyle could not go back, it was still nice of Kate to offer. Kate knew that Kyle wanted to see Cally, and she knew that Cally would want to see him, too. That is why she planned to do everything in her power to make it happen. Kyle was the one who had saved Cally's life, and he deserved to see her before he had to leave, no matter what the hospital rules were. Allowing Kyle to see Cally was the only right thing to do. Kate would not feel right doing it any other way.

"Mr. and Mrs. Smart, my name is Sharon and I'll be your daughter's nurse tonight, so if you will follow me, I'll take you back to the recovery room, so you can be with her when she wakes up," the nurse said, greeting Bill and Kate.

"Before we go back, I just want to let you know that there will be three of us, instead of two. I hope that is not going to be a problem for anyone. It is just that he is the one who saved our little girl's life tonight. I really would not feel right going back without him. I hope you understand," Kate replied, not asking the nurse, but telling her that Kyle was coming back with them.

"Well, there is a limit of two people, but since he was the one who saved her life, I do not see a problem with it. Besides, this place has been a madhouse tonight; I highly doubt that anyone will even notice him being there," the nurse agreed, after seeing how much it would mean to Kate and Kyle.

Kyle could not believe that Kate had just stuck up for him; it meant so much to him to know that Kate liked him that much. Kyle knew that Kate looked at him as if he were some kind of hero, but he did not look at himself as a hero. He had just done what anyone else in his predicament would have done. He helped a friend, a friend whom he cared a great deal about. Kyle just hoped that Cally would forgive him for telling her parents the truth about Ryan's abuse. Kyle wanted Cally to see that he had no other choice but to tell the truth about what he knew.

Upon entering the recovery room, Bill and Kate's hearts were not ready for what their eyes were about to see: their only child lying in a hospital bed with cuts and bruises all over her lifeless-looking body. Bill could not believe his eyes. He had not seen Cally until now, so he had no idea what to expect when he walked through the door. It was a father's worst nightmare, the most horrific thing that he had ever seen. Bill's emotions were running so high, he did not know what to do, let alone say. Bill wanted desperately to go up and hug his daughter, but he was terrified to. Cally's whole body was covered in cuts and bruises from head to toe. Bill hated himself for letting this happen to his little girl. How could he have been so blind and naïve? How could he have ever trusted someone like Ryan, someone so manipulative? Why did he not see through him and his lies?

"How could we have let this happen to our little girl? We should have known better! As her mother, I should have known that something was going on. All of the signs were right there in front of my face, and I was too blind to see them. It should be me lying in that bed, not her, this is entirely my fault and I'll never be able to forgive myself," Kate cried, feeling a momentous amount of guilt come over her.

Bill and Kyle knew exactly how Kate felt, because they were both feeling the same sense of guilt. If only they could have done more to prevent this tragedy, if only they had gone with their gut feelings, Cally would not be lying in a hospital bed looking as if she were near death. How could they have let the best night of Cally's life get so out of hand? Cally was supposed to be living her young life, not fighting for it. The whole situation was one big nightmare with no end in sight. Everyone just prayed that Cally would do well through the night.

"It is not your fault, Mom. Everything that has happened is my fault, and I should have told you the truth about Ryan from the start. Like a fool, though, I kept all of it a secret from you. I cannot believe that I was so foolish," Cally said in a low, weak, and disappointed voice, as she slowly opened her eyes.

"Oh Cally, thank God that you are alright! I have been worried sick about you; you gave all of us quite a scare," Kate said as she walked over and kissed Cally on her forehead.

As Kate bent down to kiss Cally, she could not help but notice that Cally was wearing a beautiful heart-shaped ring on her finger. Kate was curious as to where the ring came from; she knew what kind of jewelry Cally owned, and not once had she ever seen the heart-shaped ring before. Kate wanted to ask Cally about the ring, but she decided that it was not the time or place; she thought that it would be better to ask Cally about it when they were alone. Besides, Kate knew that Cally probably would not remember much after just waking up from surgery

"Hi, sweetheart, how are you feeling? Can I get you anything?" Bill asked, brushing Cally's bangs back off her face with his hand.

Just as Cally opened her mouth to answer her father, a loud and hurtful scream echoed throughout the hospital, sending cold chills down everyone's spine. It was a scream right out of a horror movie, a scream so horrific it could wake the dead; it was Ryan's mother, Ms. Jones. The pain in her screams filled the whole hospital, and although Bill and Kate were angry with Ryan abusing and trying to kill their daughter, their hearts still went out to her. Kate could not imagine what she would have done if Cally had been killed. Just the thought of it made her sick to her stomach.

"Maybe I should go and talk to her. After all, Ryan was her only child and she doesn't have anyone else to talk to," Kate said, feeling so much pain and remorse for Ryan's mother.

Before Kate had a chance to go and offer her condolences, the nurse came over to inform them that Cally was going to be moved into her own room. Torn between what to do, Kate let out a sigh of frustration, as tears filled her tired, bloodshot eyes. Bill knew that Kate wanted to be with both Cally and Ms. Jones, but the fact of the matter was Kate could not be in two places at once, no matter how badly she wanted to be there. Bill knew that he had to think of another way to ease Kate's mind. He had to come up with a solution to help her out, so that she could talk to both Cally and Ms. Jones.

"Look, sweetheart, everything is going to be okay. Why not just call Ryan's mother later and talk to her then? Besides, there is nothing we can really do for her right now. Only time will ease her heartache and suffering," Bill explained, hoping that Kate would see things from his point of view.

"Maybe you are right. I just hate knowing that she is in so much pain and agony and there is nothing I can do about it," Kate said, feeling numb all over her body as her heart shattered into a million pieces.

While Bill and Kate were talking, all Kyle could do was stare at Cally in sadness; he absolutely hated Ryan for what he had put Cally through. Kyle was glad that Ryan was dead. In his eyes, Ryan had gotten what he deserved—a slow and painful death. If Ryan's death had been in Kyle's hands, he would have made him suffer even longer for the way he had treated Cally. Kyle thought that Cally was the sweetest person he had ever known, and he could not understand why Ryan had treated her so badly. He really did not feel that much for Ryan's mother, either. He wondered if she knew about the abuse and allowed it to happen. Either way, Kyle could not have cared less for them both, and he did not plan on going out of his way to talk to Ryan's mother, no matter how bad she was hurting.

"Bless her heart. This girl has been through a lot tonight, it is no wonder that she cannot hold her eyes open," the nurse said, interrupting Bill and Kate's conversation as she checked Cally's IV.

"Yeah, she has been through hell and back, but hopefully things will get better now. I'm just so thankful that she came out of this with her life," Kate replied as she held on tight to Cally's hand, taking a closer look at the mysterious heart-shaped ring on Cally's finger.

Kate could not stand it any longer; the not knowing was eating away at her and driving her insane. Kate's curiosity had taken over, and she had to ask Cally about the ring, just as soon as she woke again. Every time Kate looked at the ring, she got an eerie feeling all over her body; it was a feeling that scared the hell out of her. It was almost as if the ring had its own special powers, and it was imperative that she find out where the ring came from. That way she could put her mind at rest and stop worrying about it and focus more on Cally.

"Alright, if everyone is ready, we will take this young lady up to her room, so that she can get some much-needed rest," the nurse said as she unlocked the brakes on Cally's hospital bed.

"Yes, ma'am, we are ready to go. The sooner we get Cally settled in, the better off she will be. That is all that matters to me at this point. Everything else can wait," Bill hinted, letting Kate know that she needed to put Cally first before Ryan's mother or anything else.

"I can most certainly understand that. I have a daughter of my own, about Cally's age, and if anything ever happened to her, I would go crazy," the nurse agreed as she started to roll Cally's bed down the hallway.

Bill, Kate, and Kyle followed the nurse down the long cold hallway to the elevator. To Kyle the hallway seemed as if it would never end. The bright fluorescent lights were blinding as they reflected off the shiny white floor. Kyle could not wait until they reached Cally's room; he wanted to talk to her more than anything, before he had to leave. Just the sound of Cally's voice would ease his troubled mind and help him sleep better when he got home. Kyle had learned firsthand just how much he really cared for Cally, and it amazed him that he had not seen it before. It took something horrible happening to Cally, before he saw just how much she meant to him.

"Ah, here we are, room 249. This will be your daughter's room throughout her stay with us, so if she is going to have any more visitors, just tell them that they can come straight up to her room," the nurse explained as she pushed Cally's bed into the much colder, brighter room.

"Excuse me, but do you know how long they want to keep her? Doctor Caine never discussed that with us, and I was curious to know just how long her stay would be," Kate asked, setting her purse down on the table, feeling that she could take better care of Cally at home.

"Well, I'll not know anything until I talk to the doctor. He is the only one who can make that decision. If he has not talked to you within two hours, let me know and I'll ask him myself. That way you will know," the nurse said as she continued to check Cally's vitals, making sure she was still in stable condition before leaving the room.

"Look, Kate, I know that you are anxious to get Cally home, and I'm, too, but you really should not be rushing things. Cally needs to stay here for as long as they say. There is no way that we can take care of her like they can, so would you please stop with the unnecessary questions? They will let us know when she can go home," Bill snapped, feeling irritated that Kate would ask about Cally going home so soon.

Feeling more and more uncomfortable around an arguing Bill and Kate, Kyle dropped his head to the floor and prayed that Cally would awaken soon. At this point, the only thing Kyle wanted to do was talk to Cally and then get the hell out of the hospital before Bill and Kate got into another intense argument. Kyle had heard enough arguing in his lifetime, which was why his parents divorced; they argued all the time and they could not get along, even if their lives depended on it. Kyle just hoped that Cally's parents would stop arguing before she awoke and heard them.

Without saying a word, Kate stood in the corner and stared at Bill with cold and angry eyes. She knew that Bill was going through a rough time, but so was she, and Bill needed to realize that he was not the only one hurting. Kate was so sick of him treating her as if she were a kid. That upset her more than anything, and the fact that he had done it in front of Kyle pissed her off to the limit of snapping. Kate thought about pulling Bill to the side and confronting him about his attitude, but she figured that it would not do any good. Besides, the way Bill was looking at her let her know that he was aware of his mistakes.

Bill loved Kate with all of his heart and soul; she was a good wife and a terrific mother and he would never do anything to hurt her, but he was under so much pressure and stress that he was lashing out at anything or anybody. Thinking about the way he had talked to Kate and knowing that he had upset her made him feel as if he were the biggest asshole in the world. He knew that he had to fix things between them before it was too late. Realizing his faults, Bill walked over to Kate and wrapped his comforting arms around her, as if he were apologizing to her, without saying a word.

Kyle watched as Bill and Kate comforted each other. It was so sweet to see how much in love they were. That is when Kyle realized that he wanted that kind of love, a love that was so meaningful and strong. Sure, they argued, but he knew now that they were only arguing because they were worried about Cally. A tragedy like that was enough to make any couple argue and disagree with one another, and as Kyle sat in his chair, staring at Cally, he could not help but wonder if Cally was the love he had been looking for. After all, he had known Cally since kindergarten, and he knew her better than she knew herself. To Kyle, Cally was like an open book, and that was what he loved most about her.

"Mom, are you here? Please answer me, I really need you right now," Cally moaned as she tried to open her heavy, tired eyes and look around the room to see where she was.

"Yes, sweetheart, I'm right here. How are you feeling, is everything okay?" Kate asked in a concerned voice, as she rushed over to Cally's side, letting her know she was not alone.

Kate wanted to be strong for Cally, but she could not take it anymore. She had to let some of her emotions out, before she exploded. There was no way Kate could go on pretending that everything was all right. The truth was, things were not all right, and they probably would not be for a while. The only thing Kate could do was take things slowly, day by day, and pray to God that things would work out for the best.

"Mom, why are you crying? What is wrong? Is everything all right?" Cally asked in a weak voice as she tried to hold her eyes open.

"Do not worry. Everything is going to be alright. Your mother is just a little tired, that is all, but I just want you to know that we are all here for you, so if you need anything, just let us know," Bill replied before Kate had a chance to, hoping that the sound of his voice would ease Cally's troubled mind.

Although Cally was still feeling the side effects of her concussion and the anesthetic, she was still aware of everything that had happened. She knew that she had been involved in an accident and she knew that Ryan was dead; she also knew that Kyle had saved her life. If it had not been for Kyle, Cally knew that she would have died, and that was the bottom line. Cally owed everything to Kyle, and she did not know how she could ever repay him for saving her life. The only thing Cally could really do was be there for Kyle whenever he needed her to be, and that was exactly what she planned to do.

"Mom, Dad, is Kyle here? Did he come to the hospital, too? I would really love to talk to him," Cally said as she struggled to sit up in the bed with her broken arm, so that she could have a better look around the room.

"I am right here, Cally. I have been here the whole time, waiting for you to wake up so I could talk to you. How are you feeling? Is there anything I can do for you?" Kyle asked, jumping up from his chair in the darkened corner so he could help Cally up before she hurt her broken arm.

When Cally saw Kyle's face, it was as if she started to feel better instantly. Her eyes lit up and her pale white face filled with color, as she gave Kyle a huge smile that went from one ear to the other. Cally was so touched to find out that Kyle had been there the entire time. He had missed his prom, just to be with her. It was the nicest thing that anyone had ever done for her. Cally knew in her heart that she would never forget this moment for as long as she lived. This was one thing that she would hold dear and remember forever, no matter what happened.

Bill and Kate watched in joy as Kyle and Cally talked. Sure, they wanted to talk to Cally, too, but they did not want to be rude and interrupt. They both knew that Kyle would not be there that much longer, and they wanted him to have some time with Cally before he had to leave. After all, Kyle was the one who had saved her life, and it would be undignified for them to take that away from Kyle. Kate could tell, just by looking at them, that they liked each other more than just friends, even a blind man could see the chemistry between the two. Seeing how close the two of them were made Kate wonder if Kyle had given Cally the heart-shaped ring. Maybe Kyle had put it on her finger after the accident; either way, Kate was determined to find out where the mysterious ring had come from.

"Mom, Dad, I'm sorry for lying to you and putting you through all this trouble. I swear that it will never happen again, you have my word," Cally said, realizing that she needed to apologize to her parents for lying about Ryan.

Cally felt awful for putting her parents through so much hell. If only she had told the truth from the beginning, none of this would have ever happened. The whole situation could have been avoided, just by doing one little thing: telling the truth. Although things had turned out badly, Cally was glad that everything was out in the open; it was as if a huge weight had been lifted off her shoulders. Now Cally could relax and take things day by day, without the worries of Ryan's severe punishments.

"Oh sweetheart, you do not need to worry about that right now. What's done is done. You just need to focus on getting better, so we can take you home," Kate said, comforting Cally and letting her know that she forgave her for keeping things a secret.

"I agree with your mother. Everyone makes mistakes, which is how we learn right from wrong, and I honestly think that you have learned your lesson. From now on, though, you need to trust us enough to tell us the truth, no matter what the situation is," Bill said, agreeing with Kate, but also informing Cally that the lies had to stop for the sake of everyone. Bill knew that Cally was a good girl; he just did not want Cally to go down the wrong path in life, and he wanted her to be honest with others and, more importantly, herself.

"Okay, Cally, it's time to check your vitals and take your medicine," the nurse announced as she came into the room, interrupting the conversation.

"Well, how is she? Did her vitals check out good? Is everything reading okay?" Bill asked curiously, as the nurse started checking Cally's IV.

"Yes, everything looks great, but I need to inform you that there is a limit on visitors after eleven o'clock, so someone will have to leave in about an hour. I know that is not what you wanted to hear, but that is the hospital's policy, not mine. You understand, right?" the nurse said, hoping that she would not offend or make anyone mad.

"Of course we do, and I really appreciate everything that you have done for us and our daughter," Bill said.

No sooner than the nurse walked out of the room, Cally fell fast asleep again. There was no way Cally could fight off the effects of the morphine; she was too weak and it was too strong. Cally's body was suffering a great deal from exhaustion; it was almost as if she was too tired to breathe. The truth was, Cally was lucky to be alive. Not many people walked away from a crash like that, but Cally did. Cally was truly a fighter and always had been. It was not in Cally to give up on something, especially her life. That was why she fought so hard to stay alive after the accident; Cally wanted to live her life, not lose it.

"Hey, Kyle, since Cally is sleeping, would you like to go down to the vending machines with me, so that I can get myself and Kate a cup of coffee?" Bill asked, hoping that Kyle would accept the invite, so that he could thank him for everything he had done for Cally.

"Sure, I could use a cup of coffee myself. Besides, the walk could do me some good," Kyle agreed, following Bill out of Cally's room.

5

Kate sat down in a chair beside Cally's bed and watched as Bill and Kyle walked out of the room. Kate felt so lucky to have a husband like Bill. Bill was the kind of man that any woman would love to have. He was smart, funny, kind, and caring, and he always put his family first. If only Cally would have found someone so caring, but she did not. Instead, she got someone who was cruel and abusive, with no love in his heart whatsoever. Kate did not understand how Ryan could have treated Cally so badly; she had never done anything to him except love him. Ryan acted as if he cared so much about her, but underneath the act, the truth was hidden, and Ryan did not care for Cally at all. The only thing he wanted Cally around for was to use her as a punching bag, and that absolutely broke Kate's heart.

"Don't worry, Cally. I swear that I'll never let anything else happen to you again. I'll always be there to protect you until the day I die, do not ever forget that," Kate said softly, holding on to Cally's small, cold, bruised hand.

As Kate sat there beside Cally's bed, silence filled the room. Only the ticking of the clock made a sound, a sound that played just like a lullaby. Kate could not fight it any longer. Her eyes were heavy and her body was tired. Kate felt as if she had not slept in days. The more she tried to fight off her tiredness, the weaker she got; Kate was fighting a losing battle that she would never win, no matter how hard she fought. Finally, after fighting it off as long as she could, Kate's eyes began to close, and slowly she started drifting off into a much-needed sleep.

"Hey, Mrs. Smart, why the long face? Is something wrong with your precious little daughter? Did she have an accident tonight?" a very familiar voice asked.

"Hello, is anyone in here? Have you come to see Cally?" Kate asked in a startled voice, as she rubbed her tired, bleary eyes and looked around the room, expecting to see someone standing there with her.

"Well, I guess you could say that I'm here to see Cally. She and I have some unfinished business that we need to take care of, and it is best that I take care of it now, instead of later," the voice said out of thin air, sending chills up Kate's spine.

Recognizing the low, almost whispering voice right away, Kate knew without a doubt that it was, in fact, Ryan's voice, but there was no possible way in hell that it could be Ryan, because Ryan was dead and dead people do not come back to life. Kate felt so confused. She could hear Ryan, but she could not see him. Kate even began to think that her tired mind was playing tricks on her. After all, there was no way Ryan could possibly be there. It just did not make any sense. Ryan was dead, and he was not coming back, but just to be sure and put her mind at ease, Kate decided to play along with the game her tired mind was playing on her.

"Ryan, is that you? Why are you here and what kind of business do you have to settle with my daughter? Do you not think that you have put her through enough pain already? Why are you so hell-bent on hurting her? What did she ever do to you, to make you hate her so much? Answer me, damn it. Stop being such a coward, and show yourself!" Kate demanded as her temper started getting the best of her.

"I'm right behind you, Kate, so why don't you stop being the coward and turn around and face me, or are you too damn scared to?" Ryan asked as his hot breath showered the back of Kate's neck, sending her into a frantic state of shock.

Suddenly, all of Kate's anger turned into fear. She did not want to face Ryan, but she knew that she had to do it. Kate could not, nor would not, let Ryan hurt her little girl again, dead or not; Kate was determined to stop Ryan and that was all there was to it. She had seen her family go through enough pain and suffering on account of Ryan, and she could not stand to see them hurt anymore. It was finally Kate's time, time to stand up to Ryan and put him in his place before he did any more damage to her family. Kate was so frightened; her heart was pounding and she could feel her knees begin to knock, as her face broke out into a cold, clammy sweat. Scared of what she was going to see when she turned around, Kate closed her eyes tightly and braced herself for the worst, as she slowly turned to face Ryan. Upon turning around, Kate slowly opened her eyes, to see if Ryan was indeed standing behind her.

"That is odd. My mind truly is playing tricks on me, and it is all thanks to lack of sleep. Yes, now I'm sure of it, it is just my tired, weary mind," Kate said aloud, trying to come up with a logical explanation as to why she was hearing Ryan's voice from beyond the grave.

Confused and shaken, Kate turned back around to face Cally, but instead of facing Cally, she came face-to-face with a badly burned and mangled Ryan. Kate had never seen anything that scary before in her whole life. It was as if she was staring the devil right in the face. Praying that her mind was still playing tricks on her, Kate closed her eyes and counted to three, hoping that when she opened them back up Ryan would be gone, but that was all a dream, because when she opened her eyes, there was Ryan, still staring her in the face.

"Dear God, this cannot be happening! You are supposed to be dead, Ryan. What in the hell are you doing here?" Kate asked as she stared in complete horror at Ryan's burned-to-a-crisp face.

"I have already told you. I have come back for Cally. Her place is with me, not you, so get the hell out of my way, so I can get what I came for," Ryan demanded as pieces of his burned flesh started to fall to the floor at Kate's feet.

"No, stay away from my daughter, you monster! She is not going anywhere with you. You are the reason that she is in here now, so just go back where you came from!" Kate screamed as she jumped to her feet to protect Cally.

"Kate, what in the hell are you doing? Is everything okay? Are you okay? Please answer me, I need to know!" Bill asked in a concerned voice, as he and Kyle entered the room and saw Kate lunge at something that was not there.

"Oh, thank God, it was only a dream—one big nightmare—and I'm so glad to be out of it now." Kate sighed with relief as Bill's voice brought her back to reality and made her aware of her surroundings.

Bill paused for a second, giving Kate a chance to explain herself, but Kate just stood there in silence and tried to gain her composure, as she tried to forget the horrible images she had just seen. Kate knew that she needed to say something, but she could not think of one word to say that would not make her sound crazy. Kate felt crazy enough already, just trying to figure things out for herself, and she did not need anyone else thinking the same thing. Kate would rather keep her bad dreams to herself for the time being.

"Kate, is everything okay in here? You look as if you have seen a ghost. Maybe you should go home for the night, so that you can get some sleep. I'll stay here with Cally and you can come back first thing in the morning," Bill suggested, fearing that all of the stress had finally taken its toll on Kate.

"No, everything is fine. I just had a bad dream, that is all. Besides I'm not leaving Cally's side again, so just drop it, okay?" Kate snapped, getting her point across quickly as she got up to retrieve her coffee.

Kate picked up her cup of coffee with both of her shaking hands, trying her best not to spill any before she got it to her mouth. Kate felt bad for snapping at Bill, but there was no way in hell that she was going to leave Cally, just so that she could go home and get some sleep. That was not even an option in Kate's eyes. She had promised Cally that she would be right by her side, and that was exactly what she planned on doing. Cally was Kate's whole life, and she wanted to keep her as safe as she could. The only way to do that was to never leave Cally's side again.

"So, Kyle, I never really thanked you for helping Cally. If it had not been for you, I do not know what would have happened to her," Kate said, totally ignoring Bill's offer, so he would take the hint and stop pressuring her about going home.

"Well, I'm just glad that I left prom early to go and look for her. Cally means a lot to me. I just wish that I would have called the police before all this happened," Kyle said as his light brown eyes filled with tears and his conscience ran over with guilt.

"It is not your fault, Kyle. You did the best you could to protect me, so please stop blaming yourself," Cally said softly as she struggled to push herself up in the bed with her broken arm.

"Hey girl, how are you feeling?" Kyle asked, rushing over to help her up.

"Well, under the circumstances, I feel a little bit better. How about you, is your throat okay?" Cally asked after seeing the blood-red marks on Kyle's neck, which Ryan had put there when he choked him.

"Oh, don't worry about me, I'm fine. I'm just glad that you are feeling better, that is all that matters to me right now," Kyle said with a smile, sitting down on the bed beside Cally.

Kate watched as Kyle took Cally by her hand, and she could see a familiar spark between the two of them. It was the same spark that Bill and herself had experienced years ago. Kate knew that Kyle would have to go home soon, so she decided to give them some privacy so they could talk. Kate did not know what they were going to talk about exactly, but judging by the look in their eyes, Kate knew that whatever it was, it was going to be special.

"Bill, sweetheart, would you like to join me for another cup of coffee? I think that may be just what I need to get me going," Kate said, throwing a hint toward Bill, hoping that he would catch it.

"You know, I think you're right. Another cup of coffee sure would hit the spot, and a pack of crackers doesn't sound too bad, either," Bill agreed, giving Kate a wink, letting her know that he had caught on to her plan.

"Okay, Cally, your father and I are going down to the lobby to get some coffee and snacks. We will be back in a little while," Kate said, giving Cally a kiss on her forehead.

"Thank you, Mom, for everything. You truly are the best mother in the world," Cally said softly and sincerely, as she looked at Kate with her sparkling baby blue eyes.

"You do not know how much that means to me, to hear you say that. It is the biggest and best compliment any mother could hear," Kate said, smiling at Cally, thanking God that she still had her little girl.

After Bill and Kate walked out of the room, there was an awkward silence between Cally and Kyle. Neither one of them knew what to say. It was almost as if they were complete strangers. Kyle did not want to bring up the accident, because he really did not know how Cally was taking Ryan's death and the last thing he wanted to do was upset Cally. Kyle knew that she had been through enough already, and he did not want to pile more worries on top of her. He figured that Cally would talk about things when she got ready to. Just before Cally could open her mouth, though, there was a soft knock at the door.

"Come on in, the door is open," Cally answered, expecting to see the nurse or doctor come through the door, but to her surprise, it was Ryan's mother.

"Ms. Jones," Cally said in a shocked and surprised voice.

"Oh Cally, I'm so glad that you are alright. How are you holding up?" Ms. Jones asked, walking toward Cally to give her a hug.

"Well, I guess that I'm doing okay, just a little banged up and sore. How are you doing?" Cally asked, not really knowing what to say to her.

Cally felt so uncomfortable about the whole situation. She knew that Ms. Jones did not know about the abuse or Ryan's evil plan to kill them both, and Cally knew that if she told her, it would only break her heart and send her over the edge, making matters worse. Cally did not want to hurt her anymore; she had suffered enough by losing her only child. Cally just hoped that Ms. Jones would leave before Kyle said anything about it to her, because Kyle was the type of person to say whatever was on his mind, and Cally knew that he had a lot on it.

"I did not mean to bother you. I just wanted to check on you before I went home, to make sure you were okay. I could not have slept a wink not knowing," Ms. Jones said after noticing Kyle on the bed beside her.

"Oh, you're not bothering me. I'm glad that you stopped by. It means a lot to me," Cally said reaching out to hold her hand.

"Oh my goodness, I cannot believe it. Ryan got to give you the ring before he died," Ms. Jones said, holding on to Cally's hand, staring down at the heart-shaped ring on her finger, which Cally had not yet noticed.

Cally stared down at her hand, curious to see what Ms. Jones was talking about. Cally knew for a fact that she had knocked the ring onto the floorboard of Ryan's car before they wrecked, so there was no possible way that it could be on her finger. When Cally's eyes met with her hand, though, there was the heart-shaped ring that Ryan had given her before they crashed. As Cally stared at the ring, her face turned pale; she did not know what to say. She was speechless.

"Are you okay, Cally? Do I need to get the nurse for you?" Kyle asked after seeing her response to the ring on her finger.

"No, that will not be necessary. I'm just a little tired is all. I think after I get some rest, I'll start to feel better," Cally lied as she stared down at the mysterious heart-shaped ring on her finger.

"Oh, I'm so sorry, I was not even thinking. I should not have said anything. I know that you miss Ryan, too. I'll go now, so that you can get some rest. I'll call you tomorrow with the funeral arrangements," Ms. Jones said, giving Cally a kiss on her forehead.

"I'm so sorry for your loss. If you need anything, all you have to do is call," Cally said, giving her condolences as Ms. Jones walked out of the room.

"Oh my God, there is no way that this can be happening. It is just not possible, and I know that it is not," Cally said, shaking her head in disbelief as she stared down at the ring.

"What are you talking about, Cally? You are not making any sense at all.

Are you sure that you do not want me to go get the nurse, or your parents?" Kyle asked, feeling concerned that something was wrong with Cally.

"Yes, Kyle, I'm just having a hard time remembering something that happened earlier tonight, so if you could, please give me a second to think," Cally snapped as she felt herself become more frustrated with Kyle and his questions.

Cally knew without a doubt that she had never put on the ring. It had never even touched her finger, and that is what confused her most. If she had not put the ring on her finger, then how did it get there? Cally stared at the ring and tried to come up with a logical explanation, but there was not one. There was only confusion and fear. Cally felt that she was losing her mind; nothing made sense to her anymore. Could Ryan have kept his evil promise? Had Ryan really come back from the dead for her?

"Cally, would you please tell me what is going on? Maybe it's something that I can help you with, and I'll help you, but you have to talk to me and fill me in on some things," Kyle said, eager to find out why Cally was so upset.

"Look, Kyle, I'm not trying to ignore you, but I think that this is something I need to figure out on my own. I got myself into this mess, and I need to get myself out of it," Cally said as she turned to face Kyle, but instead of facing Kyle, Cally found herself face-to-face with Ryan.

"This cannot be real! You're dead. I watched you die. There is no way that you could have survived the fire," Cally said as she stared into Ryan's devilish green eyes and watched the burned flesh peel off his face.

"I told you that I would come back for you, so why are you so surprised to see me? Did you think that I was lying?" Ryan asked as he touched Cally on the face with his ice-cold hand.

"No, this is not real. You are dead, and there is no way that you could have come back! It is not possible, so please just go away!" Cally screamed as tears rolled down her pale face.

"That does it, Cally. I'm going to get the nurse, so she can check you out and make sure everything's okay," Kyle said, jumping to his feet in fear as he watched Cally talk to someone who was not there.

"What is going on in here? Is Cally alright?" Kate asked in a panicked voice as she and Bill walked back into the room and saw Cally crying and Kyle with a frightened look on his face.

"I honestly do not know. One minute she was fine and the next, she was screaming and crying. I was just on my way to get the nurse when you guys walked in. I did not know what else to do," Kyle explained, as his heart finally started to slow down a bit.

"It was him, Mom. It was Ryan. He said that he had come back for me, and then he touched my face with his ice-cold hand," Cally cried, hoping that they would believe her and not think that she was crazy.

It did not take Kate long to put things together, because she had seen Ryan, too. Kate did not doubt Cally for a second; she knew exactly what Cally was saying. No matter how hard Kate tried, she could not get the image of Ryan's face out of her head. She did not want to tell Cally that she had seen Ryan also, because that would only upset Cally more and leave Bill and Kyle with many questions that she could not answer. The only thing Kate could do was keep Cally calm until Dr. Caine could get there.

"Oh, I'm sure that it was just a bad dream. Everything is going to be okay. Ryan cannot hurt you anymore, so just calm down, and take a few deep breaths," Kate said, trying to smooth things over for Cally and herself.

"No, Mom, you don't understand. I was wide awake, so it couldn't have been a dream. This was real. Ryan has come back from the dead for me, just like he said he would," Cally cried as Bill and Kate tried to comfort her.

Kyle did not know what to say. He felt as if he was just in the way and that was the last place he wanted to be. He knew that this was a family matter, and he was not part of the family, so without further hesitation, Kyle decided to go home for the night and let Bill and Kate spend some much-needed time with Cally. Besides, Kyle felt that he could not stay there another second without going crazy himself. All of the talk about Ryan coming back from the dead for Cally made him feel a little weird and spooked at the same time, and his night had been weird enough already.

"Well, if you do not need me any more tonight, I guess that I'm going to head home, so Cally can get the rest that she needs," Kyle said, fidgeting with his car keys, trying not to make eye contact with Cally.

"Okay, Kyle. We appreciate everything that you have done tonight. Drive safe and we will call you if anything changes," Bill said, giving Kyle a hand-shake, showing his gratitude once more.

"'Bye, Cally. I hope that you get to feeling better. I'll see you first thing tomorrow," Kyle said, giving Cally a quick hug before walking out of the room.

As Kyle got on the elevator, he could not help but wonder what Ms. Jones meant about the ring. He noticed that after she mentioned the ring, Cally got very upset and that was when she started acting out. Kyle felt his curiosity grow stronger and stronger by the second. Part of him wanted to go back and talk to Cally, but the other part told him to mind his own business and let Cally bring it up first. That way Kyle would not feel as if he were prying or being nosy.

While Kyle was on his way home, Bill was on his way to find the nurse. He hated to see his little girl going through so much hell. No matter how hard Bill tried, he still could not help her; it was the worst feeling in the world. Bill had always been able to fix things when Cally was young, but now that she was older, it was hopeless. Bill felt as if his little girl was out of reach and nothing he did could bring her closer. Everything was like one big nightmare to Bill, a never-ending nightmare.

"Excuse me, but could you please find Doctor Caine? There is something wrong with my daughter, and we do not know what to do for her," Bill explained, after he finally found the nurse.

"Sure, just give me just a second, and I'll page him directly to the room," the nurse said, picking up the phone to page the doctor.

"I found the nurse and she is paging Doctor Caine right now. She said that she would page him directly to the room, so he should be here within a few minutes," Bill said, hoping to put both Cally and Kate's mind at ease.

"I do not need a doctor, Dad, I need a priest! Ryan has come back from the dead, just like he said he would," Cally screamed as she became more and more frustrated.

"Sorry it took me so long, but I was just coming out of surgery when the nurse paged me. What seems to be the problem?" Dr. Caine asked after hearing Cally scream at her parents.

"Go ahead, Cally. Tell him exactly what you told us. I promise that everything will be alright," Kate said, comforting Cally.

Cally paused for a second and looked around the room. She really did not want to tell Dr. Caine what she had seen, because she really could not believe it herself. Cally knew that if she told the truth, the doctor would only think that she was crazy, and that was the last thing that she wanted anyone to think. Cally was so confused; she did not know what to do. Her hands were shaking and her heart was pounding. Although she wanted to lie about what she had seen, Cally knew that she had to tell the truth. It was the only way for her to get some answers.

"It is okay, Cally, just start from the beginning and tell me what happened," Dr. Caine said, pulling up a chair beside Cally's bed.

"Well, it all started when Ms. Jones came in to see me. She brought something to my attention, something that scared the hell out of me. She noticed a ring that was on my finger, this ring right here," Cally said, pointing to the heart-shaped ring on her finger.

"I'm confused, Cally. What is so scary about the ring on your finger?" Dr. Caine asked, looking at Cally as if she was indeed a little on the crazy side.

"You do not understand. There is no possible way that this ring could be on my finger. Ryan tried to make me put it on, but I threw it on the floorboard, right before we crashed. The ring never touched my finger," Cally explained, trying her best to make Dr. Caine understand what the problem was.

"Is that what upset you so badly, Cally?" Dr. Caine asked, still feeling a bit confused as to where Cally was going with her story.

"No, that is not all. I also saw Ryan. He was right here in front of my face, and I was wide awake, so you cannot tell me that it was a dream," Cally said as tears streamed down her tired, pale face.

"Oh, okay, I get it now! What you just experienced is quite normal for someone who has been through an ordeal like yours. You have been through a lot tonight. First you were in a terrible car accident, in which you had to watch your boyfriend die, and then you came straight to the hospital and went into surgery. That is a lot for anyone to take in at one time," Dr. Caine explained in a way that Cally would understand.

"So you are telling us that it is normal for Cally to see Ryan's face, even when she is awake? Well, I'm sorry, I just do not understand how is that possible," Kate said, getting a little upset with Dr. Caine's theory.

"Yes, it is called a flashback; many people who have been through a tragedy often experience a lot of them. As I said before, it is all quite normal. The only thing that I can do is give her some medicine that will help her relax, and I can refer you to a psychiatrist, so he can evaluate her and put her on a mild nerve pill to help with her anxiety," Dr. Caine said as he wrote down some things in Cally's chart.

"Oh, I get it; you do think that I'm crazy! Well, if I'm so crazy, then please explain to me how this damn ring got on my finger," Cally demanded, busting out in tears as her mind filled with so many unanswered questions.

"Just calm down, Cally. I'm sure that there is a logical explanation as to how the ring got on your finger. Maybe you should give yourself a chance to remember some things about the ring, before you go jumping to any more conclusions," Dr. Caine advised, looking at Cally's parents hoping they would speak up and agree before Cally got more upset.

"Well, what do you think, Cally? Do you need some medicine to help you rest? I'm sure that Doctor Caine has more patients to take care of, so you need to give him an answer," Bill said, interrupting before Cally or Kate could say anything else.

"I don't know. I'm feeling really confused about everything. What should I do, Mom? Should I take the medicine or not?" Cally asked, trying to get her mother's opinion on the situation.

"I think that it's a good idea. You do need to get some rest, so you will start feeling better," Kate agreed, looking at Dr. Caine, nodding her head and giving him the okay.

"Perfect. I'll order the medicine and I'll have my nurse come in and give it to you in about ten minutes. Remember what I said, Cally. Everything that you are going through is normal, so just hang in there and things will get better, I promise," Dr. Caine said before walking out of the room.

After Dr. Caine walked out, silence filled the room. Kate wanted to find out more about the ring, but she did not want to pry too much and upset Cally. Kate knew that Cally was in a fragile state, but her curiosity was running wild and she had to know more about the ring. Knowing more about the ring could answer many of the questions running through Kate's mind, and at this point, that was all that Kate wanted. Only Cally could give Kate the information she needed.

"Cally, sweetheart, are you sure that Ryan did not put the ring on your finger before the crash?" Kate asked, trying not to sound too nosy.

"Yes, Mom, I'm sure, and I really do not feel like talking about this right now. I just need some time to clear my head, so I can try to piece this puzzle together," Cally snapped as she slowly lay back down in the bed, with the help of her father.

"Okay, I'm sorry. I was only trying to help," Kate said, feeling a little offended that Cally would not open up and talk to her.

"Hello, Cally, I have come to give you some medicine so that you can get some rest. I'm just going to run it through your IV, so that I do not have to stick you with another needle," the nurse said, easing Cally's mind.

Being stuck with another needle was the last thing on Cally's mind. The only thing she could think about was the ring and how it got on her finger. Cally knew that she was not crazy and she did not need a psychiatrist. Cally had seen Ryan right in front of her face, and it was not a dream, nor was it a flashback. What Cally had seen was real; there was nothing fake about it. Ryan had kept his evil promise, to come back for her. Now the only thing to do was figure out how to send him back to the grave before he took Cally to hers.

"Alright, sweetheart, I'm all done. Now you can get some sleep. If you need anything, all you have to do is press the nurses' button on your bed and I'll be on my way," the nurse said, giving Cally a pat on her arm before dimming the lights and walking out.

Kate and Bill watched as Cally's wide-open eyes started to close as the medicine took effect. They were both glad to see their little girl getting the rest that she needed, but it still did not stop them from worrying about her. Although they were holding themselves together on the outside, they were both dying on the inside. Neither one of them wanted to bring up their feelings; they just wanted to be strong for Cally until she could regain some of her own strength. Although their family had never faced a tragedy like this one, they were not going to let it break them. They were going to stick together and fight it to the end.

"Well, I think that we should get some rest, too, while Cally is sleeping," Bill suggested with a stretch and a yawn.

"Yeah, you are right. We will be no help to Cally if we do not get some rest of our own," Kate agreed, slouching down in her chair, trying to find a comfortable position.

As Kate tossed and turned in her chair, she could hear Bill already starting to snore. Feeling a bit lonely, Kate looked at the clock on the wall. One hour had already passed, which made her wish that she had asked the doctor for something to help her sleep, too. As Kate sat in her uncomfortable chair, the only sounds in the room were Bill's snoring and the ticking of the clock. Kate desperately wanted to fall asleep, but she could not. She had so many things running through her mind that it made it impossible for that to happen. She could not stop thinking about the abuse Cally had endured while she was with Ryan, and she could not get the heart-shaped ring out of her mind, either. Kate found herself so confused about the whole situation; she just hoped that Cally would feel like talking in the morning. With different things running through her troubled mind, Kate closed her heavy eyelids and drifted off to sleep.

"Mom, are you awake?" Cally asked as she sat up in her bed, looking like a zombie.

"Yes, baby, I'm still awake. What do you need?" a very drowsy Kate asked as she tried to open her eyes wide enough to see Cally.

"It's nothing really. I was just wondering who was standing in the corner over by the sink. Is it Kyle? Did he change his mind and come back?" Cally asked, staring straight ahead at the corner, not blinking an eye.

"Kyle, is that you?" Kate asked in a trembling voice as she slowly walked over to the corner, where the black shadow stood.

As Kate got closer to the shadow, she could smell a foul odor, an odor so disgusting it would make anyone sick to his or her stomach. It smelled as if an animal had died and rotted there. Kate had no idea what the smell was, or how Kyle had slipped back inside without her hearing him, or the nurse catching him. How Kyle got back inside was not the question on Kate's mind, though. She wanted to know why he was in the corner staying hidden. It was not like Kyle to sit in one spot without talking or making himself known. Whatever the reason, Kate planned on finding out the truth.

"Kyle, sweetie, are you alright? Why are you standing in the corner? Is something wrong with you?" Kate asked, as she got closer to the foul-smelling shadow.

"No, I'm not alright. I feel and look as if I have been through hell and back, can't you tell?" a voice said, from the darkness of the corner.

"Well, maybe you should go home for the night. That way you can come back first thing in the morning," Kate said, wondering why Kyle had come back in the first place.

"I cannot go home just yet, I need to get something that I left here earlier tonight," the voice said as the shadow started moving closer to Kate.

"What exactly did you forget? Maybe I can help you find it," Kate offered as she looked around the room.

"Oh, that's okay. I know where it is. It's over there on the bed. That is what I need before I can go home," the determined voice said, as it started walking over toward Cally's bed.

"What are you talking about? There is nothing on the bed, except for Cally, and I'll not let you disturb her," Kate said in a hostile voice as she began to get irritated.

"Yes, I know, and she is exactly what I came back for. Cally needs to be with me right now. That way we can be together forever," the voice said as the tone changed to pure evil.

Confused, Kate jumped in front of the persistent shadow to stop it, but instead of stopping it, the black shadow walked right through her, as if she was not even standing there. Kate turned quickly and watched in horror and disbelief as the shadow got closer to Cally's bed. When the shadow turned around to face Kate, she could not believe her eyes. The shadow was not Kyle, it was Ryan. Chills went down Kate's spine as she stared into Ryan's horrific-looking face. Not knowing what else to do, Kate just stood there trembling.

"You cannot be here, Ryan. There is no way, you are dead!" Kate yelled out hysterically as Ryan moved closer to Cally.

"Mom, please, do not let him take me! I do not want to die!" Cally screamed as Kate tried to step in front of Ryan once more to stop him, but no matter how hard she tried, Ryan just kept moving through her.

"No, Ryan, leave her alone! Please do not take my baby, she is all I have. Please just leave her alone," Kate begged, hoping that Ryan would have pity on her and leave Cally alone, but that was not going to happen. Ryan jerked Cally off the bed, took her over to the open window, and jumped.

"No, Cally! Please do not leave me. I love you so much! Please just come back to me, I cannot live without you," Kate begged and pleaded, as she felt something grab hold of her.

"Kate, wake up. You're having another nightmare," Bill said, shaking Kate so she would wake up from her dream, before she woke Cally.

"Oh Bill, I cannot take this anymore! I keep dreaming that Ryan has come back for Cally, and every time I see his burned face, it has loose meat and skin falling off it," Kate cried out hysterically, as she put her arms around Bill for comfort.

"Listen to me, Kate. I know that you have a lot on your mind, but you are going to have to pull yourself together for the sake of Cally. She needs us more than ever right now, so we both need to stay focused, so that we can help her through this difficult time," Bill explained, hoping that Kate would pay close attention to what he was saying.

"I know that, Bill! You don't have to explain things to me. It's just that my dreams feel so real. It's as if Ryan really has come back from the dead for our little girl," Kate snapped, defending herself, letting Bill know that he was out of line with his speech.

"Look, we can finish this conversation tomorrow. Right now, we need to get some sleep while we still can," Bill said bluntly and to the point, treating Kate as if she were his child instead of his wife.

Kate felt so frustrated; she did not know why she was dreaming about Ryan coming back for Cally. Things just were not adding up, or making any sense. As Kate sat there in her uncomfortable chair, she tried to figure things out, but the more she thought, the sleepier she got. Kate did not want to go back to sleep and face another nightmare, but the steady ticking of the clock played like a lullaby, and slowly her tired eyes began to shut.

6

"Rise and shine, sweetheart, I have some good news for you. Doctor Caine came in this morning and discharged Cally, so now instead of sleeping in that chair, you can sleep in the comfort of your own bed," Bill said, waving a hot, fresh cup of coffee under Kate's nose.

"Good morning, Mom. How did you sleep last night?" Cally asked, walking out of the bathroom, looking like her old self again.

"Well, it looks like someone is feeling better, and I'm so glad to see it," Kate said in a much happier-sounding voice, as she wrapped her arms around Cally for a hug.

"Okay, Mom, just because I'm up walking around, that doesn't mean that you can squeeze me that hard when you give me a hug. I'm still kind of sore, you know," Cally joked with a big smile on her face, letting her mother know that she was not serious.

"I see that you have your sense of humor back. So how are you really feeling this morning?" Kate asked, taking a sip of her steaming hot coffee.

"Well, to be completely honest, I haven't felt this good in a long time. Sure, I'm still sore, but that should go away in a couple of days," Cally said, grabbing another bite of her blueberry muffin.

"Good for you. I knew that you would bounce back in no time. You have too much of your father in you," Kate said, feeling as if a weight had been lifted off her shoulders.

"Okay, you two, I'm ready to go whenever you are," Bill said in an anxious voice as he twirled his car keys around his finger and paced back and forth across the floor.

"Okay, Bill, just be patient. We are going as fast as we can. What is your big hurry anyway?" Kate asked, gathering her things together.

"We have to hurry up and get home, so I can finally beat Cally at a game of basketball before her arm gets better. This could be my only chance, you know," Bill joked, putting his arm around Cally.

"Dad, I hate to tell you this, but you could not beat me at a game of basketball if both my arms were broken," Cally said with a laugh.

As Cally played around with her dad, Kate was so glad to see that her little girl was feeling and looking better. All of her prayers were answered; it was truly a blessing to have her family back. Now that everything was getting back to normal, Kate hoped that the nightmares would end. With Ryan out of the picture now, the only thing Kate really wanted to see was Cally getting back to her old self again. She knew that it would not happen overnight, but no matter how long it took, Kate vowed that she would never leave her daughter's side again.

"Hey, it sounds as if someone is feeling better. I knew that you were too tough to let things get you down," Kyle said as he walked in the room and handed Cally a dozen red roses with a teddy bear balloon.

"Oh Kyle, they are so beautiful. You have really made my day. Thank you so much for everything," Cally said as she put her nose down on the roses to smell them.

"It is no problem. I'm just glad to see you up walking around. That is what makes my day better," Kyle replied, giving Cally a gorgeous smile that would make any girl weak in the knees.

As Cally stood there talking to Kyle, Kate noticed that the heart-shaped ring was gone. Although Kate was glad to see the ring gone from Cally's finger, she could not help but wonder what happened to it. She wanted to ask Cally, but she wanted to do it in a way that would not upset her, and she wanted to ask when no one else was around. Kate knew that she would get a chance to talk to Cally in private; she just had to be patient and wait for that time to come.

"Well, Kate, everyone is waiting on you now. Are you ready to go, or do you want to sleep another night in that wonderful chair you love so much?" Bill joked, knowing that Kate despised the uncomfortable chair.

"Hey, if it is okay, Kyle and I are going to go on down to the car and wait," Cally said, hoping that her parents would not object, so that she and Kyle could have some alone time.

"Well, it is alright with me, if it is okay with your mother," Bill answered as all eyes turned toward Kate, awaiting her answer.

"Of course it is alright. We will be down in a few minutes," Kate agreed with a smile on her face, still wondering about the ring, but with Cally out of the room, Kate would have the perfect opportunity to ask Bill about it.

Kate watched as Cally and Kyle walked out of the room, but just to be on the safe side, Kate looked around the corner, making sure they were both down the hallway. Kate did not want Cally to overhear her asking Bill about the ring. Kate wanted to keep things quiet for the time being, just until Cally felt more comfortable discussing the matter. At this point, it was a very touchy subject for Cally, and Kate knew that bringing up the ring so soon would only send Cally backward in her progress, not forward.

"Hey, Bill, I have something to ask you. Do you by any chance know what happened to the heart-shaped ring that was on Cally's finger?" Kate asked, in the hopes that Bill knew something about it.

"No, I sure don't. Maybe she put it in her purse or threw it away. Why do you ask?" Bill questioned as he gathered Cally's discharge papers off the dresser.

"No reason. I just noticed that it was not on her finger anymore. That is all, it is no big deal," Kate said, trying to play things off so that Bill would not question her anymore.

"Why don't you just ask Cally yourself? I'm sure that she will tell you what she did with it," Bill said curiously, wondering why Kate would not just ask Cally about it in the first place, instead of him.

"I really did not want to bother her about it; I just thought that you might have seen her put it somewhere. It is no big deal, though, so let's just drop it," Kate said, wishing that Bill would just leave things alone.

"So, are you ready to go now or what? You do know that Cally and Kyle are waiting on us, right?" Bill asked, giving Kate a reminder so she would hurry up.

"Yeah, yeah, I'm almost ready. I just have to get my purse, and I'll be ready to go," Kate answered, feeling aggravated that Bill was rushing her.

As Kate reached out to get her purse, she accidentally knocked a box of tissue off onto the floor. Feeling rushed by Bill, Kate really did not want to take the extra time to pick them up, but she did not want to leave a mess for the hospital staff, either. When Kate knelt down on the floor to pick up the tissue box, she noticed something black on the floor. Wondering what it was, Kate picked it up with a tissue and looked very closely at it. As Kate studied the mysterious black thing, she froze with fear. Kate did not want to believe her eyes, but she knew now that the black thing was not a piece of trash; it was actually a piece of burned flesh—the same piece of burned flesh that had fallen off Ryan's face the night before.

"Dear God, it was not a dream! Ryan really has come back for my little girl," Kate said aloud, as her hands started to shake with fear.

"Kate, what in this world are you talking about? You are really starting to scare me, with all of this crazy nonsense," Bill said, feeling that Cally's accident had pushed her over the edge.

"Look, Bill, this is the same burned flesh that was falling off Ryan's face last night. Now I know that Ryan really has come back from the dead—for Cally," Kate said with a nervous quiver in her voice, as she showed Bill the burned piece of flesh.

"Oh, come on, Kate, that doesn't even look like a piece of burned flesh to me. It looks more like a piece of trash that the housekeeper missed while sweeping. Now if you do not mind, I would like to end this conversation and take my little girl home, so I can take care of her. Is that alright with you?" Bill asked, shaking his head in disbelief at Kate's wild theories.

"Sure, we can forget this; we will just pretend that none of this shit ever happened. That way you can go on with your carefree life. How does that sound, Bill, would that make you happy?" Kate snapped.

"Kate, don't you think that is a bit far-fetched? You cannot possibly believe that Ryan has come back from the dead for Cally. You are a grown woman, and as such, you should start acting like it. Besides, if you tell Cally something like that, you will only scare the hell out of her. Now do you really want to do that to her, after all she has been through?" Bill asked, trying to reason with Kate before she mentioned anything to Cally.

"Look, the last thing I want to do is scare Cally or hurt her, but I think that she has a right to know that Ryan has come back for her," Kate said, walking out of the room at a fast pace.

Oh great, now I have two people to take care of. I'm the only sane parent Cally's got, Bill thought as he tried to understand Kate.

Before Bill could catch up with Kate, she had already gotten on the elevator by herself and let the door close before he could reach her. Bill knew that Kate was upset with him, but it still did not give her a reason to treat him so badly. Bill just wanted Kate to realize that she was not the only one having a hard time coping with the situation. Bill tried to look at things from Kate's point of view, but he still could not understand why she thought Ryan had come back for Cally. None of it made any sense to him, no matter how hard he tried to understand it.

"It is about damn time," Bill said aloud as the elevator finally opened for him.

Bill stepped onto the elevator and pressed the ground-floor button, as he waited for the slow, creaking door to shut. He felt the sudden drop as the elevator started going down, but before the ground button could light up, the elevator came to a complete stop, causing Bill to drop all of Cally's discharge papers. Bill felt as if his morning could not get any worse, and then, as he bent down to gather Cally's papers, the lights went out.

"Oh, wouldn't you know it, this is just my damn luck," Bill cursed aloud as the lights started to flicker.

As Bill bent down to pick up Cally's papers, he noticed what looked like a man's pair of black dress shoes right in front of his hands. Knowing that he was the only one in the elevator, Bill's mind started to wonder, as his eyes followed the black shoes up to see whom or what they belonged to. As the lights flickered back on, Bill saw the most horrifying sight he had ever seen in his life. Bill completely froze with fear as his eyes met with a set of neon-green, glowing eyes.

"Who are you, and what do you want from me?" Bill asked as his voice cracked with fear.

"I think you know what I want from you. It is your daughter, Cally. She was supposed to die with me, but she left me to die alone, and now I have come back for her, so we can be together forever," the evil voice said as the figure drew closer to Bill's face.

When the lights flickered back on, Bill could see who was in the elevator with him—it was Ryan. His face was burned to a crisp, and there was yellow pus running out of his eyes, just as Kate said. Bill did not want to believe that it was Ryan, but the facts were a little hard to ignore. Ryan looked like Satan himself. The image was far worse than any horror movie Bill had ever seen. He was so scared that he could not even breathe; it was as if the very sight of Ryan was draining him of everything.

"This cannot be happening; there is no way in hell that you are here right now. I know it is just my nerves. That is all it can be, just my nerves," Bill said, closing his eyes tightly, hoping and praying that Ryan would be gone when he opened his eyes back up. Instead of Ryan being gone, though, he was closer, so close that Bill could see the bloody flesh hanging off his devilish-looking face.

"That is right, Bill, I'm still here and I'm not going anywhere until I get what I want, and what I want is Cally," Ryan said in an evil, determined voice.

"Please, God; make him go away, just make him go away," Bill prayed aloud as his heart fell to his knees.

"Bill, what is wrong with you? Is everything alright, are you alright?" Kate asked as the elevator door opened.

"Yeah, I'm fine. It was the elevator ride. It made me a little bit nauseous is all. It is really nothing to worry about," Bill lied, trying to smooth things over so that Kate would not suspect anything.

"Well, I do not believe you for a second. Why do you have tears in your eyes? Did you see Ryan, too?" Kate asked curiously as she stared into Bill's tear-filled eyes, waiting on him to give her an honest answer.

"No, Kate, I did not see Ryan, or his ghost! I did not see anything, so can we please just drop all of this nonsense? It is getting a little old and irritating," Bill snapped, not wanting to admit to Kate right off that he had seen Ryan.

"Why are you being so hateful toward me? I have not done anything to you, except tell you the truth about what I saw," Kate said, getting angry with Bill and his sarcastic remarks.

"Look, Kate, I'm not trying to be hateful toward you. I just think that you are jumping to conclusions about this whole Ryan ordeal. I'm sure that after you get some rest, you will see that I'm right about this. Trust me, things will get better. We just have to be strong and stick together for Cally," Bill explained, feeling that his encounter with Ryan was nothing more than his nerves.

"Okay, Bill, just to save an argument, I'll do things your way for now, but if I start seeing anything out of the ordinary, I'll take matters into my own hands, whether you like it or not," Kate said firmly, getting her point across to Bill.

"Hey, you slowpokes, what is taking you so long? I'm the one who should be moving slow," Cally joked, trying to get a smile out of her mom and dad.

"Don't worry, when you get to be our age, you will turn into a slowpoke, too, I guarantee it," Bill said, putting his arm around Cally.

"So, Kyle, are you going to follow us home, or do you have other plans today?" Cally asked in the hopes that Kyle would be free so she could spend more time with him.

Cally did not know what it was, but she felt so drawn to Kyle, like a moth to a flame. She could feel her heart skip a beat every time he flashed his gorgeous smile at her; it was the best feeling she had felt in a long time. Cally was so used to being treated badly, it was kind of weird to be treated good, but hopefully she would not have to worry about that anymore, since Ryan was dead. She just hoped that Dr. Caine was right about the flashbacks. Cally prayed that there was no way for Ryan to come back from the dead.

"I do not have anything planned, as far as I know, unless my mom calls and wants me to run some errands for her. Are you sure that you feel up to having company? Because if you are not, I can always stop by tomorrow and see you. I promise that it will not hurt my feelings," Kyle said, talking to Cally, but looking more at Bill and Kate for approval on the invite.

"Do not worry, if I get tired, I'll let you know. So, is it alright if Kyle comes over for a little while?" Cally asked, giving her parents a pouty look, knowing that she always got her way when she looked like a whipped little pup.

"Well, I do not see why not, as long as your father says that it is okay," Kate agreed, staring at Bill waiting for him to give an answer, but instead of answering, he just stood there, still thinking about seeing Ryan in the elevator.

"Earth to Dad, are you going to answer me or not?" Cally asked, snapping her fingers in front of Bill's face, trying to get his attention.

"Oh, I'm sorry, sweetheart. What did you say?" Bill asked, staring at Cally with a blank look on his face.

"I asked if Kyle could come over for a little while," Cally repeated.

"Yeah sure, that will be just fine. Having a friend around just might be the medicine you need," Bill said, giving Cally a smile.

"Okay, you guys, let's not stand around here all day. Let's get going, so we can get home and relax for a little while," Kate said, after noticing the strange look on Bill's face.

Kate could almost swear that Bill had seen Ryan in the elevator, but unless Bill admitted to it, she would never be one hundred percent sure. Kate knew that Bill had a lot on his mind, too. She just wished that he would open up and talk to her. It was not like Bill to hide things from her; he was usually so open and honest. Something was definitely eating at Bill, and Kate knew that it would all come out in due time, she just had to be patient and wait for it to happen. Besides, Kate wanted Bill to see more of what she saw. That way he would know for sure that Ryan had come back, with no question in his mind.

"Okay, I'll see you at your house in a little bit," Kyle said, giving Cally a quick kiss on the cheek.

"Alright, I'll see you in a few minutes, be careful," Cally replied with a smile that went from ear to ear, as she felt a warm feeling go all over her body.

Cally could not help it. She knew for sure now that she was falling for Kyle in a big way, but she did not want to be the first one to bring it up. She wanted to see how Kyle felt about her before she said anything to him. That way she would know for sure where she stood with him. Cally did not want to jeopardize her friendship with Kyle; she valued it too much to do that. Besides Cally had been through one tragedy already, and she did not know if her heart could stand another one.

"Bill, would you like for me to drive, so you can catch a catnap on the way home?" Kate asked after seeing Bill try to open the car door with the house key.

"You know, that is probably not a bad idea. I would not want to get pulled over for a traffic violation, that's for sure," Bill said, rubbing his face as he became more and more frustrated at himself.

"Okay, guys, put on your seat belts before we get out of the parking lot," Kate said as she started the car and put it in DRIVE.

As Cally reached for her seat belt, she got a strange feeling, as if something bad was going to happen. She could feel her stomach tie in knots as her mother started to pull out of the hospital parking lot. It was the same feeling she got right before she and Ryan had crashed. Cally wondered if it was a warning, or just her nerves. No matter which one it was, Cally was scared to death. She could feel her heart trying to beat out of her chest. She knew that she had to speak up and say something before her mother got on the highway, causing her to have a panic attack, or worse.

"Mom, would it be okay if we just sit here for a few minutes?" Cally asked in a soft voice, as her heart started to pound harder with extreme fear.

"We really should not waste any more time. Remember, Kyle is going to meet us back at the house and we do not want to be late, or he will start to worry," Kate said as she continued to drive through the parking lot, not even thinking about the terrible wreck Cally had experienced the day before.

"Please, Mom, would you just stop the damn car for a second?" Cally screamed, as she started having flashbacks of the car wreck that almost took her life.

"Oh baby, I'm so sorry. I don't know what I was thinking. We can sit here as long as you want to," Kate said after realizing what was wrong with Cally.

"Yeah, we can sit here all night if you want to. Just take your time and when you get ready, you can let us know," Bill agreed, trying to comfort Cally with his words.

Bill and Kate watched with heartache and pain as a stream of tears rolled down Cally's frightened pale face. It was horrible. They hated seeing Cally go through so much hell; it was the worst thing in the world for any parent to have to watch, they both felt so helpless. They were both speechless; neither one of them could find the right words to make Cally feel better. All they could really do was give her unconditional love and be there for her when she needed them, no matter what—even if it meant staying in the hospital parking lot until she got ready to go.

"Bill, would you mind calling Kyle to let him know that we are going to be a little late getting home?" Kate asked, handing Bill her cell phone.

"Sure, I'll give him a call. I need to stretch my legs anyway," Bill answered, getting out of the car and shutting the door.

"What is wrong with me, Mom? When will all of this be over, so I can get back to my old self again?" Cally cried, as she wiped the tears from her face.

"Oh baby, I wish that I could make everything go away for you, but I can't. Truthfully, it's going to take some time for you to heal, both mentally and physically. You have been through a lot and you need to take things one day at a time." Kate advised as she reached over the seat to hold Cally's shaking hand.

"Thanks for being there for me, Mom. You don't know how much it means to me. I don't know what I would do without you," Cally said, squeezing her mom's hand and giving her a big smile.

Kate could feel her heart breaking into a million little fragments all over again, as she looked into Cally's innocent, baby blue eyes. It was something that no mother should ever have to face. Kate had always tried to protect her daughter, but this time she had failed her. She had let Cally fall into harm's way. Suddenly, Kate started to feel that guilt all over again. It was a feeling that she would live with the rest of her life. No matter what, Kate would always hold herself responsible for Cally's accident.

"Okay, I talked to Kyle and told him that we would be a little late. He said that he would wait for us in the driveway," Bill explained as he got back into the car.

Cally sat quietly in the back, taking deep breaths every few seconds, as a million thoughts ran through her troubled mind. She knew that she could not go on living this way; she had to pull herself together, so that she could overcome this tragedy and move on with her life. Things were going to get better; all she had to do was turn the negative things into positive things. Cally knew that she could do this; she was not the type of person to give up on something. Cally was determined to follow this tragedy to the end, even if it killed her.

"Okay, I'm ready to go now. I think that I'm going to be alright. No, I take that back. I know that I'm going to be alright," Cally said with a new outlook on things, as she put on her seat belt. "Are you sure that you do not need some more time, because if you do, we do not mind waiting. We just want you to feel comfortable," Bill said, offering Cally more time to prepare herself for the car ride home.

"I'm sure. I have never been more sure about anything in my life. This is going to be the first step to my recovery and I have to take it," Cally said, feeling a little more comfortable about her decision.

"I'm so proud of you, Cally. You are the bravest person I know, and I'm not just saying that. You really inspire me by the way you are handling things. For you to face your fears head-on takes courage," Kate said, feeling moved by Cally's decision to continue the journey home.

"I'm proud of you, too, sweetheart. You have a good head on your shoulders, and it shows in everything you do," Bill agreed, giving Cally an extra boost of confidence.

Kate nervously put the car in DRIVE with her trembling hand and adjusted the mirrors so that she could see well. She could not help but feel as if she were taking driver's education all over again, only this time the instructor was her teenage daughter. Kate did not want to mess up in any way, and she knew that the slightest wrong move would upset Cally and send her into another panic. She wanted to take every precaution so that would not happen, even if it meant having to pull over on the way home. Kate was willing to do anything that would help her daughter feel more at ease.

"How are you doing back there? Is everything okay?" Kate asked as she looked back at Cally through her rearview mirror.

"Yeah, I'm doing good, except for my arm throbbing," Cally answered, laying her head back on the headrest and closing her eyes.

"Well, we will stop by the drugstore and get your prescription filled. That way when we get home, you can take one of your pain pills and lie down for a little while," Kate said, wishing deep down inside that she could take Cally's pain away.

"I would rather take something that is not going to knock me out. That way I can spend some time with Kyle before he has to go home," Cally said, smiling at the very thought of seeing Kyle.

Although Cally liked Kyle a lot, she still could not help but feel saddened at the thought of Ryan's death. Sure, she was planning to end their relationship, but breaking up and dying were two different things. Cally would not wish death on her worst enemy, especially a gruesome death like Ryan's. No one deserved to die like that, no matter what they had done wrong. Watching Ryan burn to death was the most horrible and sad thing Cally had ever seen before. The images of that night would haunt Cally for the rest of her life. There was no way that she could forget something like that, no way in hell.

"You really like Kyle, don't you? I can see it in the way you look at him," Kate said, interrupting the silence and the sound of Bill snoring.

"Of course I like him. He is my best friend, and he did save my life. I could not ask for a better friend," Cally said, raising her head up, looking back at her mother through the rearview mirror.

"Are you sure that you only think of him as a friend and nothing more?" Kate asked with a smile on her face, as she saw a look of shock go across Cally's face.

"Oh, come on, Cally, you can tell me, I'm your mother. I promise that your secret is safe with me. I'll not breathe a word of it to anyone," Kate said with a giggle as she locked eyes with Cally in the mirror.

"Well, I have been thinking a lot of him here lately. Even when Ryan was still alive, I thought about how much different things could have been if I had just gone out with Kyle instead of Ryan," Cally confessed, losing herself in deep thoughts.

"I knew it, bitch! You are nothing but a damn whore and you need to die," Kate said, letting go of the steering wheel and turning her whole body around toward Cally, trying to grab her over the seat.

"Mom, what are you doing? Please stop! You are scaring me really bad," Cally begged and pleaded as her mother's skin started to bubble and her eyes turned green.

"Shut up, Cally, your begging will not help you this time. I told you that I would come back for you," Kate said, sinking her long, bloody fingernails into Cally's throat, causing her to loose air.

"Mom, please stop, you are hurting me!" Cally gasped, putting her feet on the back of Kate's seat and kicking it with what little strength she had left, causing Kate to fly forward against the steering wheel.

"What in the hell are you doing, Cally? Do you want to get us all killed?" Bill said, quickly pushing Cally's feet off of Kate's seat.

"Cally, wake up, baby. You are having another nightmare!" Kate yelled out to Cally, as she quickly pulled over to the side of the road.

"I'm sorry, I did not mean to! Please forgive me," Cally said, snapping back to reality, realizing that it was only a dream.

"It is okay, Cally. You did not do anything wrong. You just scared us a little bit, that is all," Kate replied, as she tried to hold and comfort Cally.

"I wish that I would have been killed in that wreck. That way you would not have to worry about me having nightmares and going crazy. I would be better off dead, that way Ryan could not haunt me," Cally cried out, pulling away from her mother's arms.

"Do not say that, Cally. You are my whole world and I would do anything and everything for you. We can overcome this together, we just have to be strong and give things a little more time," Kate said, pulling Cally back to her, as she started to cry herself.

"I'm sorry that I yelled at you, Cally. You just caught me off guard and scared the hell out of me. Please forgive me, I truly am sorry," Bill apologized after seeing how upset Cally was.

"It is not your fault, Dad. You did not do anything wrong. I'm the one who messed up, and it almost killed us," Cally said, trying to catch her breath.

"That is it. I'm taking you back to the hospital, so they can check you out again and give you something to help you relax," Kate said, turning back around to the front of the car.

"No, Mom, I do not want to go back. They will think that I'm crazy and lock me up. I just want to go home and rest. I'll be just fine, I promise. It was only a bad dream," Cally cried out, grabbing her mother by the shoulder with her good arm, trying to stop her from taking her back.

Kate was so scared and confused, she did not know what to say or how to handle the situation. The only thing Kate wanted to do was help her little girl, but she could not even do that, it was hopeless. Reaching the end of her short, thin rope, Kate paused for a second and looked to Bill for some much-needed advice. Waiting on him to give his opinion, Kate was shocked to see Bill just sitting there, staring out of his window, as if he had other things on his mind. Kate could not take it anymore. She felt as if she were going to explode with frustration and anger.

"Bill, would you like to help me out with this, or are you going to stay silent throughout the whole ordeal?" Kate asked, glaring toward Bill as her patience wore thin with his silence.

"Well, if you want my honest opinion, I'll give it to you. I do not think that Cally needs to go back to the hospital; I think that she will be just fine at home with us. After all, if you will remember, she had nightmares at the hospital, too. I think that if we just give things some time, they will get better on their own," Bill said, giving his honest, but stern input, pointing out that the hospital would be no different than home.

"Yeah, I agree you do make a really good point. Plus I think that I can do more for her at home than those doctors and nurses can," Kate agreed, coming to her senses after she had a chance to calm down and think about things from a different point of view.

"Okay, now that we have settled that, I think that we should continue the ride home before Kyle comes looking for us. What do you say, Cally, are you ready to try this one more time?" Bill asked, making sure Cally was comfortable with the decision to continue the ride home.

"Okay, I'm ready. I'll just crack my window a little bit, so that I can get some fresh air. Maybe it will help wake me up, that way I'll not drift back off to sleep," Cally said, rolling down her window and blinking her eyes continuously, trying to fight off the drowsiness that was quickly taking over her body.

"Alright, sweetheart, only two more miles to go, and we will be home. Then you can lie down while I fix you some dinner and your father can go back out later to pick up your medicine. Does that sound alright to you?" Kate asked, not only trying to make Cally feel better, but keep her awake, too.

"Thanks, Mom, that sounds really good. I think that being in the comforts of my own home will make me feel better, too," Cally said as her heart started to slow back down to its original pace.

7

"Now that is what I call a devoted friend. He waited out in the hot sun all this time, just to see you. That should make you feel really good, Cally," Bill said, complimenting Kyle as they pulled into their driveway and saw Kyle waiting outside his truck in the blistering heat.

Before Kate could even cut off the engine, Kyle rushed over to help Cally out of the car. He knew that Bill and Kate had their hands full with everything else, and he wanted to help them out as much as he could, so that they could get a small break in between. Kyle thought a lot of Bill and Kate. They had always been there for him, and he wanted to return the favor by doing something kind for them. Besides, Kyle loved spending time with Cally, and now that Ryan was out of the picture, he could finally get some one-on-one time with Cally whenever he wanted to.

"Thanks for waiting. I'm sorry that it took so long for us to get here. As usual, it was my entire fault," Cally said, apologizing and putting the blame on herself.

"Oh, don't be sorry, I rather enjoyed myself. I even got to take a little cat-nap, until the squirrels woke me up by dropping acorns on my head," Kyle joked as he gave Cally a wink and another gorgeous smile.

When Cally got out of the car, she froze as she glanced over at the spot where she and Ryan had had their pictures taken. She could not help but feel saddened and troubled by Ryan's death. It was slowly eating away at her, and no matter how hard she tried, she still could not shake the feeling. She could still picture Ryan, trapped under the burning car as the flames slowly cooked him alive. Cally could not imagine the pain that Ryan must have felt that tragic night. It was the most horrible thing she ever had to witness, and the worst thing about it was, Ryan had done it to himself. There was no one else to blame but him.

"Are you alright, Cally? Do you need me to carry you inside?" Bill asked, looking at Cally's weak, trembling body as she stood there staring off into the distance.

"No, I'll be fine. I just had to take a rest break before climbing the steps. That is all, but thanks for asking," Cally answered, as she started slowly walking toward the front door.

As Kate unlocked the front door and waited on Kyle to help Cally up the steps, she could see that Cally had something else bothering her besides the nightmares. Kate could not pinpoint it, but she intended on having a conversation with Cally as soon as she felt up to it. Kate had to find out as much as she could, that way she could better help Cally and her problems. It was going to be a long, rough road, but Kate was willing to do whatever it took to get Cally's life back together again.

"Would you like to go lie down in your bedroom while I get dinner ready? I'll send your father in every few minutes to check on you," Kate offered, looking at Cally's tired, bloodshot eyes.

"No, I would rather just crash here on the sofa, if it's alright with you," Cally said, gazing around the room, still smelling the lingering scent of Ryan's cologne from the day before.

"That's fine with me. I just want you to be comfortable, so that you can get the rest you need," Kate said as she fluffed the pillows on the sofa for Cally.

"Okay, sweetheart, I'm going to go get started in the kitchen while you relax and talk to Kyle. Do you need anything before I go?" Kate asked, unfolding a blanket for Cally.

"No thanks, I'm good for right now. If I need anything, I'll let you know." Cally said, snatching the remote off the table, before lying back on the sofa.

"Yeah, I think I'll go and help your mother in the kitchen. After all, I'm the real chef around here," Bill joked, excusing himself so that Cally could talk to Kyle in private.

After Bill and Kate walked out of the room, there was another awkward silence, just like the one at the hospital. Neither Cally nor Kyle knew what to say to break the silence. All they could do was sit there and stare at one another. After about five minutes of silence, Cally let out a sigh as she lay on the sofa, fidgeting with her arm cast as if she were bored. This made Kyle think she was getting tired and did not want him to stay any longer than he already had. He understood; Cally did need her rest if she was going to get any better.

"Are you getting tired? Because if you are, I can go so that you can get some rest and I'll call you tomorrow," Kyle said, thinking that Cally was getting tired of his company.

"Relax, Kyle, I'm not even close to being tired. I just have a lot on my mind right now and it is starting to get on my nerves," Cally hinted, hoping that Kyle would catch on and ask her what she had on her mind.

"Well, if you ever feel like talking, you know that I'll be right here, day or night, to listen," Kyle offered, not wanting to sound too pushy or nosy.

"I'm afraid that if I tell you what is on my mind, you will just think that I'm crazy, and I do not want anyone thinking that about me, because I'm far from being crazy. I know what I'm seeing and feeling is real. There is no question about it," Cally said with a serious look on her face, as she looked through to the kitchen, making sure that her parents were not close enough to hear what she was going to say.

Cally loved her parents with all of her heart and soul, and she knew that she could talk to them. They had always told her that she could tell them anything, but Cally felt more comfortable talking to Kyle about what was bothering her. She did not think that her parents would be as understanding as Kyle would, and she really did not want to bother them any more than she already had. Cally had put her parents through hell and back with her lies and actions; now it was time for Cally to give them a break from her screwed-up life and take responsibility for herself.

"Okay, I'll tell you, but you have to promise that you will not breathe a word to anyone, not even my parents, no matter how crazy it sounds. Do you promise? Do I have your word on this?" Cally asked, looking deep into Kyle's brown eyes, making sure she could trust him.

"Alright, Cally, just calm down. I promise you that I'll not tell anyone anything," Kyle said, hoping that he would not live to regret his promise.

"Alright, listen up, because I cannot talk loud and I don't want my parents to hear any of this," Cally whispered as she moved closer to Kyle, so that her parents would not overhear them talking.

Still staring into Kyle's eyes, Cally took a few deep breaths and paused for a second, questioning whether she could Kyle trust with her painful secret. Although they had been friends since kindergarten, she was still a bit on the skeptical side about trusting him with something so personal, but she needed to talk to someone and since Kyle was always there to listen, that made him the perfect candidate. Cally just did not want Kyle to think that she was crazy; she could not handle one more person thinking that she was, especially her best friend, the friend she was falling head over heels for!

"It is okay, Cally. I promise that you can trust me. You know that I would never do anything to hurt you, or jeopardize our friendship," Kyle said, reassuring Cally that she could trust him with anything she had to say.

"Okay, here goes. After the accident, Ryan was pinned under the car, and while I was trying to help him out, he grabbed my hand and would not let me go. He said that he wanted us to die together. After a few minutes of him holding me, I managed to get loose and push myself away from the car. When I got to a safe place away from him, he started begging me to save him again, but before I could make it to him, the car was engulfed in flames, catching him on fire. I had to sit there and watch Ryan burn to death, and before he died, he swore that he would come back for me—and I truly believe that he has done just that," Cally said as her troubled eyes filled with tears.

"I'm so sorry. I had no idea that you had to go through all that. No wonder you are having nightmares," Kyle said, taking Cally by her hand and wishing there was something he could say or do to make Cally feel better.

"That is just it, Kyle. I was not sleeping in the hospital when I saw him. I was wide awake and everything felt so real. It was almost as if Ryan were right there in front of my face. He was so close to me that I could smell his burned flesh and see the loose meat falling off his face," Cally cried, wiping tears from her eyes as her hands started to shake with fear.

"Look, Cally, I'm sure that there is a logical explanation to all of this. Maybe it is just your nerves; after all, you have been through a lot. I think that you should just give things some time before you go jumping to any conclusions," Kyle said, laying out all possibilities for Cally.

"Okay, Kyle, let's say that you are right about all of this. It still doesn't explain how the ring got on my finger, now does it?" Cally asked putting up more questions that Kyle did not have answers to.

"I really do not know. Maybe Ryan slipped the ring on your finger while he was trying to hold you there with him. I truly believe that there is an answer for everything," Kyle argued, still trying to state the obvious facts.

Cally lay back on the sofa in complete silence, as her heart dropped to the bottom of her stomach. She started to wonder if she really was going crazy. No one, not even her best friend, believed her, and that is what hurt the most. It was as if she were stuck inside one big never-ending nightmare. It was evident to Cally now that unless she had real evidence of Ryan's return, no one was going to believe a word she said. It was time for Cally to come up with a plan, a plan that would prove her sanity, not only to others, but to herself, as well.

"I hope that you two are hungry, because I have made enough food to feed an army," Kate said, walking into the living room, carrying a tray with two overfilled plates of spaghetti on it.

"Well, it sure smells good and looks great," Kyle said, complimenting Kate on her cooking.

"Let's just hope that it taste as good as it smells, because if it doesn't, we are in trouble," Bill joked, following Kate with a tray full of drinks.

"Very funny, Bill. Just remember, you helped make it, so if it tastes bad, we will just blame it on you," Kate replied with a smile as she set the tray of food down on the table in front of Cally and Kyle.

"Mom, I do not mean to be rude, but my arm is starting to throb again and I think that I should go rest in my own bed," Cally said, trying to excuse herself out of an awkward situation.

"Oh, do not worry, sweetheart. You are not being rude at all. We all understand that you need your rest," Kate replied, giving Cally a kiss on the head.

"Do you need me to help you get up?" Kyle asked, rising from his seat.

"I think that I can manage by myself. After all, I need to get used to doing things on my own," Cally said with a lonesome feeling, knowing that she was, in fact, on her own.

"Okay, I hope that you get to feeling better. Just give me a call when you get up tomorrow," Kyle said, thinking that Cally was upset with him for something that he had said, or did not say.

"That sounds good. I'll talk to you sometime tomorrow," Cally replied without so much as a look as she went upstairs.

"Alright, you two, eat your spaghetti before it gets cold. I'm going to get Cally something for her pain, and I'll be right back," Kate said, getting Cally's glass of water off the tray.

With Cally in her bedroom, Kyle started to feel a little uncomfortable again, especially eating dinner alone with her parents. It was not as if he disliked Bill and Kate, because he really thought the world of them both. He just figured that they might want some privacy, so they could discuss things. Bill and Kate had been so nice, though, that Kyle did not just want to up and leave without having a good enough reason. The last thing Kyle wanted was for Bill and Kate to think that he felt uncomfortable around them. They had been through enough, and for him to just up and leave with no good excuse would be the icing on the cake.

"Would you excuse me for a second please? I think that this is my mother texting me," Kyle said, reaching into his pocket for his cell phone and pretending to read a text.

"Sure, no problem. Take your time," Bill replied, taking another bite of his spaghetti.

"Just my luck, that was my mother texting me. She asked if I could come home and help her out with a few things, so as much as I hate to, I guess I should be heading home now," Kyle lied, hoping that his story was believable.

"Ah, that is too bad. Are you sure that you cannot stay for a few minutes and eat some of your spaghetti? It tastes really good," Bill said, wiping spaghetti sauce from his chin.

"Oh, I wish that I could stay and eat, but if I'm late getting home, my mom will just start to worry, and then I'll be in a world of trouble," Kyle answered, telling yet another lie to cover up the first one.

"I tell you what, wait right here just a second, and I'll go get you a bowl, so you can take your spaghetti with you," Bill said, getting up from his unfinished plate.

Kyle stood there in the quiet living room, fidgeting with his phone, as Bill disappeared into the kitchen. He felt so bad about lying that it made him sick to his stomach. Kyle was not big on lying—he had been raised better than that—but at this point, Kyle felt as if it was the only thing left to do. Bill and Kate were such nice people, though, they would bend over backward to help anyone out. That is what made Kyle feel so bad, but Kyle knew that he would only feel out of place if he stayed. Besides, the lie was already in motion, now the only thing left to do, was to carry it out and go home for the night.

"Here we go, Kyle, a nice big bowl of spaghetti to take home with you. I hope that you enjoy it," Bill said, handing Kyle a big bowl of spaghetti with a piece of garlic bread on top.

"Oh, do not worry about that. I know that I'll enjoy it, just by the way it smells," Kyle said, complimenting Bill on his cooking as he took the bowl out of his hands.

"And just where do you think that you are running off to, without eating?" Kate asked, walking down the stairs, catching Kyle moving toward the front door.

"Oh, my mom sent me a text and asked if I could help her out with a few things and I told her I would," Kyle said, as the lies started to choke him up.

"Well, I'll let you slide this time, but next time, you will have no other choice but to stay and eat," Kate joked with a smile on her face.

"That sounds good to me. I'll see you guys later and thanks again for everything," Kyle agreed, giving Bill and Kate a quick wave before walking out the door.

"He is such a sweet, well-mannered young man, and I absolutely love the way he listens to his mother," Kate said, sitting down on the sofa.

"Yeah, I would have to agree with you on that one. He is an exceptional young man, and I feel blessed to have him in our lives—and Cally's—too. Speaking of Cally, how is she feeling?" Bill asked with his mouth slightly full, as he helped himself to the last piece of garlic bread.

"Well, she is doing a little bit better than what she was. Hopefully that pain medicine will help her arm so she can get some sleep tonight. Which reminds me, we need to get her script filled tomorrow, since we could not do it today," Kate said, still seeing the scary image of Ryan's burned face in her mind.

No sooner than Kate stopped talking, a silence filled the room. Kate had so many things that she wanted to talk to Bill about, but she knew that he would only get upset if she mentioned Ryan's name. Just as she was secretly holding things back in her mind, Bill was doing the exact same thing. Although Bill blamed seeing Ryan's evil spirit on nerves and lack of sleep, he still could not stop thinking about it. It was the most haunting and horrifying thing he had ever seen in his whole life. Everything had seemed so real, though, it was somewhat hard to blame it all on nerves and lack of sleep completely. Bill knew that there was something more to what he had seen, and he could not, nor would not rest until he found out what it was.

"Well, how was dinner? Did you get enough to eat, or would you like for me to fix you another plate?" Kate asked, interrupting the silence as she tried to make small talk.

"No, thank you. I'm stuffed. I could not possibly eat another bite," Bill answered as he slouched down in his seat, letting out a sigh.

As Bill and Kate were talking, Cally was standing at the bottom of the stairs eavesdropping on their conversation. Cally could not help but feel as if her parents thought that she was crazy, but Cally knew that she was not crazy and she knew that she was not having flashbacks. Cally knew that what she was hearing and seeing was real. Ryan had kept his promise; he had most definitely come back from the dead for her, and now Cally's biggest problem was figuring out how to stop him. Hearing her parent's conversation come to an end, Cally tiptoed back up the stairs, so that they would not hear her.

As Cally lay awake in her bed gathering her many thoughts, she heard her bedroom door creak open. Not wanting her mother to know that she was awake, Cally just kept her head turned and stayed perfectly still, until she heard her bedroom door shut. Cally did want to talk to her mother, but she wanted to wait until she had a few things figured out for herself. That way she could better explain the things that had been happening. As Cally's thoughts cluttered her mind, she could feel her eyes starting to get heavy, but no sooner than she had closed her eyes, the phone rang. Cally could hear her mother talking to someone, but she could not make out what they were saying. Curious to find out who was on the phone, Cally slowly picked up the receiver in her bedroom so she could listen in. Cally covered the mouthpiece with her hand as she listened quietly. It did not take any time for Cally to pick up on the voice; it was Ryan's mother. Cally could not make out everything that was being said, because Ms. Jones was crying hysterically, but she could hear her mother trying to comfort Ms. Jones. The more Cally listened, the sadder she became. She felt so bad for Ryan's mother. Cally tried to think of ways to help her cope with the loss of her son, but Cally knew that no one could take the pain away, no matter what they said or did. Just the thought of her heartache brought tears to Cally's eyes; it was the worst thing to see anyone have to endure.

"Mom, could you please come in here for a second?" Cally asked when she heard her mother walk back by her bedroom door.

"Oh, I'm sorry, sweetheart. Did the phone wake you?" Kate asked, walking into Cally's bedroom and turning on the light.

"Oh, that is okay, I was starting to toss and turn anyways. So, who was that on the phone?" Cally asked curiously, pretending not to know anything.

Kate paused for a second, as she tried to decide whether or not she should tell Cally the truth about who was on the phone. She did not want to upset Cally, but she knew that she could not hide things from her any longer. Cally had every right to know who was on the phone; Kate just wanted to find the right words to tell her. Kate knew that Cally was in a critical state, and the last thing she wanted to do was set her back any. Kate wanted to see Cally make progress, not lose it. By telling Cally about Ryan's funeral made Kate fear for her daughter's well-being, but it was going to come out sooner or later, and Kate figured that now was just as good time as any to talk to her about things.

"Well, that was Ryan's mother on the phone. She just called to let us know when his funeral was going to be held," Kate answered, getting choked up at the thought of Ms. Jones having to bury her only child.

"So, when is it going to be, and where is it being held at?" Cally asked, getting a sick feeling in the pit of her stomach just thinking of the word *funeral*.

"It will be tomorrow at Corner Baptist Church. They will receive family and friends from one o'clock till three, and after that they will proceed with the funeral in the church cemetery," Kate said, sitting on the bed beside Cally, holding her hand as tears streamed down her face.

"I still cannot believe that all of this has happened. It just doesn't seem real. It feels as if I'm in one big nightmare that I cannot wake up from," Cally cried, laying her head down on Kate's shoulder as a feeling of guilt started to eat away at her, making her feel as if Ryan's death was her fault.

"Oh Cally, I wish that this was a bad dream. I hate seeing you like this. It breaks my heart to see you going through so much pain. If I could go back in time and change things, I would, but life doesn't work that way. Sometimes life can be so damn unfair, but we cannot stop living. We have to move on with our lives no matter how bad it hurts, but I do promise you, things will get better. You just have to give it some time," Kate explained, holding Cally close, letting her know that time would heal everything.

Cally wanted to tell her mother about everything that had happened after the accident. She hated to lie and keep things from her mother, but she felt as if she did not have any other choice in the matter. Cally did not know for sure if her mother would even believe her, and besides, she just assumed that some things were left better unsaid. That was all that Cally wanted, for things to get better. She just hoped that she was doing the right thing by keeping things quiet for the time being.

"Cally, I have to ask you something, and I want you to be truthful with me. What happened to the heart-shaped ring that was on your finger yesterday?" Kate asked with a concerned look on her face.

"Well, I put it in my purse for now, but I plan on getting rid of it for good tomorrow," Cally said nervously as a lump came to her throat at the very thought of her plan.

"I do not understand, Cally. Could you be a little more specific to what you are talking about?" Kate asked, looking down at Cally with a confused, but serious look on her face.

"Okay, Mom, I'll tell you, but please keep in mind that this is the only way for me to get rid of the ring. Trust me, if there was any other way, I would do it, but there is not, so just promise me that you will not try to stop me," Cally said, waiting on her mother to agree to the terms.

"Oh no, young lady, you are not going to get the upper hand on me. I have to know what you are planning to do before I can make any kind of promise, so you had better start explaining," Kate demanded in a strict tone, crossing her arms as she waited on Cally to explain.

Cally took a deep breath, wishing that she had never said anything to her mother about the ring. She knew that her mother had a tendency to make a mountain out of a molehill. What seemed harmless to Cally would be a huge deal for her mother, and that was what worried Cally the most. She did not want her mother to stand in the way of her plan. Cally knew that if she wanted to move on with her life, she had to follow through with things, no matter how bad it bothered or scared her. Cally could not let anything stop her from freeing herself from Ryan.

"Okay, Mom, my plan is to put the ring inside of Ryan's casket when no one is looking. That way the ring will be buried with him, and I'll not have the constant reminder eating away at me every single day," Cally said, waiting on her mother to object to the idea.

"Well, normally I would say no, but I think that you are right. You do need to get rid of that ring, once and for all. Maybe after the ring is gone, your bad dreams will stop, too," Kate agreed without any hesitation whatsoever.

Cally was stunned that her mother actually agreed with her on something. It almost felt too good to be true, but true or not, Cally was going to carry out her plan, even if her mother had disagreed. It would have made no difference to her. Once Cally got her mind set on something, she was going to do it or die. Ryan had ruined her life enough when he was alive, and Cally would be damned if she was going to let him do it when he was dead. There was no way in hell that she was going to let that happen. Something had to give, and it was not going to be Cally.

"So, Mom, in your honest opinion, do you think that my plan will work?" Cally asked, looking for more reassurance.

"You will not know unless you try, and personally, I think it is worth a shot," Kate said, boosting Cally's spirits.

"Thank you for everything, Mom. You do not know what it means to me," Cally said as she started to get tears in her eyes again.

"It is no problem, Cally. You are my little girl, and I'll always be there for you, so do not ever forget that. Now, I'm going to let you get some much-needed rest. I'll see you in the morning," Kate said, bending down to give Cally a kiss on the cheek.

"That sounds like a good idea for everyone, including me," Bill said, walking into Cally's bedroom.

"Oh, what is wrong, Dad? Are you getting tired already?" Cally joked with a smile on her face.

"You know it, that is why your mother and I are going to leave you alone now, so you, too, can get some sleep. But if you need anything, no matter what time it is, all you have to do is let us know," Bill said, giving Cally a kiss on her head.

"Would you like for me to tuck you in before I go to bed?" Kate asked, looking down at Cally.

"No, that is alright. I'm pretty comfortable the way I'm. Good night, Mom. I love you," Cally said, rolling over to her side.

"Good night, sweetheart. I love you, too. Pleasant dreams," Kate said as she slowly closed Cally's bedroom door.

8

As Cally moved around in her bed, trying to get comfortable, she heard her parents' bedroom door shut. For some reason, the pitch-black darkness in her room seemed to bother her greatly. She got an odd feeling that someone was in the room with her. Scared of what she would hear or see, Cally pulled the blanket over the top of her head, as if it were some kind of protective shield. Only ten minutes had passed, but it seemed like an eternity for Cally. She could feel herself starting to smother underneath the heavy blanket as she lay there with it pulled tightly over her head. Cally did not want to stick her head out from under the covers, but she really did not have much of a choice in the situation. She had to get a breath of fresh air some way.

"Okay, on the count of three, I'll stick my head out long enough to take a few good breaths, and then I'll come back under before I have a chance to get spooked again," Cally said to herself, as her heart started to pound with fear.

When Cally got to three, she started to slowly pull the blanket off her head. As Cally pulled the blanket down, uncovering her face, she could feel the cool air rushing toward her. The cool, crisp air felt so good brushing against her hot, sweaty face. It was the best feeling she had felt in a long time. Still feeling paranoid, Cally kept her eyes shut tightly, as her body got the relief it needed. Cally did not know why she was so scared; it was a feeling that she could not explain. It was as if her sixth sense was trying to tell her something, but she just did not know what it was.

This is much better, Cally thought as she slowly and bravely stuck her head out farther and inhaled more of the cool air.

"Wait a minute, what in the hell am I doing? I have got to stop acting like a scared little girl who thinks that there are monsters under the bed," Cally said to herself as she opened her eyes and pulled the covers down the rest of the way.

This is not so bad, Cally thought as she felt a much colder breeze hit her hot, flushed skin.

"That is odd. I do not remember it being this cold before," Cally said as she scanned the pitch-black room, looking for anything out of the ordinary.

As Cally lay in the bed with her eyes wide open and her heart pounding, she could hear all kinds of creaks and pops in the house. It was almost as if the house had a voice of its own. Cally tried to ignore the sounds, but it was hopeless. The more she tried to ignore them, the louder they seemed to get. Every time the house creaked, it seemed to echo throughout the whole house, making Cally cringe at the very sound of it. Cally knew that she had to be brave, but with everything that had happened, it was hard to overcome her fears.

"Oh, this is just great, now I have to go pee. Could my night get any worse?" Cally asked herself, as the urgency to pee got worse.

Cally slowly pushed herself up in the bed with her good arm, as she continued to look around the cold, dark, room. Feeling more paranoid than ever, Cally quickly swung her legs over the side of the bed and put her feet on the ice-cold floor. No sooner than Cally's feet hit the floor, she could feel an enormous draft coming from under her bed; it was as if someone had turned a fan on. There was no doubt in Cally's mind that the temperature in the room had dropped dramatically. Instead of the room being a comfortable cool, it suddenly felt like a giant freezer.

"Whoa, I'll probably die of hypothermia before I make it to the bathroom," Cally said as the ice-cold floor chilled her to the bone.

Cally walked quickly to the bathroom and sat down on the toilet. While Cally sat there, she noticed that the bathroom was not nearly as cold as her bedroom was. Cally could not help but wonder why there was so much difference in the temperatures of the two rooms, unless her bedroom window was open. Cally tried to think of a logical explanation, as she pulled up her pajamas and stared into her bedroom from the doorway. Cally felt so confused and freaked out that she almost decided to just sleep on the bathroom floor, but she knew that the hard floor would be uncomfortable for her broken arm, and she most definitely did not want to be up all night with her arm throbbing. Knowing that she did not have any other choice, Cally slowly walked back to her bed, squinting her eyes at both of the windows to see if they were open. As Cally got a little closer she noticed that both windows were shut. With her heart pounding and her legs shaking, Cally took a quick dive into her bed, not caring if she hit her broken arm or not. Cally was only worried about one thing, and that was making it to her bed. Breathing a sigh of relief, Cally pulled the blanket over her head.

"Well, so much for being brave and fearless. I guess that I'll always be a scared-to-death little kid," Cally said quietly to herself, as she made a slight opening in the blanket just big enough to stick her nose out of.

Cally desperately wanted to go to sleep, but she had too many things running through her mind, and they were bothering her more than her broken arm was. Cally felt as if she were trying to put a puzzle together that had missing pieces. No matter how hard she tried to sort through her problems, she just could not do it. It was like trying to find a needle in a haystack—virtually impossible. As Cally lay there in bed with her head still covered, she heard what sounded like a voice. Startled and scared, Cally just lay there holding her breath, trying not to make a sound.

"Oh God, please let this be my imagination playing tricks on me," Cally prayed as her heart started to pound again with fear.

"Cally, come over here and let me in the window before I fall," the voice said, getting much louder and clearer.

"Who is there, and what do you want?" Cally asked, raising the blanket up enough to get a good look at both of the windows.

"It is me, Kyle. I need to talk to you, so would you please open the window for me?" the voice said, sounding more convincing to Cally.

"Kyle, what in the world are you doing at my bedroom window, and what do you need to talk to me about?" Cally asked, as she slowly made her way to the window, still confused as to why he was there in the first place.

Out of all the years Cally had known Kyle, not once had he ever tried to come through her bedroom window. Kyle had always been the type of person who called before he came over. This was not like Kyle at all, and Cally had a strange feeling that something was not right. As Cally got closer to the window, a voice inside her head told her to go back, but Cally had to know if it was really Kyle or her imagination playing tricks on her. Cally knew that she was taking a big risk by going to the window, but her curiosity had taken over and she could not rest until she found out who was out there.

"What window are you at?" Cally asked, as she glanced back and forth from window to window.

"I'm over here, Cally, at the window to your right. Now hurry up and let me in, before we wake your parents," the voice said, urging Cally to open the window.

Cally took a deep breath and proceeded to the window, but suddenly, she stopped dead in her tracks as her common sense took over, reminding her that there was no possible way Kyle could be at her window. Cally knew that her window was too high and there was nothing for him to climb up on. Panicked and scared, Cally found herself unable to move. She had never understood the expression *scared stiff* until now. Cally wanted to turn around and run like hell back to her bed, but she could not. Her feet felt as if they were stuck in concrete. All she could do was stare straight ahead at her window and pray that whatever was there would go away and never come back, but something told Cally that the chances of that happening were slim to none.

Just as Cally's leg muscles started to loosen up, a bloody hand slapped the window, followed by Ryan's bloody and burned, horrific-looking face. Cally could not believe her eyes; it was as if Satan himself were staring at her through the window. Cally was so scared; she did not know what to do. She wanted to scream for her parents, but she could not even open her mouth. It was as if Ryan had her in some sort of a trance, a trance that she could not get out of, no matter how hard she tried.

"Come on, Cally, aren't you going to let me in?" Ryan asked, scratching down the window with his bloody, chipped fingernails.

"You are not real; it is all in my mind. I'll close my eyes and count to three, and when I open them, you will be gone," Cally said, closing her eyes tightly as her knees started to knock with fear.

As Cally stood in the pitch-black room with her eyes shut, she could feel another dramatic change in the temperature. It felt as if someone had turned up the heat. It was suddenly so hot that it felt like an oven. Just as Cally started to open her eyes, she could feel heavy breathing on the back of her neck. With cold chills shooting down Cally's spine, she burst out into tears. She knew now that it was too late to scream or run back to her bed. Ryan was already in the house, and she knew what he had come to get.

"Why are you doing this to me? Why don't you just leave me alone, so I can get on with my life? It is not my fault that you died, so please just go away and leave me alone," Cally cried, falling to her knees as if she were begging Ryan to have mercy on her.

"Oh Cally, stop crying like a little bitch, because it is not going to do you any good. I told you that I would come back for you, so why are you acting so shocked to see me?" Ryan asked with an evil laugh that echoed throughout Cally's bedroom.

"No, God, please do not let him take me. I do not want to die. Please just make him go away and leave me alone," Cally prayed as the walls felt as if they were closing in on her, leaving her trapped with no place to go.

"Enough with the drama, Cally. It is time to finish what we started. It is time for you to join me in death," Ryan said, moving to the front of Cally, holding out his burned, maggot-infested hand for her to take.

Cally was at the end of her rope; there was no place to run and no place to hide. Cally took a deep breath and held out her ice-cold, trembling hand as she stared in horror at Ryan's glowing green eyes. Just the look of Ryan's horrible, burned face made Cally feel as if she were going to pass out, and the smell of his burned flesh was absolutely sickening. Cally's stomach churned at the foul odor coming off of him; it was the worst smell she had ever encountered, and the worst part of everything was knowing that she had no other choice but to go with him.

"Well, come on, Cally, I do not have all night. You belong to me now, so let's get going before I run out of patience," Ryan ordered with an evil laugh.

"Go where? Where are you taking me, and why are you taking me there?" Cally asked with tears running down her face.

"We are going to our funeral. Now, let's go, bitch. You have wasted enough of my time," Ryan said, grabbing Cally by her hand and pulling her up to her feet.

Cally tried to pull away from Ryan, but it was no use. Ryan was so much stronger than she was. Ryan dragged Cally across the floor toward the window as if she were a rag doll. This was it; Cally could see her whole life flashing before her eyes. She knew without a doubt that this was going to be the end of her young life. There was no escaping Ryan and his deadly grip this time. He was more determined than ever to take her life, and the only thing

Cally could do was let him.

"Well, this is it, Cally. You know what you have to do, so get on with it," Ryan said, pushing Cally to the window ledge, waiting for her to jump and end her own life.

"Please, Ryan, do not make me do this. I do not want to die, so please just leave me alone," Cally begged as she felt her fingertips start to slide off the window frame.

Cally could feel her feet starting to lose their balance as she tried to steady herself, but it was no use, no matter how hard she tried to hang on and keep her balance, she just could not. Her only other option was to let go and fall to her unwanted death. Cally closed her eyes as the warm summer breeze blew through the trees, hitting her in the face, almost taking her breath away. It all seemed so strange to Cally. Here she was, about to die, but yet she had never felt so alive in her whole life. It was as if her mind and body were in a peaceful and calm place, a place where nothing really mattered to her.

"Alright, Cally, you have wasted enough time. Just do it already, so we can be together forever," Ryan demanded, giving Cally a slight push, trying to rush her to her death.

Ready for everything to be over and done with, Cally leaned forward and took a deep breath, as she prepared herself for the jump. Cally did not know what was going to happen after she hit the ground; she just hoped that the afterlife would not involve Ryan. If she could not be happy and peaceful in life, she hoped at least she could be happy in death. Cally knew that her parents would be heartbroken, but at least they would not have to worry about Ryan and his evil ways anymore. They could finally get some peace of their own.

"No, Cally, do not do it! Please just stay still and I'll help you back inside," Kate yelled, running over to Cally before she plummeted to her death.

"Mom, is that you? Please hurry and help me," Cally begged as her grip loosened and her balance became more unstable, causing her to slip.

"Hang on, Cally, I have got you. Just try to push yourself up with your feet, so I can get a better grip and pull you back in," Kate said in a frantic voice, as she pulled on Cally with all of her might.

"I cannot do it, Mom. I'm losing my grip and I do not have the strength in my legs to push myself back up," Cally said as her hand started slipping out of Kate's.

Kate started to panic. She did not know how she was going to pull Cally back inside. It felt as if something was pulling her down, and the more Kate struggled, the weaker she got. It was hopeless; there was no way that Kate could pull her back in, she just was not strong enough. Cally was too heavy and Kate was too weak. Kate knew that Cally was going to fall to her death, but just as Kate started to lose her grip completely, Bill came running into the room and grabbed on to Cally, pulling her back in safely.

"Oh my God, Cally, what were you thinking? You could have been killed just now," Kate cried as she held on to Cally tightly.

"Where is he? Where did he go? Didn't you guys see him trying to push me out of the window?" Cally asked as she looked around the room, trying to find Ryan.

"See who, Cally? Who are you talking about? There is no one else in here but us," Kate explained as she looked around the room herself.

"It was Ryan; he came back again and tried to kill me. I swear to you that I'm telling the truth. It was without a doubt Ryan, I saw him with my own two eyes," Cally cried, laying her head down in Kate's lap, hoping and praying that her parents would believe her.

"Alright, Cally, this nonsense has to stop before you end up getting hurt or killed. Ryan is dead, and there is no possible way that he could come back for you. Ryan is gone, and you need to accept that so that you can move on with your life," Bill said in an angry tone, as he gave Cally a look of disappointment.

"I do accept the fact that he is dead, and I know how crazy this sounds, but I'm telling you the truth. I would not lie about something like this, you have to believe me," Cally argued, trying to convince her parents that she was telling the truth.

"Everyone needs to just calm down so that we can figure this out, because we are getting nowhere by arguing," Kate advised, looking at both Cally and Bill.

"I'm sorry, Cally, but I'm having a hard time believing you. It is just not logical, so would you please stop blaming everything on a dead person and take some responsibility for your own actions? You need to pull yourself together before you drive yourself insane," Bill said, scolding Cally for the second time.

Although Bill had seen Ryan in the elevator, he still blamed it on lack of sleep and his nerves. Bill was not going to lead himself to think that Ryan had come back from the dead. Bill knew there was no way in hell that could be possible; it just did not make any sense to him. Bill just wished that Cally and Kate would see things from his point of view. It was very hard for Bill to hold the family together all by himself. He needed for Kate to back him up and support him on things, so he would not have to do it alone. Bill could not wait until things got better for Cally; it could not happen soon enough for him.

"Bill, come back here and apologize to your daughter. She has been through enough, and here you are, putting more on her. That is not right," Kate demanded in an angry voice as Bill walked out of Cally's bedroom.

"It is okay, Mom. Dad is right. Even I think that I'm going crazy," Cally said, agreeing with her dad and acting as if his comments did not bother her, so that her mother would calm down and stop arguing with him.

Cally hated to see her parents argue. It made her feel as if she was the one at fault. Although what Bill said did hurt Cally's feelings, she was not about to let her mother know, because that would only add fuel to the fire and that was the last thing Cally wanted to do. Cally just wanted for things to get back to normal. It was killing her inside to know that she was putting her parents through so much heartache and pain. She had never seen her parents like this before. It was so sad to see them going through so much agony. Cally just prayed that things would get better after the ring was gone.

"I cannot believe that he would say something like that to you. He was completely out of line, and he needs to know that," Kate said, staring at the door, as if she wanted to go after Bill and tell him what she thought about his hurtful remarks.

"I only said those things because I love you and I do not want to see anything bad happen to you. When I found out that you had been in a car accident, my heart fell to my feet. I was so afraid that you were going to die, all I could do was think about how empty my life would be without you," Bill said, walking back into Cally's bedroom, feeling bad for the things he had said to her.

"It is okay, Dad. You do not have to explain. I understand why you said the things that you did, and believe me when I tell you that I'm not mad or upset. I could never get mad at the two of you. You guys are the best parents in the whole world, and I'm very lucky to have you," Cally replied, hugging both Bill and Kate, thanking God for blessing her with two caring and loving parents.

"I truly am sorry. Can you find it in your heart to forgive your old man?" Bill asked, wrapping his arms around Cally, as his eyes started to fill with tears.

"Of course I forgive you. It is water under the bridge, so let's just forget about it, okay?" Cally said, hugging her father in return, letting him know that there were no hard feelings.

Kate was glad that Bill had come back in and apologized to Cally, but she was still furious with him and it showed in her eyes. Bill could see the fury in her eyes as she stared coldly at him without so much as a blink. Bill knew that he had not heard the last from Kate. He had a strong feeling that she was really going to let him have it whenever they got some alone time. There would be no way for him to talk his way out of this one. All he could do was sit back and enjoy the fireworks, because like it or not, they were coming.

"Cally, sweetheart, would you like for me to sleep in here with you tonight?" Kate asked, still keeping her eyes glued on Bill.

"No, Mom, I think that I'll be alright now, but thanks for the offer. If I need anything I promise that I'll let you know right away," Cally said, trying to sound convincing, when deep down she was really dreading being by herself.

Although Kate was scared to leave Cally alone, she realized that she could not keep treating Cally like she was a baby. Cally was a young woman, not a ten-year-old little girl, and that was what Kate wanted to treat her like—a young woman. Besides, Kate knew that she could not protect Cally forever; the car accident had proved that to her. The fact was, Kate had to let go of Cally and let her grow up, and Kate felt that now would be the perfect time to do so. No matter how much it bothered her, it had to be done.

"Okay, sweetheart, but if you need anything, just yell and I'll be right in," Kate said, looking at Cally, hoping that she would change her mind and take her up on the offer.

"Well, come on, dear, let's go so Cally can get some sleep. I'm sure that she is tired and wants to lie down so she can rest," Bill said, rushing Kate out of the room, almost as if he were telling her that visiting hours were over.

"Hey, Mom, do you think that you could tuck me in before you go? I do not know why, but I always seem to sleep better after you tuck me in," Cally said, letting her mom know that no matter how old she got, she would always need her in some way or another.

"Anything for my little girl, it would be my pleasure," Kate answered with a smile on her face, feeling as if she was needed and appreciated.

"Remember, sweetheart, if you need us for anything, we are right down the hall," Bill said as he blew Cally a kiss and walked out of the room.

"Sleep tight, and remember, no more bad dreams. Just think of happy things and you should have nothing but sweet dreams all night long," Kate said, adjusting Cally's pillow and giving her one more kiss.

As Kate walked out of the room, she got an eerie feeling that someone or something was watching her. Kate could not help but feel a little uneasy about leaving Cally alone in the room by herself, but she did not want to bring up anything and startle Cally just based on an eerie feeling. Kate was afraid that the slightest event might trigger more bad nightmares for Cally, and she did not want to see her daughter go through anything else. Kate only wanted Cally to get better, not worse.

As Kate shut Cally's bedroom door, Cally could feel her heart starting to pound again with fear. For Cally, being scared was the worst feeling in the world. It made her feel as if she were trapped and helpless. Cally could not help but wonder if she would live in fear the rest of her life, because the way things were going, that was a big possibility. With everything on her mind, Cally lay quietly in her bed, listening to the house creak and pop, as her eyes got heavier and heavier. Desperately wanting to fall asleep, Cally did not fight the exhaustion that took over her body; instead, she just closed her eyes tightly and went with it. Five minutes later, Cally was sound asleep, and just as she started to snore, Kate slowly cracked the door open so she could check on Cally one last time before going to bed herself. As Kate stared at Cally, she realized just how lucky she was to be blessed with such a wonderful daughter, and although Kate hated to see Cally going through so much pain, she knew that Cally was a strong person and in time, she would overcome all of her problems.

9

With Cally resting well, Kate quietly closed the door and started down the stairs to fix herself a cup of warm herbal tea. While Kate stood at the stove heating the water, she could feel someone or something coming up behind her, so she quickly spun around to find out who or what it was. As Kate turned around, expecting to see something bad, she already had her guard up just in case it would be Ryan, but much to her surprise, it was only Bill. Glad to see Bill instead of Ryan, Kate let out a sigh of relief as she gave him a smile.

"Oh, I'm sorry, honey. I did not mean to startle you. I just heard some noises down here, so I came to investigate," Bill said after seeing the surprised look on Kate's face.

"That's okay. I was feeling a bit restless, so I came down to fix myself a cup of tea. Would you care to join me?" Kate offered, feeling that Bill was having trouble sleeping, too.

"Sure, I'll join you for a cup, that is, if it's no trouble for you," Bill said politely, as if he were trying to make up for something.

As Bill and Kate sat at the table, silence filled the room. Kate wanted to talk to Bill about the things he had said to Cally, but the more she thought about it, the more she realized that Bill probably had a reason for saying the things he said. Kate knew without a shadow of a doubt that Bill loved Cally very much and he would never say or do anything that would hurt her intentionally. He was not that kind of father, and besides, Kate figured that Bill was probably feeling pretty bad about the things he had said, so she decided to keep quiet and let things blow over on their own.

"Wow, that stuff really works. I'm feeling sleepy already," Bill said with a huge yawn, as he stretched his arms out over his head.

"Yeah, I'll agree with you on that. I can barely hold my eyes open. They feel as if they have ten-pound weights on them," Kate replied, rubbing her tired eyes as she took the last sip of her tea.

"Well, since the tea is doing its job, maybe we should go upstairs and take advantage of it. After all, I figure that we'll have another busy day tomorrow, so we should get some sleep while we can," Bill said, getting up from his chair.

"Say no more, I'm right behind you. I'll clean this mess up in the morning, when I'm feeling a little better," Kate agreed, putting her arm around Bill and giving him a hug as they started upstairs to their bedroom.

"Okay, sweetheart, you go on to bed, and I'll go in and check on Cally one last time, just to make sure she's alright," Bill said, volunteering so that Kate could have a little break from things.

Kate watched in awe as Bill walked into Cally's room. Although Bill tried to act tough, Kate knew he was still the same loving and caring man she had fallen in love with and married years ago. Kate knew without a doubt that she was the luckiest woman in the world, and while she was counting her blessings and getting ready for bed, Bill was busy checking on Cally, making sure that she was alright. Not only was Bill concerned about Cally, he was also concerned about the windows in her room. Bill wanted to make sure that her windows were locked and secure before he went to bed. That way he would not be up all night worrying about things.

"So, how is our little girl doing? Is she still sleeping?" Kate asked, as Bill climbed into bed.

"Oh, Cally is just fine. She's sleeping like a baby. I don't think that a bomb going off would wake her up tonight. She didn't even move when I opened the door," Bill said, cuddling up to Kate and giving her a kiss.

"Well, that's good. I hope that she gets some good rest tonight. Lord knows she needs it, and so do we," Kate said with a yawn, as she slid closer to him, wrapping her arms around him as if he were a teddy bear.

Suffering from exhaustion, it did not take long until both Bill and Kate were sound asleep in each other's arms. With everyone sound asleep, it was almost too good to be true—and it was. Suddenly, out of a dead sleep, Bill was awakened by a loud beating sound coming from downstairs. Not knowing who or what was making the noise, Bill reached and grabbed his 45 Mag out of his nightstand, just to be on the safe side. Bill did not want to walk into a burglary without some sort of a weapon. He had a family to protect and that was what he was going to do.

Trying not to wake Kate up, Bill picked her arm up slowly and carefully slid out from underneath her. Before starting downstairs, Bill took the safety off and cocked the gun, putting one bullet into the chamber, just in case he had to protect himself from a burglar. On the way downstairs, Bill tried to be as quiet as he could, but with the stairs creaking every step he took, being quiet was hard to do. As Bill stood at the bottom step, he slowly poked his head around the corner, so he could check the living room out. Seeing that everything was okay, Bill started toward the kitchen.

As Bill approached the kitchen door, he could hear dishes being moved around as if someone were cooking a meal. Not knowing what he was walking into, Bill stuck the gun out in front of him and pushed the door open quickly, hoping to catch whomever or whatever off guard. Upon opening the door, Bill quickly scanned the room, only to see Cally standing in front of the fridge with the door open. Bill did not know what Cally was doing down there, but he intended to find out.

"Oh Cally, you almost gave your old man a heart attack. I thought that you were a burglar," Bill said, letting out a sigh of relief as he laid the gun down on the kitchen table.

Bill stood there at the kitchen table and waited on Cally to respond, but she never said a word. She just kept on looking in the fridge, as if she did not even hear him. While Bill stood there, he wondered why Cally had not answered him yet. He knew that he had spoken loud enough for her to hear him, and then it dawned on him—maybe Cally was sleepwalking. Although she had never done it before, there was still a possibility that it could happen. Knowing that sleepwalking could be a possibility, Bill started walking over toward Cally to wake her, but right when he got close to her, Cally closed the fridge and started walking toward the kitchen table.

"Hey, Cally, did you hear a word I just said?" Bill asked, as he started walking over to the kitchen table where Cally was standing.

Bill thought for sure that the tone in his deep voice would have gotten Cally's attention, but it did not. Cally just kept on doing what she was doing, not even acknowledging the fact that her father was talking to her, let alone in the room. Bill could not help but feel a little confused about the way Cally was acting. One minute she was sound asleep in her bed, and then the next, she was downstairs in the kitchen. Knowing that his voice was doing no good, Bill started walking a little closer toward her, but as Bill got closer, he noticed that Cally had her hand on the fully loaded, ready-to-use gun that he had laid on the table earlier.

"No, Cally, put that gun down before you get hurt, or hurt someone else. It is nothing to play with. Now put it down before something bad happens," Bill demanded as he tried to get the gun out of Cally's tightly gripped hand.

"Stop, Dad, and leave me alone. This has to be done. It is the only way for me to escape Ryan's evil," Cally said, turning to face Bill, still not letting go of the gun or loosening her grip.

When Cally turned around, Bill was so startled by her appearance that he quickly started backing away from her. Cally had blood and pieces of burned skin all over her face; she looked as if she had been in a horrible accident. Confused and frightened by what he was seeing, Bill closed his eyes tightly and then reopened them, hoping that what he was seeing would go away, but nothing had changed. Cally was still covered in blood, and she still had the loaded gun in her hands. It was the worst thing Bill had ever encountered in his entire life.

"Cally, sweetheart, please put the gun down before you hurt yourself. You do not have to do this. Ryan is dead, and he is not coming back for you. It is all in your mind, there is no possible way that someone can come back from the dead. It is just not possible," Bill said, trying to convince Cally that everything was going to be okay, so she would give him the gun back before she ended up shooting herself.

"You are not listening to me, Dad. Ryan has come back from the grave, and he will not stop until I'm dead. If you do not believe me, just turn around and look behind you, then you will see that I'm telling the truth," Cally said as she stared directly behind Bill in complete horror.

Scared to see what was behind him, Bill turned around very slowly and braced himself for the worst, but instead of seeing Ryan, or anything else, Bill just saw the kitchen wall. Bill had no idea what Cally was talking about, or why she was acting so strange, but he knew that it was time to get Cally some professional help. Whether Cally wanted help or not, she really did not have much of a choice. Bill could not take another chance like this one. Cally needed help and she needed it as soon as possible. There was no other way around it.

"You see, Cally, it is just like I said. There is no possible way that Ryan can come back from the dead. It is all in your mind, sweetheart," Bill said, feeling relieved as he turned back around, only to find Cally with the barrel of the gun stuck in her mouth and her finger on the trigger.

"No, Dad, it is true, and I have to end this before Ryan does," Cally mumbled as tears rolled down her bloody face.

"Cally, please stop. Do not do this. It is not worth it, so please just give me the gun," Bill pleaded as he reached for the gun.

Before Bill could get his hands on the gun, Cally had already pulled the trigger, splattering blood and brains all over the kitchen table. Bill watched in horror, as Cally fell to the floor with the smoking gun still gripped tightly in her hand. Bill could not, nor did he want to believe his eyes; his only child was lying on the floor dead. Cally had killed herself with the gun that he had brought downstairs for protection. Traumatized and deeply saddened by what he saw, Bill fell to his knees beside Cally and prayed that he would just wake up from this bad dream.

"Oh God, no, this cannot be happening. My little girl cannot be dead. Please, just let this be another bad dream," Bill cried as he picked up Cally's lifeless body and held it close to his.

"Nice work, Bill. I did not have to kill her after all. You did it all by yourself, and I must say, you did a hell of a job," a deep and evil voice spoke from behind Bill.

When Bill heard the voice, he knew right then that it was Ryan. Feeling angry and frustrated by Cally's suicide, Bill turned around to face the demon that had taken his little girl. As soon as Bill's eyes met with Ryan's, all he could think about was how he could kill the demon that was standing in front of him. All of a sudden, without any warning, Bill totally lost it. All he could feel was anger running throughout his body, and before he knew it, he had grabbed the gun out of Cally's lifeless hand and aimed it at Ryan.

"Go ahead, Bill, fire away with your little pathetic gun. It is not like you can kill me. Besides, I got what I came for and that is your little bitch of a daughter, lying there with her brains blown out," Ryan said as he started walking closer toward Bill and the gun, showing no fear whatsoever.

Without saying a word or blinking an eye, Bill gave Ryan a quick smirk and started firing the gun, hitting Ryan with every single shot. At this point, the only thing Bill wanted to see was Ryan full of bullet holes and bleeding. Bill knew that there was no bringing Cally back, but he hoped and prayed that he could at least send Ryan back to hell. Ryan had taken his only child, and now it was time for him to pay for what he had done. Bill had no plans of stopping until he did just that.

"Bill, what in the hell are you doing and what are you shooting at?" Kate asked, jerking the gun out of Bill's hands.

"It was Ryan, Kate. He killed our little girl, so I had to send him back to hell. Please believe me. I did not have any other choice," Bill cried with tears streaming down his face, as if he were scared to death.

"What are you talking about, Bill? Cally is just fine, she is right behind you," Kate said, pointing to Cally so that Bill could see her and know that she was alive and well.

"Oh God, Cally, is it really you? Please tell me that I'm not dreaming again," Bill said in a confused but happy voice as he wrapped his arms tightly around Cally.

"Cally, sweetheart, now that your father knows you are okay, why don't you go back upstairs and get some sleep?" Kate said, motioning for Cally to go so that she could talk to Bill in private and find out exactly what was going on.

Kate watched as Bill stared at Cally with tears in his eyes. She had no idea what was going on, and she did not know what to say to Bill. Just the thought of seeing Bill with the gun in his hands made her very nervous. She knew that something had spooked him and spooked him badly. At this point, though, the only thing Kate could think about was getting to the bottom of everything. She just hoped that Bill would be honest with her so she would not have to pry and seem nosy.

"Why don't you sit down for a little while so we can talk about things?" Kate suggested, pulling out a chair for Bill to sit in.

"I'm so sorry, Kate. I do not know what got into me. At first, I thought that we were being robbed, so I got the gun out, but when I came downstairs, all I saw was Cally, and the next thing I knew, she had already killed herself, and after she killed herself, that is when I saw Ryan—" Bill was getting tongue-tied and confused at what he was saying.

"Oh Bill, it's okay. I believe you. You do not have to explain it to me," Kate interrupted before Bill had a chance to say anything else.

Kate was so glad that Bill had admitted to seeing Ryan. That made her feel so good inside. Now that Bill had seen Ryan, too, Kate knew for a fact that she was not going crazy. Finally Kate could talk to Bill about everything she had bottled up inside, without hearing him condone her. It was as if Kate's prayers had been answered. Now that everyone was on the same page, they could work together and find a way to stop Ryan before he ended up hurting or killing someone. Kate knew that Ryan was not going to go away that easily, but the next time Ryan showed his face, Kate planned on being ready for him.

"We have to do something about Ryan before he does something else to hurt our little girl. He has to be stopped and that is all there is to it," Bill said, giving Kate a serious look, as if he expected her to have all the answers.

"Well, I hate to say this, but I told you that I had seen Ryan and you did not believe me. You just played it off as if I was crazy or something, and I have to be honest with you, it really hurt me that you did not believe me," Kate said, feeling a little angry that Bill did not forgive her in the first place.

"Okay, Kate, you win, but this is not about who is right and who is wrong. This is about our little girl, and if we do not think of something fast, we may end up losing her forever," Bill said as he racked his brain for ideas that would help them save Cally.

"Well, I talked to Cally earlier, and I think that she has come up with a pretty good plan that just might work. At Ryan's funeral tomorrow, she is going to put the ring inside of Ryan's casket, so that it will be buried with him forever. Who knows? After the ring is gone, maybe things will get back to normal," Kate said as she noticed all the bullet holes in the kitchen wall.

"You know something, that just might work. It is at least worth a shot. I mean, what do we have to lose by trying? Either it works or it doesn't," Bill said surprising Kate that he was willing to go along with the plan.

As Bill and Kate continued to talk, Cally was standing at the door eavesdropping for the second time. Although her mother had told her to go back to bed, there was no way she could sleep knowing that her dad had just shot up the kitchen. Cally wanted some answers; she had to know what was going on with her parents. Cally knew that her parents would not give her the whole truth about what was going on, because they wanted to protect her, so she had to get it the best way she could, even if that meant having to listen in on their conversation.

"So, how are we planning on doing this without anyone seeing us? You do know that it will be a closed casket, there is no way that they are going to let anyone see Ryan's burned body," Bill said, already putting the plan into motion.

"Well, I suppose Cally could ask for a few minutes of privacy, and when no one is looking, she could raise the lid and drop the ring inside. That way no one will suspect anything, it will just look as if Cally wanted a few minutes to say her good-byes," Kate said, as she, too, racked her brain for more ideas.

"Yeah, that sounds like the best way of doing things. Just make sure that you talk to Cally about everything and explain to her what she needs to do. We have to get this right the first time, because there will be no more chances after he has been buried," Bill advised, as he started to nervously bite his fingernails.

"Okay, but I don't think that you'll have to worry about Cally messing anything up. After all, she was the one who came up with the plan," Kate said, trying to make Bill realize that he needed to have a little more faith in Cally.

As Cally continued to listen in on her parents' conversation, her stomach started to churn with fear. She did not like the fact that she would have to see Ryan's burned body again. To Cally, everything felt like one long, never-ending nightmare. Cally could not wait until everything was over with, and she knew that her dad was right about things needing to be done right the first time. Cally had only one shot, and she knew that she could not afford to screw it up.

"Well, I know this much is true, if we do not get some sleep, we will not be a bit of help to Cally tomorrow, so what do you say that we give this sleep thing another try?" Bill asked, as he slid his chair back across the floor.

"Well, Bill, I *was* sleeping just fine, until you killed the kitchen wall," Kate joked, trying to ease some of the tension, hoping that she would get a smile or a laugh out of Bill.

"Hey, you know me, if a kitchen wall looks at me the wrong way, I'm going to let it have it," Bill joked back, giving Kate the smile she'd hoped to see.

When Cally heard her parents push the chairs back underneath the table, she knew that she needed to hurry back upstairs to her bed and pretend to be sleeping. Cally did not want her parents to know that she had been eaves-dropping on their conversation. Cally knew that her parents were just trying to protect her, but she still wanted to be a part of the conversation in some way, even if it meant having to eavesdrop. Cally walked as quickly as she could back up the stairs, trying not to make any noise, and then jumped into her bed, pulling the covers up over her head.

"That is a shocker. I figured that she would be up all night, after what happened in the kitchen," Kate whispered to Bill, as they walked softly out of Cally's bedroom, pulling the door shut halfway.

As Cally lay awake in bed, she heard her parents' bedroom door shut. Knowing that they would not check back in on her for a couple of hours, Cally sat straight up in her bed and tried to go over her plan again for the hundredth time, mapping out any shortcuts that would help her get things done faster. Cally absolutely hated the idea of getting that close to Ryan's dead body again, but she knew that putting the ring inside his casket might be the only way for the terror to stop. While sorting through her problems, the darkness of the room was interrupted by a sudden flash of blue lightning. Startled by the sudden flash, Cally quickly slid down into her bed and pulled the covers up over her face.

"Oh great, as if my night could not get any worse, now I have to endure this loud, horrible storm," Cally said softly to herself, as an enormously loud rumble of thunder shook the whole house, sending cold chills down her spine.

Normally Cally loved a good thunderstorm, especially at nighttime. Just the sound of the rain beating down on the rooftop would put her to sleep in no time. It was like one of nature's many lullabies, but after being in the car accident and having the heavy rain hit her in the face as she lay on the cold, wet ground, everything had changed. Now all the rain did was make her feel depressed and scared, and those were two feelings that Cally could live without. Cally just wanted everything to go back to normal, because she did not know how much longer she could deal with everything. Cally tried her best to think about different things, so it would take her mind off the storm and everything else that had happened, but nothing seemed to work. It was as if she was fighting a losing battle. Just as Cally started feeling helpless, her bedroom door slowly creaked open.

"Mom, is that you?" Cally asked, raising her head up and looking at the doorway.

"Oh, I'm sorry, sweetheart. I did not mean to wake you. I was just checking in. I got a little worried when I heard the big rumble of thunder. I'll get out of here now, so that you can get back to sleep," Kate said, apologizing for the intrusion as she started to close Cally's door.

"You are not bothering me, Mom. I have been awake for a while now. I'm actually glad that you came in here, because I have a favor to ask of you," Cally said quickly before Kate could close the door.

"Sure, just name it, you know that I would do anything for you," Kate said, turning on Cally's bedroom light so that she could see her better.

"Well, do you think I could sleep in your room, just for the night? I could make a pallet on the floor, and I promise that you will not hear a peep out of me all night," Cally said, feeling a bit childish, but still hoping that her mother would say yes.

"Of course you can, sweetheart. That is the sweetest favor you have ever asked of me. Just grab your pillow and you can sleep in my bed. I'll sleep in the middle and you can sleep on my side," Kate answered, smiling from ear to ear.

"Thanks, Mom. I knew that I could count on you. You are the best mother in the world," Cally said, grabbing her pillow off the bed.

"Well, do not get too excited. You have not heard your father's snoring lately. He sounds just like our garbage disposal," Kate whispered, giving Cally a playful nudge.

"Do not worry, Mom. I'm so tired right now I think that I could sleep through a nuclear bomb," Cally replied, rubbing her half-closed, tired eyes.

"Good night, sweetheart, and remember, if you need anything, all you have to do is wake me up," Kate said, assuring Cally that she would always be there for her.

Kate pulled the covers up over Cally and noticed that her little girl was already sound asleep. As Kate lay there between Cally and Bill, she could feel her own tired eyes starting to close. The sound of the heavy rain beating down on the rooftop made her feel as if she were melting into the bed. Feeling that Cally was safe for the night, Kate rolled onto her side and closed her eyes. Not wanting to fight the tiredness any longer, Kate drifted off to sleep.

10

"Okay, girls, rise and shine. I've been up since ten o'clock fixing you two the best breakfast in the world, and if you don't at least get up and try it, then my feelings will be hurt all day," Bill said jokingly, figuring that Kate and Cally needed some cheering up.

"Well, it sure does smell good, and I'm so hungry that I could eat a horse," Kate said with a yawn, as she stretched her arms out.

"Cally, sweetheart, you should come down and eat some breakfast before it gets cold. I made your favorite: bacon, eggs, toast, and pancakes," Bill said, rubbing Cally's head, trying to get a response out of her.

Cally turned her head to Bill and slowly opened her tired eyes, giving him a smile that would light up any room. It was the first time since the accident that Bill had seen her look so peaceful and happy. It was as if she was back to her old self again, which made Bill very thankful. He just hoped and prayed that Cally's plan would work, because if it did not, he did not know what to do. Bill just knew that he did not want to come face-to-face with Ryan ever again, because the next time he might not be so lucky.

"Good morning, Dad. Good morning, Mom. Thanks again for letting me sleep in your bed. I haven't slept that good in a long time," Cally said, feeling refreshed and energetic.

"Well, come on, slowpokes. Let's go downstairs and eat before it gets cold. After all, I put a lot of hard work into making this breakfast for my two best girls," Bill said with a smile as he helped Cally up out of bed, so that she would not have to use her broken arm.

"Come on, Cally, you heard your father. Let's go eat this wonderful breakfast he has prepared for us," Kate said, grabbing Cally by the hand.

"Wow, Dad, you really did go all-out on this. It looks and smells delicious. I cannot wait to dig in," Cally complimented her dad, as she pulled out a chair and sat down in front of a huge plate of pancakes.

"I have to agree, dear. This looks like a breakfast fit for a king," Kate said as she helped herself to a piece of bacon.

"Well, don't just sit there like a knot on a log. Dig in before it gets cold," Bill said, pouring Kate and Cally glasses of freshly squeezed orange juice.

"This is really good, Dad. I'm impressed. You could be a chef in a fine restaurant, and I'm not even exaggerating," Cally said, complimenting her dad once more as she scarfed down two pancakes covered in maple syrup.

"She is right, dear. You have truly outdone yourself, and now that I know you can cook so well, I may have you do it more often," Kate joked, giving Bill a wink as she poured herself another cup of coffee.

As Bill, Kate, and Cally sat at the table enjoying their breakfast, they could not have been happier. It was the first time in a long time that they actually felt like a happy family. Although Ryan had tried his best to break them up, he had not succeeded. If anything, Ryan had brought them closer together, just by doing the hurtful and selfish things that he was so good at. Bill was so happy to see both of his girls smiling and having a good time, but his happiness was interrupted by the sound of the phone ringing.

"I'll get it!" Cally said, as she quickly jumped up from the table and ran toward the phone, hoping that it was Kyle on the other end so she could apologize for being so rude to him the night before.

"Hi, is this Cally?" a woman asked, pausing as she waited for an answer.

"Yes, this is Cally, who is this?" Cally asked curiously, as she tried to place the voice.

"It is Ms. Jones. How are you feeling today?" Ms. Jones asked in a soft and caring voice.

"Oh, hi, Ms. Jones, I didn't recognize your voice. How are you doing?" Cally asked, knowing already that she was not doing well at all.

"Well, I guess I'm doing alright. Time has a way of healing all things, and right now, that is all I have. I actually called to tell you that if you did not feel like coming to the funeral, you do not have to. I know that you loved Ryan very much, and I just wanted to let you know that I'll not get upset if you decide not to come. It is totally up to you, and I'll respect your decision," Ms. Jones said, getting choked up at just the mention of Ryan's name.

As much as Cally wanted to take her up on the offer, she could not. Cally knew that she had to go and at least try her plan. Whether it worked or not, Cally could not leave herself wondering. She would love nothing more than to never see Ryan's disgusting face again, but the plan had to be carried out. Cally had to put the ring into Ryan's casket—it was the only chance she had and the only way to find out if the plan would put a stop to Ryan and his evil ways.

"Well, I thank you for being so understanding, but I would really like to come and pay my last respects, if that is alright with you?" Cally lied, knowing that if it was not for the plan having to be carried out, she would not go at all.

"That is really sweet of you, Cally. I'm so glad that Ryan had you in his life. You were the best thing that ever happened to him, and I know that he felt the exact same way, but I know that you are probably busy, so I'll let you go and I'll see you in a little while," Ms. Jones said before hanging up.

"Who was that on the phone?" Kate asked, pretending as if she did not know.

"That was Ms. Jones. She just called to tell me that I did not have to come to the funeral if I did not feel like it," Cally answered, staring down at the floor, feeling her stomach tie in knots as her pancakes felt as if they were making their way back up her throat.

"Look, Cally, I know that things are hectic right now, but you need to focus on the real reason for going to Ryan's funeral. You have to get rid of that ring before something really bad happens. After all, this could be your only chance to rid yourself of Ryan's evil spirit," Bill said, hoping that Cally was not having second thoughts about going.

"Do not worry, Dad. I know how important this plan is without you telling me, and besides, who told you what I was planning on doing with the ring? Oh, let me guess. Mom probably filled you in, right?" Cally snapped, wishing that just for once her parents would treat her like an adult, instead of a little kid.

"Knock it off, Cally. Your father is just trying to help, and you should not talk to him that way. He loves you very much, and I think that you should show him a little respect," Kate demanded firmly, letting Cally know her place, as she jumped to Bill's defense.

The last thing Kate wanted was to be harsh to Cally after all that she had been through, but she did not want Cally thinking that she could just run over them any time she felt like it, either. Kate wanted Cally to realize that they were only trying to help her, not hurt her, and the only way to do that was to stand her ground as a mother and be firm with Cally, no matter if it upset her or not. Although Cally had been through an ordeal, she still needed to know her place and have respect for her parents, and Kate knew that if she gave her an inch, Cally would end up taking a mile. That was something Kate was not going to let happen.

"You are right. I'm sorry for talking to you like that, Dad. I promise that it will not happen again, and from now on, I'll start letting you know things, too. That way you will not have to hear it from Mom," Cally said, apologizing with tears running down her face. She gave Bill a hug.

"Oh sweetheart, I forgave you the minute you said it. I know that you are going through a lot right now, but hopefully after today, things will start getting better," Bill replied, letting Cally know that he was not upset with her.

Kate watched as Bill and Cally made up. She knew that Cally was going through a very stressful time, and she wished a million times that she had just gone with her gut feeling and made Cally stay home on prom night, but instead, she believed Ryan and his countless lies. Kate could not help but feel one hundred percent responsible for everything that had happened. If only she would have done things differently, Cally would not be going through pure hell. The only thing that made Kate feel better was knowing how strong Cally was. She knew that Cally would pull through this tragedy and return to her old self again. All it was going to take was a little bit of patience and time.

"May I be excused now, so that I can go call Kyle? I feel as if I was rude to him last night, and I just want to apologize to him before we go to the funeral," Cally asked, planning on more than just an apology.

Cally knew that Kyle would do anything for her, including going to Ryan's funeral. Throughout all the years Cally had known him, he had never turned his back on her, no matter what the reason. It was as if Kyle were her security blanket. She just felt so much safer with him around, especially after the accident. Although Cally's parents were going, it was not the same as Kyle going with her. For some reason, and Cally did not know why, she just felt empty when Kyle was not around. It was almost as if a piece of her was missing.

"Well, it is alright with me, if it is okay with your mother. After all, you did eat most of your breakfast," Bill said as he looked over at Cally's half-empty plate.

"Oh sweetheart, you know that you do not have to ask if you can call Kyle. I think having Kyle around has been good for you, and I can tell that he cares a lot about you. It is practically written all over his face," Kate said, giving Cally a smile and her permission to call Kyle.

"Thanks again for everything that you do for me. I feel as if I'm the luckiest daughter in the world," Cally said before walking out of the kitchen.

As Cally walked upstairs to her bedroom, she could not help but think what it would be like to have Kyle as a boyfriend. Every time she was around him, her stomach filled with butterflies. She was like a lovesick schoolgirl. She knew that it was wrong of her to be thinking about another guy on the day of Ryan's funeral, but she could not help it. Her feelings had grown stronger for Kyle, a lot stronger. Kyle had given her something that Ryan failed to give her, and that was love. As Cally sat on the edge of her bed holding the phone, she could feel the palms of her hands starting to sweat. Never before had Cally been this nervous about calling Kyle.

"Okay, Cally, get it together. You are not thirteen anymore. It is just a simple phone call to your best friend," Cally said to herself as she started to dial Kyle's number.

"Hello," Kyle said after the phone barely had a chance to ring.

"Hey, Kyle, it is me, Cally. Look, I know that I'm the last person that you want to hear from, but I really need to talk to you about something," Cally said nervously, as she waited on Kyle to hang up on her.

"Yeah, I kind of gathered that, when your number showed up on my phone. So, what is up? What do you need to talk to me about?" Kyle asked curiously, as he waited on Cally to start talking.

"Well, first of all I want to apologize for the way that I acted toward you last night. I had no right to treat you like that. You have been nothing but nice to me, and I feel just awful for being so rude to you," Cally said, apologizing right away, hoping that he would accept it.

"Oh, that is okay, you do not have to apologize for anything. I know that you were tired and your arm was hurting. If I were in your shoes, I would have done the same thing, but enough about that. How are you feeling? Did you get a good night's sleep?" Kyle asked, showing Cally that he still cared about her and her well-being.

Cally cared a lot about Kyle, and although Kyle was her best friend and she trusted him with her life, she still could not bring herself to tell him the truth about how her night really went. Cally knew that if she told him, he would only think that she was crazy, and that was something Cally did not want anyone thinking about her. It was hard enough knowing that her parents thought she was crazy, let alone Kyle. Cally knew that if her plan did not work, she would eventually have to tell him everything, but for the time being, Cally just wanted to keep everything to herself in the hopes that her plan would get rid of Ryan.

"Honestly, Kyle, I slept like a baby. I do not think that I have ever slept that good in my whole life. It was like heaven," Cally lied, trying to sugarcoat things so that Kyle would believe her.

"Well, that is really good. I'm so glad to hear that you are doing better. I honestly did not think that you would bounce back this soon, but this is one time I'm glad that you proved me wrong. And who knows? Maybe one day in the near future, you will feel good enough for me to take you out to lunch," Kyle said, hoping that Cally would pick up on his hint and take him up on his offer.

Kyle really liked Cally and he always had. He had been so devastated when Cally started going out with Ryan that he did not know what to do, but now that Ryan was out of the picture, he was going to try in every way to let Cally know just how much he really liked her. Kyle had missed out one time before, and he was not about to do it again. He cared too much about Cally to just give up and walk away. She was the most important thing in his life, besides his mother, and she was definitely worth waiting for, no matter how long it took. Kyle just hoped that Cally felt the same way about him.

Oh great, Kyle. You just had to open your big mouth. She probably just likes you as a friend and nothing else, Kyle thought as he waited on Cally to break the awkward silence.

"You know what, Kyle, I would love to go out and have lunch with you. I think that it may be good for both of us, what do you think?" Cally asked, as a huge smile lit up her face.

"Well, just let me know when you get ready, and I'll be at your front door with bells on, that much I can promise you," Kyle said, glad that Cally had accepted his offer.

"Hey, Kyle, before we get off on another subject, I have to ask a favor of you, and if you say no, I swear that I'll understand, so do not be afraid to tell me no," Cally said, completely changing the subject.

"Okay, Cally, now you have got me curious. Tell me what this favor is and I'll let you know if I can do it or not," Kyle said cautiously, not wanting to make a promise he could not keep.

"Well, you have always been there for me when I needed you the most, and that is why I'm asking you to go to Ryan's funeral with me. I know that it is a lot to ask of you, but it would mean so much to me if you would go and be by my side during this time. I promise that I'll make it up to you, just name your price," Cally said, crossing her fingers, praying that Kyle would say yes.

Kyle was completely speechless. He did not know what to say. He never dreamed in a million years that Cally would have asked him to go to the funeral. He did not even know why Cally wanted to go herself, after everything Ryan had put her through. Normally, Kyle would have done anything for Cally, but this time he was not so sure. After all, Ryan was the one who had mistreated Cally, and he was also the one who had almost killed her. Kyle could not help but wonder what was going through Cally's mind.

"Forgive me for asking, but why in the hell would you even want to go to that asshole's funeral in the first place? Have you forgotten how he treated you? I mean, come on, Cally, this is the same guy that beat you up throughout your relationship, and he tried to kill you, so why on earth would you want to go and pay your last respects to someone like that?" Kyle asked bitterly, thinking that Cally still might have some feelings for Ryan.

"Just forget that I even asked. I do not have time to explain this shit to you. As a matter of fact, I do not even know why I called you in the first place," Cally snapped, feeling upset that Kyle would even question her to begin with.

"Okay, look, I'm sorry that I upset you. I should have never opened my big mouth. You have every right to be mad at me. I just hope that you can find it in your heart to forgive me," Kyle apologized, after seeing how upset he had made Cally.

"I'm not mad at you, Kyle, just a little disappointed. I thought that I could count on you to be there for me, but I guess I was wrong. Anyways, I'll let you go so that you can get back to whatever it was you were doing. I'm sorry that I bothered you, but do not worry, it will not happen again. This is the last time you will ever hear from me," Cally said, as if she were threatening him with their friendship.

"No, Cally, just hear me out before you hang up. I'm sorry for being such a jerk to you. It is just that I cannot find it in my heart to forgive Ryan for what he did to you. No matter how hard I try, I just cannot do it, but if you need me there by your side for support, I'll be there, no matter what my feelings are toward Ryan. I said that I would be there for you, and I'm not about to go back on my word now. I care too much about you, and all I want is for you to be happy," Kyle said with tears in his eyes, worried that he might lose Cally forever.

Cally did not know what to say. She felt so bad for the things that she had said to Kyle. She had totally lost her cool and had taken it all out on him. Cally knew that Kyle was only saying those things because he cared about her. It was not like her to be short-tempered with him. It was as if Ryan had turned her into a cold, heartless person just like he was, and Cally did not want to be anything like him. All Cally wanted to do was go to Ryan's funeral and follow through with her plan, so that she could rid herself of him once and for all and get on with her life.

"Hello, Cally, are you still there?" Kyle asked, concerned that Cally had already hung up on him.

"Yes, I'm still here. I'm just feeling a little confused is all. I think that you and I need to have a long talk about some things, but I do not want to discuss it over the phone. I think that we should talk face-to-face, that way I can fill you in on some things, so that you will have a better understanding of what is going on. Is there any way that you can come over before it gets any later?" Cally asked, hoping that Kyle could come over before the funeral started so she could explain things to him about her plan.

"Well, I guess that I can come over now, but I'll have to take a quick shower before I do, because I just got done changing the oil in my truck and I'm covered from head to toe in oil and dirt," Kyle said, looking down at his hole-filled, stained jeans.

"Okay, that is fine. I'll see you in a little while. Drive safely," Cally advised before hanging up.

Upon waiting for Kyle to arrive, Cally paced nervously back and forth through her room, as she tried to think of a way to explain everything to Kyle so that he would not think that she was the craziest person on the face of the earth. Although she did not know exactly how to tell Kyle, she knew that she could not keep it a secret from him anymore. Kyle had to know the truth. Tired of pacing, Cally sat down on the edge of her bed and stared out the window, while biting her already chewed-down nails.

"Cally, sweetheart, is everything okay? I heard a lot of movement up here and I got a little worried about you," Kate said, walking right into Cally's room without so much as a knock, fearing that Cally might have seen Ryan again.

"Yeah, I'm okay. I'm just trying to think of a way to tell Kyle about my plan without him thinking that I'm crazy," Cally said, still chewing on her nails.

"Why would you tell Kyle about your plan? He doesn't have anything to do with this, so you really should not drag him in on it," Kate advised, in the hopes that Cally would listen to her.

Kate knew that Cally and Kyle were friends, and she knew that Cally trusted Kyle with her life, but she still did not want Kyle knowing that much information about what was going on. She feared that Kyle would only think that Cally was crazy, and she did not want to see Cally go through any more heartache, especially if it was not necessary. Kate just wanted Cally to take things slow and wait for a while before she told Kyle anything. That way she could at least have a little time to think about what she was going to say, and maybe Kyle would understand things a little better.

"Look, Mom, I think a lot of Kyle, and I don't want to keep any more secrets from him. This is something that I think he should know and I'm going to tell him, no matter what he might think. Besides, if he truly is a good friend to me he should understand why I have to do this, plus I need him at the funeral for moral support," Cally said, feeling a little worried about Kyle's reaction to her confession.

"Okay, Cally, you know Kyle better than I do, so if you feel like you should tell him and you think that he will understand, then go ahead. But if I were you, I would not tell anyone else about this. It's not something to broadcast to the whole world," Kate said, worrying that Cally might be making a huge mistake by telling Kyle the truth.

"Please don't worry, Mom. I know that Kyle will understand, and besides, I'm so sick and tired of lying and keeping secrets. I just want to be truthful with everyone from now on, so please do not be mad at me," Cally begged, hoping that her mother was not disappointed or angry at her.

"Oh Cally, I'm not mad at you. I just do not want to see you get hurt any-more. I do not know what I would do if something were to happen to you again. I just want you to be careful and take things slow," Kate said, giving Cally advice, hoping that she would use it.

"Mom, I have to ask you something, and I want you to be absolutely hon-est with me. Do you think that this nightmare will end, or do you think that it will keep going until it gets the best of me? Because, to tell you the truth, I feel as if I cannot fight this much longer. My body is getting tired and weak, and I think that I'm losing my mind," Cally cried, as tears rolled down her pale, gaunt face.

"Cally, I know that it is hard right now, but you have to stay strong and positive about things, because if you do not, then you might as well say that Ryan has won. And we cannot let Ryan win, we have to send him back to hell where he belongs. Do you understand me?" Kate asked, making sure that she got her point across.

"Yes, Mom, I understand and I promise you that I'll stay strong. I'll not let Ryan take anything else from me. It's time to put a stop to him and his evil ways," Cally answered in a serious voice, letting her mother know that she was not about to give up.

Kate hated to see Cally struggle with her problems and emotions, but she knew deep down that there was a way to get rid of Ryan's evil spirit, and she was not going to stop until she figured it out. Kate knew that Cally had a lot more fight in her. She just prayed that Cally could find it before it was too late. Ryan was coming at Cally with everything he had, and Kate just wanted to make sure she was ready for him. Kate knew for a fact that Ryan was de-termined to get Cally. She just hoped that Cally was as determined to get rid of him.

"Cally, could you please come down? Kyle is here," Bill yelled out, inter-rupting Cally and Kate's talk.

"Sure, I'll be right down, give me just a minute," Cally called out, letting her dad know that she heard him.

"Well, come on, sweetheart. We don't want to be rude and keep Kyle wait-ing. Besides, I bet your father has talked the poor boy into a coma by now, so right now might be the best time to go in and save him," Kate joked, giving Cally a big smile.

"Yeah, you are probably right about that. I just hope that Dad did not take him into the kitchen to see all of the bullet holes in the wall. Although I'm sure that Dad had his reasons, but still you have to admit it is a little embarrassing," Cally said with a giggle, showing her mother that she had not lost her sense of humor.

Kate and Cally walked side by side downstairs, giggling the whole way down to the living room. Kate was so glad to see that Cally was feeling better. It made her feel as if her little girl was getting back to her old self again, and that absolutely thrilled her. From the day Cally was born, the only thing Kate wanted was to see her happy. Kate prayed that this plan would work, for Cally's sake. Kate knew that she could not bear to see Cally unhappy for the rest of her young life. To Kate that was not even an option.

"Oh no, it is worse than I thought, now both of them are in a coma," Kate said after walking into the living room and seeing both Bill and Kyle with their eyes glued to the TV.

"Well, at least they are watching something educational," Cally said after seeing that they were watching a nature program.

"Hey, Bill, why don't you follow me into the kitchen, so that we can give Cally and Kyle some privacy to talk. I'm sure they have a lot of catching up to do," Kate said while giving Bill a slight nudge.

"Oh, that is okay, Mom. Let Dad finish his program. We can go outside to talk. After all, it is a beautiful day and I do not feel like wasting it," Cally said, taking Kyle by his hand.

"Do not worry about a thing, Kyle. I'll let you know what happens when you come back inside," Bill said, keeping his eyes glued to the TV as if he were afraid that he might miss something.

Kate sat down on the couch beside Bill and watched as Cally and Kyle walked out the door. No matter how much she wanted to, she still could not help but worry that Kyle would not believe Cally, and if he did not, then it would only lead to more heartache for her. Fifteen minutes went by, and Kate could not take the anticipation any longer. She did not want to be nosy, but she did want to look out of the window and check on Cally. Not wanting to be noticed by Bill, Kate slowly and casually got up from the couch and walked over to the window, taking a peek out just to see if Cally was okay. While Kate was busy spying on Cally and Kyle, she did not notice that Bill was spying on her.

"Kate, honey, is there a reason why you are looking out the window at

Cally and Kyle? Don't you think that you should give them some privacy and stop being so nosy? I mean, after all, they are just right outside," Bill said catching Kate totally off guard.

"Oh, you are absolutely right, Bill. I really should not be nosy, but I cannot help but feel that it is my job to protect her from now on. It seems like only yesterday, I was holding her in my arms, and now she is all grown up. Where did the time go? It feels as if the years have flown by," Kate cried as she sat back down on the couch and laid her head on Bill's shoulder.

"Well, like it or not, our little girl is growing up quickly and there is no way to slow it down or stop it. We just have to take things one day at a time and hope that she never leaves home," Bill joked, trying to make Kate feel better before Cally and Kyle came back inside and they sensed that something was wrong.

Although Bill put on a good front, he was really scared to death on the inside. He did not know what to do if Cally's plan failed. All he knew was that they were dealing with something that was powerful, evil, and very determined to take their daughter away from them. Bill racked his brain constantly, trying to come up with ways to get rid of Ryan, but nothing good came to mind. It was as if the more he thought, the more confused he became, and Bill could not let Kate and Cally see him frustrated. Bill knew he had to be strong for the both of them, because if he did not, the whole family would come unplugged and fall apart and he was not about to let that happen. While Bill was in the house, trying to make Kate feel better, Kyle was outside with Cally, trying to understand what she had just told him.

"Look, Cally, we have known each other for a long time, and I have never once heard you talk this crazy before. Do you have any clue as to how ridiculous and crazy you sound right now? I mean, you do not even act like your old self anymore. I really hate to say this, but you are really starting to worry me a little bit with all of this nonsense you are telling me," Kyle said as he stared down at the ground and pulled up sprigs of grass, acting as if he was getting irritated with Cally's stories.

Cally sat in silence with tears streaming down her saddened face, as she tried to cope with Kyle's reaction. Cally never dreamed in a million years that Kyle could be so hurtful and cold. Kyle had always been there for her through thick and thin, and he never once questioned her sanity. He had always believed everything that she had told him, no matter what it was. Cally desperately wanted Kyle to believe her, or at least give her the benefit of the doubt, but Kyle seemed too set in his ways and it did not look as if he was going to budge anytime soon. Feeling like there was nothing else to say, Cally got up and started slowly walking toward the front door.

"So that is it, huh? You are just going to walk away without saying a word? I swear, Cally, for the life of me I do not understand you. One minute you are acting normal, and then the next, you are acting like a crazed lunatic. I'm completely lost right now, so would you please explain to me what it is you want me to do?" Kyle asked, following behind Cally as she kept walking without any hesitation.

"I do not want you to do a damn thing for me, except get the hell out of my life and leave me alone. Do you think that you can handle that, or do I need to help you out a little bit?" Cally asked bitterly as she stopped dead in her tracks and spun around to face Kyle, so that she could look him eye-to-eye and get her point across.

While Cally and Kyle were outside arguing, Kate could not help but over-hear their voices being raised. She could tell that something was wrong with Cally, just by the tone in her voice, and although she did not want to butt in, she knew that she had to—just in case things were getting out of hand. Kate promised Cally that she would never leave her side again, and that was a promise that she was not going to break. Kate was going to set things straight with Kyle once and for all, no matter if it made Cally mad or not. It had to be done.

"Look, Cally, I know that I told you that I would stay out of this, but I'll be damned, if I'll stand by and watch another boy treat you like shit, or talk to you as if you were some stray dog. He has no right whatsoever to talk down to you, and you know that as well as I do. So with that being said, Kyle, I think that you should be going now, before you get me really upset. Do you understand what I'm saying to you, or do I need to call the cops and let them explain it?" Kate snapped, looking at Kyle with a crazed look in her eyes, as if she could kill him.

Cally was speechless. She did not know what to say. She had never seen her mother jump to her defense like that before. It was as if Kate had turned into an attack dog that was ready for anything or anyone. Cally could even see the fear in Kyle's eyes. He looked like a whipped, scared-to-death little pup. Cally herself was a bit concerned for Kyle's well-being. At this point she did not know what her mother was capable of, and she really did not want to find out. Scared of what her mother might do, Cally quickly stepped in between them, as if she were the referee.

"Okay, Mom, I think that you should just calm down before you do something that you are going to regret. Just take a few deep breaths and try to relax," Cally said, coaching her angry mother before things got out of hand.

"I cannot help it, Cally. You opened up to him and poured your heart out, only to have him treat you as if you were some kind of crazy person. You know, Kyle, I hate to be the one to tell you this, but you are no different from Ryan," Kate said, still staring at Kyle as if she could kill him.

Kyle could not believe what he was hearing. It hurt him so badly when Kate compared him to Ryan. It was like a knife stabbing him right in the heart. Overcome by what Kate had said, Kyle just stood there in silence. He knew that he had angered Kate, but what bothered him most was realizing how badly he had hurt Cally. Kate was right; he had never treated Cally so badly, it was almost as if he had a little bit of Ryan in him. Ashamed of what he had said to Cally, Kyle just stood there quietly and dropped his head in shame. Kyle desperately wanted to apologize to Cally and Kate, but he could not find the right words to say to them at the moment. Not wanting to cause any more pain or trouble, Kyle turned around and started walking toward his truck.

"Kyle, wait. I'm sorry that I compared you to Ryan. I had no right to do that. Sometimes I just let my anger do the talking, and that is what ends up coming out. I hope that you can forgive me for the mean and cruel things that I said. I know that you are nothing like Ryan. I just don't want to see Cally get hurt any more. She's been through enough," Kate called out, stopping Kyle dead in his tracks.

"No, you're right. I shouldn't have been such an asshole. I should have been a little more open-minded and understanding toward Cally. I was the one who didn't have the right to say the things that I said, and I'm sorry for that. I just hope that you can forgive me, so we can move past this," Kyle explained, hoping that Cally and her mother would forgive him for the things that he had said.

"Look, Kyle. I know that it sounds crazy and it seems impossible, but everything Cally told you was the truth. I give you my word on it, from one man to another," Bill said, joining in on the conversation.

Kyle did not want to believe that Ryan had come back from the dead for Cally. This was something that could only happen in a horror movie, not real life. This all seemed virtually impossible to him, but the more he stared into Bill's worried eyes, the more it became evident that Bill, Cally, and Kate were telling the truth about seeing Ryan's ghost. The reason he knew this was because Cally and her parents would have absolutely nothing to gain from lying. Things were starting to clear up and make more sense now, but Kyle still had two questions that were weighing heavy on his mind: How did Ryan come back from the dead? And how could they stop a ghost from hurting or taking Cally?

"Look, Kyle, I know that this is a lot to take in at one time—it was for us, too—so if you still want to leave, I promise you that there will be no hard feelings. But if you want to stay, your help would be greatly appreciated," Kate explained, letting Kyle know that he had more than one option in the whole matter.

"Well, I appreciate the offer, but I have got my mind made up and I want to help you guys out as much as I can. Please remember, though, all of this is brand-new to me and I'll need for you to show me what to do, because right now I'm still feeling a little bit confused," Kyle warned them, so that they would not expect too much from him right away.

Cally could not believe what she had just heard; it was like a slap in the face. Cally was completely shocked that Kyle had actually agreed to help, after having her mother jump all over him. It was almost as if Kate's talk had actually opened his eyes and done him some good. Cally usually did not like it when her parents nosed in on things, but this time, she was glad that they did, because if it had not been for them, Kyle would have walked away and their relationship would have fallen apart, causing nothing but more heart- ache and pain.

"Thank you so much, Kyle. You do not know how much this means to me. You truly are a wonderful friend, and I feel blessed to have you in my life. I don't know what I would do without you," Cally said as tears of joy streamed down her worried-looking face.

"Well, I hate to be the bearer of bad news, but it's already eleven o'clock and we need to go inside and get ready to go to Ryan's funeral. After all, if we show up late, Cally's plan will be ruined," Bill said, trying to get the show on the road.

"Sounds good to me. I don't know about the rest of you, but I'm ready to send Ryan back to hell, where he belongs," Kate said, hoping the whole time that Cally's plan would work.

"I'm more than ready. I have sat back for months and watched Ryan mistreat you while he was living, and I'll be damned if I let him hurt you when he is dead," Kyle said with a bold yet manly look on his face, as he stared directly into Cally's baby blue eyes.

Cally was moved by Kyle's kind words; they made her feel so safe and protected. Even her parents did not make her feel that safe; it was as if Kyle was her very own protective shield, ready for anything. It truly amazed Cally to find out just how much Kyle cared about her; she felt so lucky to have Kyle in her life. He was a godsend, an angel from heaven that was sent to watch over her and keep her safe from anything and everything that could or would ever harm her. It all started to make sense now. It was crystal-clear that Cally was, in fact, in love with Kyle, no questions about it. She could feel it in her heart, and Kate could see it on her face.

"Okay, you guys, I think we should head in the house now so that we can get ready before it gets any later," Kate said, reminding everyone again.

"Mom, is it alright if Kyle and I stay out here and talk for a few minutes while you and Dad get ready? I promise that it won't take long and as soon as we are finished, we will come straight in and start getting ready ourselves," Cally asked politely, giving her mother one of her famous begging looks, thinking that it might give her a better shot at getting her way.

"Well, I guess that it's okay, but don't stay out here too long. I want to be ready to go by at least twelve thirty. That way we can make it on time, without having to rush ourselves," Kate said, looking into Cally's love-struck eyes, hoping that Cally would not get in over her head with Kyle.

Cally watched nervously as her parents walked back into the house. No sooner than the front door slammed, Cally got an incredible feeling of excitement all over her body. This was the perfect time to tell Kyle how she really felt about him, before she chickened out again. Cally did not know exactly how she was going to tell Kyle that she was in love with him, but she was going to do it or die. Cally felt as if she should have done it a long time ago, but it was better late than never. She just hoped that Kyle felt the same way about her, because if he did not, then Cally did not know what she would do.

"Okay, Kyle, I really don't know how to say this, so please just be patient and hear me out before you say anything. Because once I get started, I want to finish. I'm falling in love with you. I know that this is a lot to put on you at one time, and I don't expect you to give me an answer right away, but I could not take it any longer, I had to tell you," Cally explained as she dropped her head down, fearing Kyle's response would not be the one she wanted.

"Wow, you were right, this is a lot to put on me in one day, but I'm glad that you did, because I feel the same way and I have for years. I just didn't have the courage to tell you, and when you started dating Ryan, I lost all hope of us ever getting together. But now that I know you feel the same way, I think that we can make a go of things. What do you think?" Kyle asked as he put his hand under Cally's chin and raised her head, so he could get the kiss he had been waiting on for years.

Cally felt so relieved to find out that Kyle felt the same way as she did. It was like a dream come true. Cally felt like a princess who had just met her Prince Charming. This was the best feeling Cally had ever felt. It was as if she and Kyle were destined to be together, and as Kyle gently leaned forward to kiss Cally, her heart started racing with excitement again. Cally could feel his warm minty breath on her face, as his lips slowly touched hers. As they continued to kiss, Cally could not help but put her arms around him and think how magical everything felt. If only for a moment, before reality kicked back in, this was a real-life fairy tale, and Cally could not have been happier.

"I hate to cut this short, but I think we should go inside and start getting ready. I just saw your mother looking out of the living room window, and I'm guessing that is her way of telling us to come in. What do you think?" Kyle asked, still caressing Cally's soft, yet still bruised-up face, letting her know that it was not his idea to end the kiss early.

"You know, I think that you just might be right about that. If you're ready, we can go inside now and start getting ready," Cally replied with a half smile on her blushing face, wondering if her mother had just witnessed the first kiss between her and Kyle.

"Here, Cally. I found this dress while I was digging through my closet. It has wide arm openings, so you should have no problem getting your arm cast through it. Now hurry up and go get ready. The clock is ticking, you know, and as for you, Kyle, you can go change your clothes in my bathroom," Kate said, pointing the way.

At twelve thirty on the dot, Cally came walking down the stairs looking absolutely beautiful in her velvet black dress, with her long blond hair curled to perfection. With her hand gliding down the banister, she started having a flashback of prom night, especially when she saw Kyle in his suit and tie waiting on her at the bottom of the stairs. Cally wished that she could go back in time and change things, but she could not. All she could do was accept the bitter truth and try to move on with her life. Cally knew that no matter what happened, she had to be strong in order for her to survive this whole tragic ordeal.

"Wow, Cally, you look really pretty. Black is definitely your color," Kyle complimented her with a smile on his face that went from ear to ear. He looked into Cally's baby blue, sparkling eyes, almost getting lost in them.

"Why, thank you very much. You don't look so bad yourself," Cally said, giving Kyle a wink, as her face blushed a bit at Kyle's compliment.

"Well, since you two are ready, I guess it is about that time," Kate said after seeing both Cally and Kyle standing at the bottom of the stairs.

As Cally stared into her mother's worried eyes, she could not help but feel at fault for everything. She hated to put everyone through so much trouble and pain; it was as if she had caused this whole catastrophe on her own. Cally could not wait to get everything over and done with. She just prayed that her plan would work, because she knew that if it did not, then her life would be miserable forever. Ryan would make sure of that. He had made a promise, and Cally knew that he would keep it. There was no doubt in her mind about that.

"Thank you so much for everything that you have done for me. You do not know how much it means. I feel as if I cannot thank you enough," Cally said, wrapping her arms around her mother as tears came to her baby blue eyes, making them look like the deepest blue ocean.

"Oh Cally, you don't have to keep thanking me. I'm your mother and I would do anything for in this world for you. I would even walk through the depths of hell, just to reach you on the other side," Kate said, returning the hug and giving Cally a kiss on the cheek.

"Okay, you two, I hate to break up the party, but it is already a quarter till one, so we should be getting a move on if we want to make it there on time," Bill said anxiously, as he rattled the car keys around in his pocket.

"Oh goodness, I didn't know that it was that late. I let time slip away from me. You are absolutely right, we should get going. Cally, do you have the ring?" Kate asked in case Cally had forgotten it upstairs.

"Yes, it's right here. I put it in my pocketbook, so that I wouldn't forget it," Cally said, patting her pocketbook with her trembling hand.

"Good girl, now let's go get this finished, so we can put this nightmare to rest and hopefully get back to our normal lives," Kate said, taking Cally by the hand, letting her know that she would be right by her side the whole way.

As Cally held on to Kate's hand, she could not help but feel a little bit scared. She had so many things running through her mind that she could not even see straight. Her hands were shaking, and her heart was pounding. Cally knew that the task ahead of her was not going to be an easy one. She had to do things right the first time, because there was not going to be a second chance. This was Cally's one and only shot of getting rid of Ryan, and she would be damned if she was going to screw it up. Cally had to be strong for herself and her family.

"I should have known. It seems as if every time there is a funeral to go to, it is always raining. Just a few minutes ago, the sun was shining bright and the birds were chirping, and now there is nothing but this gray, rainy sky to look at," Bill said, as the cold raindrops hit his head in a steady falling beat.

"Yeah, that's usually the way it goes. It's almost as if the sky itself is depressed," Kate said, backing out of the driveway.

On the way to the church, everyone was quiet, so quiet that the only thing you could hear was the sound of the engine and the heavy rain beating down on the rooftop. Although the heavy rain did not seem to bother anyone else, it did Cally. All she could do was think about prom night, the prom night that almost took her life. Every time the rain got heavier, Cally would cringe with fear. All she could do was picture herself lying on the ground while the heavy rain hit her in the face. That was a night that Cally would never forget as long as she lived. It was a terrible memory that would scar her forever.

"Okay, Cally, before we get any closer to the church, are you sure that you want to do this, because if you don't, I'll take you back home, no questions asked," Kate advised, as she pulled into an empty parking lot, giving Cally one last chance to change her mind.

"Thanks, Mom, but this is something that I really need to do. I think that once I put the ring inside Ryan's casket, things will get back to normal—or at least I hope so," Cally said as her hands started to shake and sweat at just the thought of putting her hand inside Ryan's casket.

"Don't worry. I'll be right there for you the whole time, and I promise that I'll not let anything happen to you," Kyle said, hoping that his words would ease some of the tension for Cally.

"Alright, if you're sure that this is what you want to do…" Kate said, stalling, giving Cally another second to think things through.

"I'm sure, Mom. I just want to get this over and done with, so I can finally move on with my life," Cally said, sticking to her plan as Kate pulled out of the parking lot.

"Well, there is one thing about it. There is no turning back now, so let's just all take a few deep breaths and try to relax before we get out," Bill said as Kate pulled into the church parking lot.

"I have never felt so bad about a funeral in my whole life. I cannot imagine what that poor woman is going through. She has got to be the strongest person I know. I wish that there was something I could say or do to make her feel better, but only God and time can mend her broken heart," Kate said with a sad look on her face as she gave Ms. Jones a quick wave.

Cally sat in the backseat and held on to Kyle's hand as she gave some thought to what her mother just said. Cally knew that Ms. Jones was hurting. There was no question about that, and although Ryan was a bad person, he still did not deserve to die. Cally wished a million times that she could go back and change things, but she had to face the bitter truth. There was no way to go back and change anything. Cally had to accept things the way they were, not the way she wanted them to be, and move on with her life. Cally knew that things would work out over time. She just had to be patient and wait on that day.

"Well, we aren't getting anything done just sitting here, so let's go inside and get this over with before I change my mind," Bill said, interrupting Cally's thoughts as he noticed a break in the rain.

"Yeah, we really do need to get in there before any more people show up and crowd the place. Who knows, maybe it won't be as bad as we think," Kate said, trying to keep a positive attitude about things as she glanced back in the rearview mirror at Cally.

"Are you absolutely sure, without a shadow of a doubt, that you want to do this? Because it is perfectly fine if you do not want to," Kyle whispered, as he started to feel a little uneasy about the whole situation.

"It is okay, Kyle. I'm ready to do this, so let's just go inside and get this over and done with," Cally said, opening her car door.

11

Walking toward Ms. Jones, Cally got an eerie feeling all over her body; it was almost as if Ryan was right behind her. Scared to look back, Cally picked up her pace and kept her eyes focused on Ms. Jones and the church. As Cally approached Ryan's mother, her eerie feeling was replaced by a sad one. She felt so confused, and she did not know what to say to her. It was if she could not speak at all. Cally wondered what she could possibly say to someone who had just lost their only child. Bottom line, there was nothing Cally or anyone else could say to help with the pain.

"Oh Cally, I'm so glad to see that you made it. How are you feeling today? Is your arm doing any better?" Ms. Jones asked, reaching her hand out to Cally's.

"I'm doing okay, but I'm more concerned about how you are doing. How are you holding up?" Cally asked. The words flowed effortlessly, as if her mouth had a mind of its own.

"Well, I'm taking it slow, but there is still a lot of hurt. Still, I'm sure that things will start looking up for me," Ms. Jones replied, wrapping her arms around Cally, as Kate, Bill, and Kyle walked up.

"You have got the sweetest daughter in the whole world. I have never met anyone as loving and caring as she is. Now I know why Ryan loved you so much," Ms. Jones said, complimenting Cally and letting her know how much she really cared about her.

"Speaking of Ryan, would it be okay if I went inside and had a few minutes alone with him—before anyone else gets here? It would really mean a lot to me. I promise that I'll not be long," Cally said, hoping that Ms. Jones would not have any objections.

"Of course you can, Cally, and do not be in a rush. Take as much time as you need. I'll keep everyone else out here until you finish saying your good-byes. I know that Ryan would have wanted it this way. But there is one thing before you go: the casket is closed, due to all of the burns, so please do not try to open it. Trust me, it is for your own good," Ms. Jones warned before letting Cally go.

As Cally got closer to the church doors, her heart started to pound and her legs turned to Jell-O, making it difficult for her to walk. Despite being scared, though, Cally knew that she had to do this for her sake and the sake of her family. Ryan had done enough damage, and it was time for Cally to put a stop to his reign of terror, once and for all. Taking a deep breath, Cally opened the church doors and walked inside. Upon entering the church, the first thing she saw was a huge wreath, followed by Ryan's black shiny casket. Cally was terrified at the sight of Ryan's casket, so terrified that she could feel her knees starting to buckle. With all of the things Cally had been seeing, she did not know what to expect when she opened the casket, but whatever happened, she had to be prepared for it.

Cally closed her eyes tightly and swallowed hard as she tried to brace herself for the most frightening, gut-wrenching thing she would ever do in her life. Cally was so scared that she could feel the hair on the back of her neck starting to rise as she neared Ryan's casket. It was absolutely the worst feeling in the world, and Cally could not wait until it was over with. In a hurry to get everything over and done with, Cally reached into her purse and took out the ring. With her hands shaking nervously, Cally opened the casket up just wide enough to drop the ring in.

"Come on, Cally. You can do this. You have to do this. It is the only way to get your life back," Cally said to herself as she tried to find one ounce of courage in her terrified body.

Without further hesitation, Cally stuck her trembling hand inside and dropped the ring. She wanted to be happy about the way everything had gone, but she knew that she was not out of the woods yet. At this point, anything could happen, and the last thing Cally was going to do was under-estimate Ryan. Cally knew how evil and powerful Ryan was, and she was not about to let her guard down for any reason. Cally was too close, and she knew that she could not afford to screw anything up.

Just as Cally turned to walk away, she heard something hit the floor and bounce twice before stopping. Cally was petrified. She did not want to turn back around and face Ryan's casket again, but she knew that she had to. She could not just walk out without knowing what had hit the floor. After all, she had come to the funeral for one purpose and one purpose only, and that was to carry out her plan so that she could get rid of Ryan once and for all. Terrified of what she would see, Cally turned around slowly, keeping her eyes focused on the floor. There, only inches away from her, was the heart-shaped ring, which she had just put in Ryan's casket. Cally was scared stiff. Her heart started to pound, and her hands started to shake. She could not believe what had just happened. Cally knew there was no possible way that the ring could have bounced out by itself, so that left only one other option: it was Ryan, without a shadow of a doubt.

"Come closer," a voice called out in a whisper, startling Cally so bad that she nearly fainted.

Cally did not know where the voice was coming from, but she knew it was Ryan calling for her. Cally started shaking so badly that she could not control herself; it was almost as if she was having a seizure. Cally wanted to scream out for help, but she knew that if she did, then people would hear her and start to come inside the church before she had a chance to put the ring back in Ryan's casket. Cally had come too far to turn back now. She had to regain her courage and finish the plan before it was too late.

"Why are you doing this to me, Ryan? What do you want from me? Why don't you just let me get on with my life?" Cally asked as she scanned the church, looking for Ryan.

"I'm over here, Cally. Come closer so I can see you," the voice said, as Cally heard the hinges squeak on Ryan's casket.

Cally automatically looked at Ryan's casket and noticed that the top of it was opening slowly. Cally wanted to run out of the church screaming, but she could not. Her whole body was frozen. All she could do was stand there and watch in horror as Ryan's casket opened up. Cally prayed to God that He would give her the strength to make it out of the church before Ryan could hurt her. Finally, after what seemed like forever, Cally could feel her legs start to loosen up, and without any hesitation, Cally took a few steps back, still keeping her eyes focused on Ryan's casket.

"Come on back, Cally. I have got you. Do not worry. This will be over soon, I promise," a voice said from behind Cally, as an ice-cold hand touched her on the shoulder, sending chills down her spine.

Cally knew that her only way out was to turn around and run toward the door as fast as she could, and at this point, she did not care who saw her run out. All Cally cared about was getting away from Ryan before he killed her. It was all evident to Cally now; there was no getting rid of Ryan. He was on a mission, and he was not going to stop until he completed it. Cally knew that she was trapped and helpless. Ryan was going to take her with him. At the end of her rope and not knowing what to do, Cally took a step forward and turned around quickly, plowing right into her mother, knocking her straight to the floor.

"Oh Mom, I'm so sorry. I was trying to get away from Ryan. Are you okay? Did I hurt you?" Cally asked, as she helped her mother up off the floor.

"Yes, Cally, I'm fine. I should not have snuck up on you without letting you know that it was me. It is just that you were taking so long in here. I decided to come in and check on you, just to make sure that Ryan was not hurting you in any way," Kate explained, still feeling a little shocked as to what had just happened.

"Well, he is back to his evil ways again, because after I put the ring in his casket and started to walk out, the ring fell out of the casket and hit the floor," Cally said as she scanned the floor, trying to locate the ring.

"Okay, let's just find this ring so that we can do what we came to do, before people start crowding in. Ms. Jones cannot hold them out there forever," Kate said as she started to look for the ring herself.

As Kate helped Cally look for the ring, her heart started to flutter and her hands started to shake with fear. She could not help but feel a little worried that Cally might have lost the ring for good, and that was one problem Kate was not ready to deal with. Although Kate wanted things to go smoothly, she had one of her gut feelings that something was going to go wrong—and it did. It seemed as if nothing was going to go right for them, no matter how hard they tried. Kate was so afraid that people would start coming in before they had a chance to find the ring, but just when she had given up all hope, Cally called out the words she had been longing to hear.

"Here it is, Mom. I found the ring, it is right over here," Cally said with relief as she picked the heart-shaped ring up off the floor and showed it to her mother.

"Good, now drop the ring inside of the casket and let's get out of here before Ms. Jones starts getting suspicious," Kate said, keeping a close eye on the church doors, making sure that no one was coming in on them.

"Okay, Mom, it is done. We can go back out now," Cally informed Kate as she grabbed her mother by the hand and pulled her toward the door.

"There you two are. I was beginning to get a little worried about you. Is it okay to start now, or do you need some more time alone? Because if you do, then I would be more than happy to wait as long as you need me to," Ms. Jones said sincerely as she took Cally by the hand.

"No, that won't be necessary. I got a chance to say my good-byes, and for that I thank you from the bottom of my heart. It really meant a lot to me," Cally lied, as a feeling of guilt swept through her entire body.

Saying good-bye to Ryan was the last thing on Cally's mind, but she did not want Ms. Jones to know that. The only thing Cally had needed was the opportunity to go inside and get rid of the ring, and now that it was done, all she had to do was wait to see if her plan had worked. Cally felt bad for feeling this way, but she could not wait until they put Ryan's casket and his ring in the ground. To Cally, saying good-bye to either one would not be hard to do. Ryan had tortured Cally long enough, and now it was time to send him back to hell where he belonged.

"Okay, everyone. We're ready now, so let's go inside before it starts raining again," Ms. Jones said, taking Cally and Kate by their hands as they followed Preacher Ron inside.

As soon as everyone was inside, Kate decided it would be better if she and Cally sat with Ms. Jones, especially since she did not have anyone to sit with her. Kate knew that Bill would understand that she was only trying to be there for Ms. Jones in her time of need. As soon as everyone grew quiet, Preacher Ron started his sermon, and during the sermon, Cally could not help looking around the room. It made her feel so uncomfortable to sit and stare at Ryan's black shiny casket. Just the color of it reminded her of just how dark and evil Ryan really was. While looking around the room, Cally noticed that there was not a dry eye in the whole church, which confused her. Cally began to wonder if she was the only one whom Ryan had treated badly. Judging by the looks on everyone else's face, she concluded that she must have been the first and only one.

Cally was so caught up in her thoughts that she did not hear when Preacher Ron asked everyone to bow their heads and pray. If it had not been for

Kyle tapping her on the shoulder to get her attention, she would have kept on with what she was doing. After the prayer was over, the pallbearers picked up Ryan's casket and started carrying it out of the church to the graveyard. When Ryan's casket passed by Cally, she shut her eyes tightly and tried to imagine that she was somewhere else, anywhere else but there. When the pallbearers had gone out the door, everyone stood up and started to follow them. On the way out the church doors, Cally felt a feeling of peace and joy. She was so glad that the funeral was almost over. She could not wait until they put Ryan in the ground and covered him up, along with the ring. That would be the closure she needed to move on with her life.

"Here we go. Just a little while longer and all of this will be a thing of the past," Cally said to herself as she moved a little closer to Kyle.

Cally was so excited about starting a new relationship with Kyle, every time she thought about it, her heart skipped a beat. It was like a dream come true for Cally—a dream that she had waited so long for. The only thing Cally regretted was not going out with him sooner. She felt as if she had wasted too much time with Ryan and his controlling ways. Cally was so caught up in her thoughts that she did not notice that the funeral was almost over. Preacher Ron had just instructed everyone to take a red rose from the basket so they could be dropped into Ryan's grave. Cally could not have cared less about dropping a rose in Ryan's grave. If it was up to her, she would have thrown a boulder in on top of him, but Cally wanted to look and act sincere for Ms. Jones's sake. Although Ryan was a cruel and evil person, it did not mean that his mother was. In fact, she was one of the nicest people Cally had ever met, and she did not want to do or say anything that would upset her. Cally just wanted to put everything behind her, so that she could move on with her life.

"Cally, would you like to go first?" Ms. Jones asked kindly, snapping Cally out of the daze she was in.

"No, that's okay. I'll take my turn after you," Cally replied with a nervous stutter as she pricked her finger on one of the thorns.

Everyone formed a line behind Ryan's mother and waited patiently on their turn to drop their roses in the grave. While standing there, Cally glanced back and noticed that the line was long—it seemed to go on forever. Cally dreaded having to look at Ryan's casket again. It was like one big, never-ending nightmare. She started to wonder how much longer the funeral was going to last. She had never been more ready to leave. Just standing there was like torture to her, and Kate could sense it, too. Kate just prayed that Cally could hold out for a little while longer and make it through the rest of the funeral without any problems. After everyone had dropped their roses in, Preacher Ron called for one last prayer before the crowd was to depart.

This had better be the last prayer or I swear that I'm just going to start walking to the car, Cally thought to herself as she bowed her head and gritted her teeth together.

Cally did not see how one evil person could have that many people who cared for him. It seemed ridiculous, and it was obvious they did not know the same cruel and heartless Ryan that she did. When Cally heard Preacher Ron say "amen," it was music to her ears. She hated to be so impatient, but she had put up with Ryan long enough. Now all she wanted was to erase him from her life completely. Cally did not even want to remember the good times they had, because to Cally, no memories were good ones.

"Well, I guess we should be going now. After all, it's almost time for Cally's medicine, but if you should need anything or just someone to talk to, you know that you can always count on me to be there for you day or night," Kate said to Ms. Jones, trying to give her a good reason for leaving so soon and hoping that it would not offend Ryan's mother in any way.

"Oh, I understand, and thank you again for everything that you have done. It means a lot to me to know that I have a friend like you. I know that Ryan would be thankful too. Cally, please remember that you are welcome over at my house anytime, so don't be a stranger," Ms. Jones replied, wrapping her arms around Cally to give her a hug good-bye.

"Sure thing. I promise just as soon as I start to feel better, I'll come and visit you," Cally replied, quickly ending the awkward conversation.

12

"Thank God that is over with. I was starting to feel uncomfortable. I just hope that Ms. Jones did not pick up on any of it," Kate said, unlocking the car doors as the rain started to pour heavily again.

"I think everything will be alright for Ms. Jones—and us, too. We just have to let time heal everything and be patient as it does," Cally said, sounding more positive than ever as she slid quickly into the backseat, so they could hurry up and get out of there before something else came up.

"So, how did everything go? Did you put the ring inside Ryan's casket?" Bill asked curiously as the anticipation was eating away at him.

"Yeah, everything went smoothly. The ring is now six feet under, right along with Ryan, and personally, I could not be happier. Now maybe things can get back to normal." Cally answered, feeling positive that Ryan could not come back now that the ring was in the grave with him.

"Well, we should not count our chickens before they hatch. After all, there is still a possibility that things could go wrong. We don't know for sure if the plan is going to work, so don't get ahead of yourself," Kate advised Cally before she got too excited.

"I'm proud of you—it took a lot of guts to do what you did. But I agree with your mom on this one. We need to wait and make sure that Ryan is not going to come back before we get our hopes up," Kyle said, taking Kate's side on things, merely giving Cally his advice, too.

"Well, let's just keep our fingers crossed and maybe everything will work out for the best. But if it doesn't, then we will just cross that bridge when we get to it," Bill said, trying to make things seem like no big deal.

While Cally was still trying to be positive, Kate was not. Kate had an eerie feeling about things, and she was not about to let her guard down until she was one hundred percent sure of things. Kate would have loved to look on the positive side of things, but she could not—the feeling was just too strong and her gut told her that they had not seen the last of Ryan or his evil ways. Kate had no idea when or where Ryan was going to show up, but this time she planned on being ready for him. Kate was not going to let Ryan get the upper hand this time. Cally was her only child, and she would do anything to protect her, even if it meant dying for her.

"I don't know about the rest of you, but I'm starting to get hungry. Maybe we should go out and get something to eat before heading home. What are you guys in the mood for?" Bill asked, interrupting the silence that filled the car.

"You know, Dad, I could really go for some pizza right about now. What would you like to eat, Kyle?" Cally asked politely as she took Kyle by the hand and gave him a warm, smile.

"It doesn't matter to me; I'll eat just about anything. What about you, Kate? Does pizza sound alright to you?" Kyle asked, looking at Kate through the rearview mirror.

"That sounds great to me, so if everyone agrees, I'll take us to that little Italian restaurant in town. They have got the best pizza around, and their prices are good, too." Kate said as she kept her focus on the road.

Kate proceeded to drive to the restaurant. She was glad Bill had brought up the idea of getting something to eat; she thought that everyone could use a change of scenery, especially after all they had been through. And the thought of someone else waiting on her did not sound too bad, either. Kate could not help it. She wanted to be strong for her family, but all of the extra work and extra stress had finally taken its toll on her, both mentally and physically. Kate knew that she had to slow down and take some time for herself, so that she would have the strength to take care of Cally and Bill.

"Wouldn't you know it? I bet that every red light in town will catch us before we get there," Bill said impatiently as Kate had to stop for the third time.

While waiting for the light to change, Cally noticed a very familiar-looking car right next to them. It was a black Mustang, just like the one Ryan had before he crashed it. Cally stared hard at the car, trying to see who was driving it, but it was no use. The windows were tinted too dark and the heavy rain made it difficult to see inside. But after seeing the car, Cally's positive feelings started to go away; it was almost as if no matter where Cally turned, she would always have some kind of reminder of Ryan. Cally found herself wondering if she would ever get back to her old self again.

"That's a nice car. It looks as if someone has put a lot of money and hard work into it. I bet that it's super fast, too. You can tell by the way that the motor sounds. What do you think, Bill?" Kyle asked, right out of the blue, which frightened Cally a bit.

Cally had known Kyle for a very long time, and during that time, he had never been into cars. Kyle had always been a truck person; he had even said it himself on numerous occasions. Cally could not believe that he would say something like that, especially knowing that Ryan's car was just like the one next to them. Not only did Cally find it hard to believe, but so did Bill and Kate. They both turned their heads to see what Kyle was talking about, and when they saw the car, they were speechless. Both Bill and Kate could not help but wonder why Kyle would blurt something like that out, unless he was just trying to make small talk. To Bill and Kate, though, it was like a sign, telling them that Ryan was still with them.

"Mom, what are you waiting for? The light is green. You can go any time now," Cally said, rushing her mother through the stoplight so that they could get away from the black Mustang.

"Oh, I'm sorry. I don't know where my mind is today. You know what it is like when you have a lot on your mind, the smallest things can distract you," Kate explained, trying to play everything off as she gave the car some gas and proceeded down the road to the next red light, only to see the same black Mustang stopped there, too.

"Well, Bill, you never did tell me what you thought about the car. Do you like it or not?" Kyle asked for the second time, this time a little pushier.

"I've never really been into muscle cars. I think they are overrated and a bit loud, too," Bill answered in an irritated voice, letting Kyle know that his questions were starting to piss him off.

The conversation between Bill and Kyle was getting a little heated; Kate could tell by the sound of Bill's voice that he was beginning to get a little agitated with Kyle. Kate could not understand for the life of her why Kyle was acting so strange. It was not like Kyle to be so outspoken. It was as if he were a different person. Kate wanted to change the conversation before Bill said something out of anger toward Kyle, but she could not think of anything to say. It was as if her mind had gone completely blank. All she could think about was getting to the restaurant so they all could get out of the car before something bad took place between Bill and Kyle.

"Oh, thank goodness we are here. It is about damn time," Kate said aloud before she even realized she had cursed.

"Wow, I have never seen anyone get this excited over an Italian restaurant before. You must be really hungry, huh?" Kyle asked sarcastically with a laugh, poking fun at Kate as she circled the parking lot. She was looking for a close place to park so that they would not get drenched by the heavy rain as they walked inside.

"Okay, on the count of three I say that we make a run for it so that we do not get soaked," Kate said after parking. She totally ignored Kyle's sarcastic remark, as if she did not even hear him.

"Mom, you and Dad go ahead. We will catch up to you in a few minutes," Cally said as she viciously glared at Kyle, letting him know that she was upset with him.

"All right, sweetheart, but don't be too long. We do not want to keep anyone waiting," Kate said, feeling a little uneasy about leaving Cally alone with Kyle, with the way he was acting.

Cally stayed quiet as she watched her parents walk away. She was so upset with Kyle and the way he was acting. She had never known Kyle to be so rude to anyone, especially her parents. Cally could not believe that things had gone from good to bad so quickly. It seemed as if her life was meant to be a living hell. Cally thought a lot of Kyle, and before he had acted out, she had also respected him, but now she was not so sure. Cally tried to find the right words to say to Kyle, but the more she thought about things, the madder she got. She was so upset that she knew she had to say something before she exploded.

"What the hell is your problem? Why are you acting like such an asshole toward my parents and me? You know that we have been through a lot the past couple of days, so why on earth would you act this way?" Cally asked in a hostile voice, as she grabbed Kyle by his arm.

"What are you talking about, Cally? I have not been an asshole, nor have I said anything out of the ordinary to you or your parents. I would never disrespect them like that, so why don't you just chill out and think about what you are saying before you say it?" Kyle replied with a snap, as if he had no memory of what Cally was talking about.

"Oh, you know good and damn well what I'm talking about, so do not play dumb with me. First, you bring up the black Mustang that was beside us, knowing that Ryan's car was just like it. Then, like an idiot, you asked my dad what he thought about it, and you do not think that there was anything wrong with that?" Cally asked in an angry voice as she started to get very irritated with Kyle and his sorry excuses.

"Not in the least bit. It was only a car, and besides, I was only trying to make small talk to break the uncomfortable silence," Kyle explained, taking up for himself before Cally could fire back at him.

"Okay, I get it now. This is your way of telling me that you do not want anything to do with me anymore, right? Well, let me tell you something. If you do not want anything to do with me, all you had to do was say so, and I would have left you alone, no questions asked," Cally said, raising her voice as she broke down and started to cry.

"No, Cally, that is not it at all and you know that. You are just taking things to a whole new extreme. I really do care about you, and I would like for us to start acting more like a couple, but if you are going to take everything I say the wrong way, then I do not see any point in us being together, and that is my honest opinion. I do not know any other way of saying it." Kyle reached for his door handle so that he could get out of the car and away from the argument.

When Cally saw that Kyle was going to get out of the car and leave, she started to panic; she could feel her heart crumbling into a million little pieces. It was as if a part of her was dying, and that was a feeling she could not handle. All Cally wanted was to get her life back and spend it with Kyle, and now she felt as if she had blown her chances completely with him. After seeing how upset he got when she confronted him, Cally knew that he was telling the truth. Knowing that she had made a terrible mistake, Cally felt that she had to apologize and set everything straight before Kyle walked out of her life for good.

"Wait, where are you going? Please do not leave me when I need you the most. I'm sorry, I did not mean to make you mad, please forgive me," Cally begged hysterically as she grabbed hold of Kyle's jacket, trying to stop him.

"Look, Cally. I know that you have been through a lot, and I think that maybe you should get better before we jump into anything serious. Trust me, it is for your own good. I'm just thinking of you and your well-being," Kyle explained as he pulled away from Cally and reached for the door handle again.

"No, Kyle. You do not understand. I need you so that I can get better. You mean everything to me, and I do not want to lose you over some misunderstanding. Please just give me another chance. I promise that this will never happen again," Cally begged and pleaded for the second time, hoping that she could get through to him before he left.

"Okay, Cally. One last time. But I swear if you start flipping out again, I'm walking. Do you understand what I'm saying? Now we really should be getting inside before your parents come looking for us," Kyle said bitterly, as if he were talking to a small child.

On the way inside the restaurant, Kyle stayed ahead of Cally as if he were trying to punish her in some way. Cally knew that Kyle was upset with her, but she did not understand why he was still being so mean to her. It just did not make any sense. Cally felt so confused. She had already apologized to Kyle, and yet he was still acting ugly toward her. Cally was at a dead-end road, and there was nothing more that she could do or say to Kyle to make him understand just how sorry she was. The only thing Cally could really do was wait patiently and let Kyle cool off before she talked to him again.

"There you two are. I was beginning to get a little concerned. Is everything okay?" Kate asked curiously as Cally and Kyle sat down at the table.

"Yeah, everything is just fine. We just needed a few minutes alone so that we could talk about a few things," Cally explained, feeling as if she had just lied to her mother again.

"She is right. We just had a misunderstanding about some things, and I would really like to take this time to apologize to both of you for bringing up the black Mustang. Honestly, I did not mean anything by it I was only trying to start a conversation, but I see now that I was completely out of line. I hope that you can accept my apology," Kyle said sincerely.

"Of course we forgive you. We all make mistakes, and after all, we are only human. At least you admitted your wrongdoing, and it takes a real man to admit when he is wrong," Bill said, giving Kyle a nod of approval.

"It sure is, so do not be so hard on yourself. It has been a rough day for everyone. We are all entitled to make a few mistakes," Kate said, agreeing with Bill as she motioned for the waiter to come over.

"Hello, I'll be your waiter this afternoon. Are you ready to order now?" the waiter asked as he clicked his pen as if he were rushing them to make a decision.

"I believe so. I think that we will have the buffet and a large pitcher of sweet tea," Kate said, ordering for everyone.

"Was it just me, or did that waiter seem a bit pushy?" Bill asked, as he unfolded his napkin.

"Oh, he is probably just having a bad day. After all, we did keep him waiting awhile," Kate said, taking up for the busy waiter.

"Speak of the devil, here comes our pushy waiter again, with our tea, and he doesn't look happy to see us," Bill joked, hoping to ease some of the tension that Kyle was probably feeling.

"Oh Bill, would you stop and leave that poor boy alone? He looks like a sweet kid, so stop trying to give him a hard time. Remember, you waited tables when you were around his age, too," Kate said and gave Bill a playful smack on the leg.

"You are right. I sure did, and people gave me a hard time, too, so I think I should repay the favor. After all, it is only fair, right?" Bill replied, giving Kate a wink and a smile to let her know that he was only playing.

"Well, while you give the waiter a hard time, Cally and I are going to the bathroom to wash up before we eat," Kate said, motioning for Cally to go with her.

Kate wanted to get Cally alone so that she could talk to her about Kyle, and she thought that this would be the perfect time to do so without being obvious. Kate just had to know what was said between them, and most importantly, she wanted to hear Kyle's excuse for bringing up the black Mustang. Kate knew that there had to be a reason; she just wanted to find out what that reason was. As soon as Kate and Cally walked into the bathroom and Kate saw that there was no one else there, she jumped in.

"Okay, Cally. I have to know what is going on between you and Kyle. Is everything okay? Because you look as if you have been crying," Kate asked as she stared into Cally's red, swollen eyes.

"Yes, Mom, everything is just fine. I thought that Kyle was being rude on the way over here, but when I confronted him about it, he said that he was only trying to start a conversation with Dad," Cally explained, hoping that her mother would also understand Kyle's reason for bringing up the car.

"You know, I thought that was what he was doing, so that is why I did not say anything to him. You can just look at him and tell that he is nervous as can be. The poor guy has taken on a lot today, and that could take its toll on anyone. I think he just needs a little time to adjust to things," Kate said, letting Cally know that everything would get better.

"Thanks, Mom. I'm so glad that I have you to talk to. You are like my mother and my best friend combined. I do not know what I would do without you," Cally said, giving her mom a hug.

"Do not mention it, sweetheart. I'm always glad to help, but I think that we should get back out there before your dad and Kyle get into trouble," Kate said, opening the bathroom door for Cally.

As Kate and Cally walked out of the bathroom, Cally felt as if a huge weight had been lifted off her shoulders. She was so relieved that her mother did not get upset about the things Kyle had said. Cally really enjoyed the conversations that she had with her mother. She felt as if she could tell her anything, and that was exactly what she wanted to do from now on. Cally never wanted to lie to her mother again, or hide things from her, because she knew that lying would get her nowhere. All Cally wanted to do was be honest with her mother—and herself.

"Well, would you look at this? I do not believe my eyes. I figured that you two would have been in trouble by now," Kate said, joking with both Bill and Kyle and managing to get a laugh out of them both.

"You girls should go to the buffet and fix a plate. They just brought out a fresh pizza and some delicious lasagna," Bill advised as he devoured a hot slice of pepperoni pizza almost in one bite.

"Wow, Dad. You should really slow down before you choke. I'm sure that they will bring out more food in a few minutes," Cally said, insinuating that Bill was eating like a pig.

"We really cannot help it. It tastes so good that you do not want to put it down," Kyle sided with Bill as he stuffed a slice into his mouth also.

"Cally, I think that we should go get some pizza before these two decide to go back for seconds," Kate said, watching Bill and Kyle scarf down their food like wild animals.

"Just our luck, Mom. We waited too long, and now there is only cheese and mushroom pizza left," Cally complained as she scanned the buffet table, hoping to see something that caught her eye.

"Oh no, look behind you," Kate said, watching the waiter bring out another pepperoni pizza.

Curious as to what her mother was talking about, Cally turned around quickly, only to find herself face-to-face with the pushy waiter. After almost plowing into the waiter, Cally could not help but notice his eyes; he had the exact same color of eyes that Ryan did. Frozen dead in her tracks, suddenly Cally found herself wondering if she was having another bad dream. Everything seemed so strange to Cally. She did not remember the waiter's eyes being that color before, but then again she did not remember observing them that closely. Finally after snapping back to reality, Cally knew that it was not a dream—it was real.

"Excuse me. I'm so sorry. I did not mean to get in your way," Cally apologized to the waiter, who had a pissed-off look on his face.

"That is okay. I'm used to dealing with bitches like you," the waiter replied, as he stared Cally down with his dark green eyes.

"What did you just say to me?" Cally asked in complete shock, as she stared him down also.

"I said that is okay. Why do you ask?" the waiter replied after picking up on Cally's unnecessary hostility.

"No, you did not. You just called me a bitch. I heard you plain as day, so do not try to deny it," Cally argued as she stared him down.

"Cally, sweetheart, maybe you and I should go outside and get some fresh air," Kate suggested with a confused look on her face, as she took Cally by her hand.

"No, Mom. I want to see the manager of this place so that I can tell them what a pathetic loser they have working for them," Cally said, raising her voice in anger at both her mother and the waiter.

"I'm so sorry. I do not know what has come over her. She is usually not like this at all," Kate explained, feeling a little embarrassed by Cally's outburst.

"That is okay. There is no need to apologize. It is not the first time that I have been yelled at, and I'm sure it will not be the last," the waiter replied gracefully as Kate tried to get Cally to go outside until she calmed down.

"No, Mom, I'm not going anywhere, and do not apologize to this asshole.

You do not owe him anything," Cally said, still not budging.

"Knock it off, Cally. Enough is enough. You completely misunderstood what he said, and if anyone needs to apologize, it should be you. Now let's go before they call the cops on us," Kate demanded, still feeling confused as to why Cally would just go off on the waiter for no good reason.

Finally, after putting her foot down firmly, Cally followed her mother outside, leaving Bill and Kyle clueless as to why they were walking out. Kate was so upset and frustrated with Cally that she did not know what to do. She could not understand why Cally was acting out; it was almost as if she had two different personalities. Kate did not like having to be so firm with Cally, especially after all she had been through, but Cally was causing a scene, and Kate did not want the waiter to get into any trouble over something he did not do.

"What has gotten into you, Cally? Why did you make such a scene in there?" Kate asked, still trying to figure everything out.

"Look, Mom, I know that I'm not hearing things. I heard what he said as plain as day, and he called me a bitch. This much I'm certain of. I just cannot believe that you turned everything around on me, just to save his job," Cally said with a mean glare in her eyes as she raised her voice, showing no respect whatsoever to her mother.

"Hey, what is going on out here? Is everything okay?" Bill asked, walking out of the restaurant and noticing the tension between Kate and Cally.

"It was the waiter, Dad. He called me a bitch, and now Mom is taking his side, just so he will not lose his job," Cally blurted out, putting all the blame on her mother and the waiter.

"Well, it looks as if I need to go and have a little talk with this waiter. I could tell that he was a pushy asshole as soon as we walked in," Bill cursed, feeling angry and upset that someone would disrespect his daughter that way.

"You will do no such thing, Bill. You do not even know what happened, and I'll not stand by and let you go in there and cause him to lose his job over something he did not say," Kate said with an aggressive attitude as she grabbed Bill by his arm and looked at Cally in complete disbelief.

"Is there anything that I can do to help?" Kyle asked, walking out the door as the chaos started.

"Actually, there is. Could you take Cally to the car while I go back inside and pay the bill before they call the cops on us for skipping out on the check?" Kate asked, still holding on to Bill's arm tightly as she tried to find her wallet with her other hand.

Kyle had no clue as to what was going on. At first he thought that Cally might have gotten sick, but after seeing how upset Kate was, he knew that something else had to be wrong. Kyle wondered if the waiter had anything to do with Kate and Bill being mad. He knew that the waiter had gotten under Bill's skin by being so pushy, but he still did not know what that would have to do with Kate sending Cally to the car before eating. Still clueless as to what was going on, Kyle took Cally by her trembling hand and started walking her to the car, in the hopes that Cally would fill him in before her parents returned.

"Okay, Kate, moment of truth. Why did you let that waiter get by with calling our daughter a bitch?" Bill asked, still feeling angry about the whole ordeal.

"Listen, Bill, I have already told you. He did not say one harmful word to her. All he said was that it was no big deal after she apologized for almost running into him, and after that, Cally totally flipped out, for no good reason. She started accusing him of saying something that he did not say. Trust me, Bill, if he had called her a bitch, I would have taken care of him myself. I swear, I do not know what got into her, but whatever it was, it made her go absolutely ballistic," Kate explained, stressing the truth to Bill so that he would not go back inside and start more trouble with the waiter.

"Are you absolutely, positively sure that you heard him correctly? Because it was awful loud in there, and Cally was standing closer to him than you were." Bill questioned, giving Kate a chance to think about things.

"Stop trying to change my mind, Bill. I know what I heard, and it was not remotely close to what Cally said. I think she is just stressed out and needs some rest, and that is exactly what she is going to get when she gets home, even if I have to tell Kyle to leave and come back tomorrow. As of now, though, I'm going back inside to pay the bill. I'll be out in a second," Kate snapped, giving Bill a mean and powerful look as she walked back inside.

Bill felt so torn, he did not know what to do, or who to believe. He wanted to believe Cally, but he wanted to believe Kate also. Bill knew there was a possibility that Cally had misunderstood what the waiter had said. After all, she had been through a lot, and it would not be hard to misconstrue words. That was something Bill had to take into serious consideration before making any rash decisions. Bill loved Cally with all of his heart, and he hated that she had to go through so much. It was as if their lives were being turned upside down, and there was nothing he could do about it. Bill felt so helpless. He wanted to protect his family and keep them safe, but that was hard to do when he did not know who to believe.

"Why are you still standing out here? I thought that you would be in the car by now. Is something wrong?" Kate asked after looking into Bill's worried eyes.

"Oh no, there is nothing wrong. I was just trying to collect my thoughts before going back to the car. I cannot help but feel sorry for her; this whole damn situation has really taken a toll on her—and us," Bill said as his eyes started to fill with tears.

"Look, Bill. I know that you love Cally and you want to make everything better for her—so do I—but we cannot help her unless we work together on this. Common sense will tell you that we have to come together and be strong for her," Kate explained, hoping that Bill would understand and pull himself together for Cally's sake.

"I know, Kate. You do not have to tell me how important this is, because I already know. I want you to know that I'm on your side, and I'll back you one hundred percent from now on," Bill said, wrapping his arms around Kate.

"Mom, Dad, is everything okay?" Cally asked as she walked up behind them, feeling once more that everything was her fault.

Cally did not like to see her parents fight—it was the most unpleasant thing to see. Cally knew that she had caused the argument between her parents because she had put all the blame on her mother. Cally felt terrible about the whole thing. She had never disrespected her mother like that before. Cally could not figure out what was wrong with her. She thought she had heard the waiter call her a bitch, but her mother saying that he did not confused Cally even more. Cally felt as if she was at her breaking point, and she started to think that maybe she did need that psychiatrist after all.

"Oh Cally, you scared me. I did not even see you walk up. Are you feeling better now?" Kate asked, as she let go of Bill to comfort Cally.

"Yeah, Mom. Everything is fine. I just wanted to say that I'm sorry. I should not have talked to you like that. I had no right whatsoever to say the things that I said. Can you please forgive me?" Cally asked, bursting into tears.

"Of course I forgive you. I could never stay mad at you. You are my whole life, and I love you with all of my heart," Kate said, holding Cally close.

"Okay, girls, we really should be getting to the car, because it is starting to rain again," Bill advised, putting his jacket over Kate and Cally's head as the rain started to pour.

Kate was thrilled to see that Cally was feeling better. It absolutely killed Kate to see her daughter struggling every minute of every day. It seemed as if this nightmare would never come to an end, and that was what Kate was worried about, not for herself, but for Cally. Kate hated to argue with Cally, because it left her feeling absolutely wretched. Kate missed the way things used to be so much, and she could not wait for things to get back to normal. For Kate it could not come soon enough.

"Hey, there you guys are. I was beginning to get worried," Kyle called out, pretending not to know what was going on as he held the car door open for Cally.

"Wow, that rain is really pouring down. I did not think that it was supposed to rain today. That just goes to show you how much the weatherman knows," Bill said, drying his head off with his handkerchief.

"Yeah, they did not say a word about rain being in the forecast last night when we watched the news after dinner," Kate agreed as she started the car.

"Whoa, speaking of dinner, you and Cally did not get a chance to eat anything. I bet you guys are starved to death, aren't you?" Bill asked, remembering that they had walked out of the restaurant before getting to eat anything.

"That is right. I have not had a chance to eat, and I'm beginning to get a bit hungry," Kate said as her stomach growled like an angry dog.

"I'm so sorry, Mom. It is my fault—if I had not caused a scene in there, you could have eaten," Cally said as a feeling of guilt swept over her.

"Oh no, sweetheart. It was not your fault. We have all had a rough day. It is only natural that something would go wrong," Kate said, looking back at Cally and giving her a big smile to let her know that it was not her fault.

"I have an idea. Why don't I just go back inside and order you girls a pizza to go? That way you will not have to worry about cooking anything when you get home," Kyle suggested as he pulled out his wallet.

"That is a good idea, Kyle. I could not have said it better myself," Bill agreed, pulling out a twenty and handing it to Kyle before he had a chance to take any money out of his wallet.

"Okay, I'll be right back with one large pepperoni pizza," Kyle said, jumping out of the car and running inside.

Cally watched in awe as Kyle ran inside to get their pizza. She thought it was so sweet of him to even suggest it. Cally felt so lucky to have someone in her life who was as loving and caring as he was; she just hoped that her crazy behavior would not scare him off. Kyle meant everything to Cally, and she did not want to lose him. Just the thought of it made her stomach churn. Cally wished she could control things better—for her sake and for the people around her—but she could not. It was something that would take time and patience, and Cally prayed that Kyle would just bear with her long enough to get things together.

"Wow, that was fast. I thought it would at least take fifteen minutes," Kate said, shocked to see Kyle so soon.

"Yeah, it surprised me, too. It was almost as if they knew we'd be coming back," Kyle said, passing the pizza and change back to Bill as he tried to buckle his seat belt with one hand.

"Well, it looks as if we will get to enjoy some pepperoni pizza after all, and the best part is, I do not have to cook when we get home," Kate said, putting the car into DRIVE.

"Hey now, do not get ahead of yourself. Kyle and I might still be hungry—you never know with us guys," Bill joked, trying to put a smile on Kate and Cally's faces.

"Do not even think about it, because as hungry as I'm right now, I would probably fight you for it, and trust me, you do not want that to happen," Kate said with a laugh as she slid the pizza closer to her.

13

"Oh man, what a day! I cannot believe it is finally over with. I don't know about the rest of you, but I could really use a nap right about now," Kate said, pulling into the driveway, trying to throw a hint Kyle's way so that he would leave before she had to ask him to.

Kate liked Kyle. As a matter of fact, she thought the world of him, and she did not want to hurt his feelings by asking him to leave, but Kate knew that Cally needed her rest and she was willing to do anything to make that happen, even if it meant sending Kyle home and making Cally mad at her. Kate knew that Cally would hit the roof if she told Kyle to go home, but Kate did not care how mad Cally got. It was time for Kate to be the parent and not the best friend. Kate had made a promise to take care of Cally, and that was one promise that she was not going to break. Kate had a job to do, and she was not going to stop until it was done.

"Yeah, I'm feeling a little sleepy too. Now that my stomach is full, I feel as if I could go into hibernation," Bill agreed with a huge yawn as he got out of the car.

"Well, I'm not tired at all. I'm just now starting to wake up. As a matter of fact, I have never felt more rested," Cally said, disagreeing with her parents and hoping that they would go inside and take a nap so that she and Kyle could have some time alone with each other.

"You know, this day has been hectic for us all, and I'm starting to feel the effects myself, so I guess that I'm going to head home now. I'd like to take a nap before my mom gets home from work. Besides, Cally, you need to get some rest yourself. Maybe tomorrow we can go do something, that is, if it is alright with your parents," Kyle said, waiting on Bill and Kate's approval.

"Well, maybe you two could do something around here tomorrow, like go swimming in the pool or fishing in the pond behind the house. You know, we just turned some big catfish loose in there a few weeks ago," Kate suggested, feeling a little nervous and uneasy about letting Cally leave the house again without her supervision.

As much as it worried Bill to think about Cally leaving the house again without himself or Kate being with her, he also knew that they could not keep her caged up like some animal. Cally was not a little girl anymore; she was a smart young lady with a good head on her shoulders. Bill knew that he had to start trusting her sometime to do the right thing whether he wanted to or not. He knew he needed to let Cally go so that she could live her own life. Although Bill found himself wanting to do the right thing, he was not so sure about Kate. Bill knew without a doubt in his mind that Kate was going to be the hardest one to convince, and he did not think that Cally could convince her on her own, so Bill had to do the right thing and help Kate understand Cally's needs.

"Well, maybe we should leave that up to Cally and Kyle to decide," Bill said. "After all, they might not want to hang around here all day with us old people." Bill hoped that Kate would back off before she embarrassed Cally too badly.

"Don't be silly, Bill. There are more things to do around here than any-where else, plus I'm sure they will have just as much fun hanging out over here, and they won't have to worry about spending money," Kate said, sugar-coating things to make it seem like the best thing to do even though she knew deep down that it was the wrong thing to do.

Kate could not stand the thought of Cally leaving the house again; it scared the hell out of her and made her stomach tie in knots. For Kate, everything was moving way too fast and there was nothing she could do, to slow it down or stop it. All Kate could do was picture Cally getting hurt again, or worse, killed. Kate knew that it was not fair to Cally, but she could not help it. All Kate wanted to do was to protect Cally in case Ryan decided to make another comeback, which was very possible. Although Cally's plan seemed to be a success, Kate had no intention of letting her guard down until she was one hundred percent sure that Ryan was gone for good.

"Whatever you decide, Kate. After all, you know what is best for everyone," Bill smarted off in a sarcastic tone, feeling angry with Kate because of the way she was treating Cally.

"Well, as much as I hate to, I guess that I should be going now before my mom comes home and starts to worry," Kyle said, feeling a little out of place as the tension grew stronger between Bill and Kate.

"Are you sure that you cannot stay a little while longer? There is something that I need to talk to you about and it is really important," Cally said, praying that Kyle would agree to stay for at least another hour.

"Come on, Kate. Let's go inside so these two can talk. I think you have chaperoned enough for today," Bill hinted, hoping that Kate would see just how nosy she was being standing there next to Cally and Kyle.

"Okay, I'll give you a few minutes to say good-bye, but after that, Cally, you need to come inside and eat so that you can take your medicine and lie down for a while," Kate ordered in a firm tone, directing her words straight toward Cally.

Kate could feel her blood starting to boil as she walked inside the house. She felt as if Bill had totally undermined her, and she could not believe he had done so right in front of Cally and Kyle. Kate could not understand why Bill was going against her. It was as if he wanted to look like the good parent and leave her looking like the bad parent. Kate walked into the kitchen with Bill following close behind, and as soon as she got to the bar, she slammed her purse and keys down, causing the sound to echo throughout the whole house. Bill knew right then that he would be getting an earful from her. It was only a matter of time before she started in on him, but Bill truly believed that his case was worth arguing.

"Okay, Bill. Just out of curiosity, when did we start going against each other? Please tell me, because I'm dying to know," Kate said sarcastically, giving him a look that would scare any man, no matter his size.

"Look, Kate, I know you don't want to hear this, but there comes a time in life, when we just need to step back and let our little girl grow up. And that time is now. It's not as if she is ten years old anymore. She is almost a grown woman, and we need to start trusting her so that she will trust us in return," Bill said, putting it into terms that Kate would better understand.

"What are you talking about? Cally *does* trust us, and there is no doubt in my mind about that. You're just trying to look like the good guy and leave me looking like the bad parent," Kate said in a loud voice, trying to make Bill see that she was right about everything.

"Kate, please lower your voice and listen to what I have to say. If you do not start giving Cally some space, then you will lose her forever. Trust what I'm telling you. I know that you want to protect Cally and keep her safe, but you cannot be there all the time for her. It is just not possible. Please just give her the space that she needs, and do not keep her caged up like some animal. Let her go places with Kyle and live her life," Bill pleaded, hoping that Kate would not continue to punish Cally for Ryan's mistakes.

When Kate saw how emotional Bill was, she started to think that maybe she was taking things a little too far and being a little too strict with Cally. Kate did not want to be that way, nor did she want to hurt Cally. All she wanted to do was protect her, but she saw that her protective ways would only drive Cally further away, and Kate did not want for that to ever happen. Although Kate was not happy with the idea and she had a bad feeling about things, she knew that she had to start trusting Cally and make things right with her before it was too late. Kate had almost lost Cally before, and she was not about to take another gamble.

"You're right, Bill. Now I see the point you were trying to make. If you'll excuse me, I'm going to go fix things with my daughter. I'll be back in a few minutes," Kate said, dropping her head in shame as she walked out the door toward Cally and Kyle.

"Cally, could I please have a word with you? I promise that it won't take long," Kate called out, trying to keep her distance so that Cally would not think that she was trying to be nosy.

"Oh great, I wonder what she wants now. I swear, sometimes she can be so annoying and nerve-racking," Cally said, rolling her eyes and shaking her head in embarrassment.

"Come on now, don't give your mother such a hard time. She is only trying to help because she loves you, so be nice and go see what she wants," Kyle said, giving Cally a slight push in Kate's direction.

"Hey, Mom, what's up? Is everything okay?" Cally asked nervously as she approached her mother and noticed that tears were in her eyes.

"Don't worry, sweetheart. Everything is just fine. I just wanted to talk to you for a minute. I actually should have told you this before, but I was being selfish, and I hope that you can forgive me," Kate said, as tears streamed down her face.

"Mom, please tell me what is wrong. You are starting to scare me. Are you sure that you're okay?" Cally asked for the second time as she grew more concerned about her mother.

"Yes, Cally. I'm sure that everything is okay. I just wanted to apologize for the way that I acted. I should have never tried to run your life. You are a young woman now, not a toddler, so you should be able to go out and do things without me having to tag along, and you should take a nap when you get ready to, not when I say so," Kate said, feeling more ashamed of herself by the second for treating her daughter the way she had.

"Mom, are you saying what I think you are saying?" Cally asked, as her eyes lit up with happiness.

"Yes, dear, you heard me right. Now get out of here before I change my mind," Kate said, feeling a sudden urge to take back what she had just said.

"Thanks, Mom. This means more to me than you will ever know," Cally said, giving her mother a kiss on the cheek.

Kate watched as Cally walked off with a smile on her face. Although she had done the right thing, she still felt there would be some regret on her part, but she did not want to drive Cally away. All she wanted to do was make her happy, and by the look on Cally's face, Kate knew that she had succeeded. As Kate turned to walk back in the house, she saw Bill looking out of the window with a huge smile on his face. He gave her a thumbs-up on her good deed. While Kate was praying that her decision would not come back to haunt her, Bill was feeling good about the way everything turned out. He knew that it was killing Kate now, but in the end, it would only bring them closer to each other.

"You did a very good thing just then. You have now made your daughter the happiest person in the whole world," Bill said, complimenting Kate as she walked through the front door.

"It may have been a good thing, but I'm not sure that it was the right thing. I guess only time will tell," Kate said, feeling more worried than relieved.

"Well, I just want you to know that I'm really proud of you. You should be proud of yourself, too. It took a lot of guts to do what you just did," Bill said, hoping that Kate would eventually feel the same way.

"Hey, Mom. Is it okay if Kyle and I go out for a little while after we change our clothes?" Cally asked, interrupting Kate and Bill's conversation.

As soon as the words came out of Cally's mouth, Kate's heart dropped to the pit of her stomach. Kate had dreaded this moment, and it had come a lot sooner than she thought it would. Kate did not think that Cally would react so quickly, but she did, and Kate knew that she could not go back on her word, no matter how much it bothered her. Cally was growing up, and Kate had to face the bitter truth. It was now time to let go of her little girl and let her live her own life—a life that Kate prayed would turn out beautifully.

"Well, I suppose that you can, as long as you are back by ten o'clock and no later," Kate said, giving Cally a curfew that she thought was reasonable, considering the circumstances.

"Thanks, Mom. You are the best. I promise that I'll make that curfew," Cally cheerfully said as she wasted no time to go and change.

"So, Kyle, where are you planning on taking Cally this evening?" Bill asked, since he figured that Kate would not.

"Oh, I was going to take her to the ice cream shop in town to get a banana split. She had mentioned that she would like to have some ice cream, so I told her that I would take her to get some, if that is okay with you guys," Kyle said, double-checking one last time to make sure that it was alright with them.

Although Bill had told Kate to back off and give Cally her space, he did not see anything wrong with asking where they were going. As Cally's father, he felt as if he had the right to know where they were going and what time they would be back. That was why he did not hesitate one bit about asking Kyle where they he was planning on taking his daughter. Bill could not have been more pleased about Kyle and Cally's destination. The ice cream store was only a few minutes away, and it was a nice environment for Cally to be in. Bill knew that getting out of the house would be good for Cally, and that is what he wanted the most for his little girl—for her to be happy and free, without the constant worries of Ryan and the horrible things he had done.

"Well, don't you look beautiful? All this just for some ice cream," Bill said, as Cally walked down the stairs in a pair of cut-off jean shorts and a tank top.

"Do not worry, Mom. I'll wear my seat belt, and I promise that I'll call you every twenty minutes to check in," Cally said, after seeing the worried look on her mother's face.

"No, that will not be necessary. Just promise me that you will be safe and if you need me for anything, anything at all, just call and I'll be on my way," Kate said, hugging Cally so tightly that her arms began to ache.

Bill and Kate watched nervously as Cally and Kyle got into his truck and drove away. Neither of them wanted to see her go, but it was too late. They had already given Cally their permission to go with Kyle. While Bill was keeping his emotions hidden, Kate was not. She was biting on her nails and pacing the floor. For Kate, ten o'clock could not come any sooner. It seemed as if the clock had stopped completely. Kate just prayed to God that Cally would make it back safely.

"Bill, what if something bad happens to our little girl again? I would never be able to forgive myself," Kate said, as she stared out the window, hoping to see Cally and Kyle pulling back in the driveway.

"Kate, please stop worrying. I promise that everything will be just fine. Cally will be back home before you know it," Bill said, trying to ease Kate's troubled mind.

14

While Bill and Kate were at home worried about their little girl, Cally was having the time of her life. She could not believe that she and Kyle were finally together as a couple. For once in Cally's life, everything started to fall right in place; it was almost as if their relationship was meant to be. Cally had always been a firm believer that things happened for a reason, and she was so glad that Kyle was now a part of that reason. Cally just wished that she had picked Kyle over Ryan long before. Maybe then Ryan would still be alive instead of haunting her every thought.

"Wow, can you believe this is really happening? I never thought that you and I would be going out as a couple," Cally said with a smile on her face.

"Well, to be honest, I figured that you would end up marrying Ryan and moving away, never to be seen or heard from again. But just to let you know, I'm really glad that you are here with me now," Kyle said, taking Cally's hand and kissing it.

"Thank you so much. That is really sweet, and just to let you know, I'm so glad that we are together, too. You have made me the happiest girl in the world, and I hope that I have made you happy also," Cally replied, leaning her head over and resting it on Kyle's shoulder as he pulled into the ice cream store's parking lot.

"You are quite welcome. To answer your question, yes, you have made me very happy, too, but you can probably tell that by looking into my eyes," Kyle said, turning his head slowly in Cally's direction.

Cally knew automatically that Kyle was coming in for a kiss because her whole body started to tingle. As soon as Cally felt his warm breath on her face, she closed her eyes tightly, and his soft lips pressed up against hers. Cally's whole body felt like hot, melting butter. She was practically putty in his hands. The kiss was absolutely magical, and she wanted it to last forever, but unfortunately, her fairy-tale kiss was interrupted by the loud sound of sirens. Startled, Cally opened her eyes quickly only to see that Kyle's eyes were not brown anymore—they were green, as in Ryan green...

"Oh my God, Kyle! What is wrong with your eyes? Why are they a different color?" Cally cried out as she stared in horror at Kyle's changing eyes.

"What in the hell are you talking about, Cally? There is nothing wrong with my eyes. They are the same color that they have always been," Kyle replied as he looked into the rearview mirror, trying to figure out what Cally was talking about.

When Kyle turned to face Cally again, shockingly his eyes were brown again, with absolutely no hint of green whatsoever. Cally could not believe her eyes. It was as if Kyle had just pulled off the ultimate magic trick. She knew that she was not seeing things, nor was she crazy. Without a doubt in her mind, she knew that Kyle's eyes had been green. She just could not figure out how or why they had changed, but she planned on getting to the bottom of it. Confused and not wanting Kyle to think that she was crazy, Cally played it off as best she could.

"My mistake. It was only the sunlight shining in your eyes, making them look a little bit green," Cally explained as she checked the color of his eyes one last time, just to be sure.

"That is okay. Sometimes the sunlight can do that. So what do you think is going on up the road? There sure were a lot of cops and ambulances that passed by," Kyle said, cutting short the conversation about his eyes.

"I don't know what it could be, but I got an eerie feeling a few minutes ago. Maybe we should go and check things out," Cally suggested, worrying that something might have happened to her parents.

"Are you sure that you want to go before getting any ice cream? If you can hang on a few minutes, I'll go up there and order a banana split to go for you," Kyle offered, feeling bad that Cally did not get to enjoy any ice cream.

"No, that is okay. We can always come back tomorrow. Besides, I'm curious to know what is going on," Cally said, as her heart started to pound with fear.

Just as Cally and Kyle were pulling out of the parking lot, her cell phone rang, sending a chill down her spine. Cally shuddered at the very thought of answering it. She just had one of those gut feelings that something was wrong. First, it was the sirens, and then it was Kyle's eyes changing colors. It was as if one big terrible puzzle was putting itself together. Cally could not believe it—just when she thought her life was coming together again, it slowly started to crumple right before her eyes. Cally was so afraid to answer her phone—she had a feeling that it was going to be bad news, and Cally did not know how much more bad news she could handle. She was already at her breaking point.

"Hello…" Cally answered in a frightened voice, praying that nothing was wrong with her parents.

"Hi, Cally. It's Mom. I hate to bother you, but I was wondering if you could come straight home after getting your ice cream?" Kate asked, trying her best not to sound too upset or scare Cally.

"Well, actually, we were on our way right now. Is everything alright? You sound as if something is wrong," Cally said, as her heart started to rapidly race, making it hard for her to breathe.

"Look, don't worry. Everything is just fine. I'll talk to you when you get here," Kate said, cutting Cally off before she could ask another question.

"Something is wrong. I just know it. I knew that all of this was too good to be true," Cally said, closing her cell phone.

"What are you talking about? Who was that on the phone?" Kyle asked, curious and concerned.

"It was my mother. She told us to come straight home, but she wouldn't tell me the reason why. The sound in her voice makes me think that something bad has happened," Cally answered, rolling down her window so that she could get some fresh air.

"Well, don't worry. I'm sure that nothing is wrong. Your mom just probably got to missing you," Kyle replied, trying to make Cally feel better.

As Kyle pulled into Cally's driveway, the first thing Cally noticed were two cop cars sitting there with their lights on. Cally knew right then that something was terribly wrong. She did not know what exactly, but she knew that it was something bad. Her gut feeling told her that much. Cally prayed that nothing had happened to her parents. She did not know what she would do if she lost them. It was something Cally did not want to think about, much less experience. Confused and panicked, Cally jumped out of Kyle's truck before he even had a chance to park and ran into the house.

"Mom, Dad, where are you guys at? Please answer me!" Cally yelled out in a panicked voice, as she searched from room to room, trying to find her parents.

"We are in the kitchen, sweetheart," Kate called out as she walked through to the living room to find Cally after hearing her frantic cries.

"Mom, please tell me what is going on. Why are there two cop cars out front? Are you and Dad okay?" Cally asked, looking her mother over as Kyle walked through the front door, curious himself as to what was going on.

"Calm down, sweetheart. Your father and I are alright, but there is something that we need to tell you, so why don't you come in to the kitchen and sit down so that we can talk," Kate said, trying to calm Cally down so that she could tell her the reason behind her phone call.

Cally had a million things running through her troubled mind; she did not know what was going on. She was so scared that her heart felt as if it was beating out of her chest. Cally did not know what to expect when she walked through the kitchen door. It was one bad thing right after another. Cally knew in her heart before walking through the kitchen door that Ryan had something to do with all of this, and that told her that her plan had not worked. Cally was at the end of her rope. She had tried the one and only thing she knew might get rid of Ryan, but it had failed, and now she had no idea what she was going to do next.

"Cally, are you okay? Do you need to sit down in here while I get you something to drink?" Kate asked after noticing how pale Cally's face was.

"No, Mom. I just want to know what is going on and why the cops are here," Cally answered quickly as she started to grow impatient with what she thought was a guessing game.

"Alright, Cally, but you need to come in to the kitchen and have a seat beside your father," Kate ordered, taking Cally by the hand, leading her in to the kitchen where the two police officers and her father were waiting.

"Okay, you guys, enough with the guessing games. Someone needs to tell me what is going on, because I do not know how much more of this I can take," Cally snapped as she looked around the room, waiting for someone to speak up and fill her in.

"Well, sweetheart, I hate to tell you this, and there is really no easy way to say it, so I'm just going to say it. Ms. Jones killed herself about an hour ago. That is what the cops are doing here. Before she committed suicide, she wrote you a letter, and before the police can continue with their investigation, they had to come by to talk to you," Kate explained as she started to get choked up at the very thought of Ms. Jones taking her own life.

Cally could not believe it. She had just seen Ms. Jones at Ryan's funeral, and now, hearing about her suicide was like a slap in the face. It absolutely chilled Cally to the bone. Not knowing what to say, Cally dropped her head to the floor and started to cry. Cally wondered how many more things could go wrong. While Cally was trying to cope with the bad news, Kate was questioning whether she should even let Cally read the letter. Although the letter was addressed to Cally, Kate feared that letting her read it would only result in more confusion and pain, and Kate definitely did not want to see that happen.

"Hey, Mom. Is there any way that I could read the letter, or do I have to wait until the investigation is over?" Cally asked, directing her question more toward the police officers than her mother.

"I'm not sure about that, sweetheart. Maybe we should just let the police handle this matter. After all, you don't need any more stress," Kate suggested in the hopes that Cally would feel the same way.

"No, Mom, the letter was written to me, and I think that I have every right to read it without anyone objecting," Cally argued, desperate to find out what the letter said.

"Are you sure that you want to do this, Cally? Because I honestly think that you're making a big mistake," Kate said, hoping that Cally would change her mind.

"Yes, Mom. I'm sure that I want to do this. I have to know what Ms. Jones wrote before she killed herself," Cally said, reaching for the blood-spattered letter.

Dear Cally,

*I'm so glad that you came into my life one year ago.
Ryan could not have picked a better girl to go out with.
You have brought so much joy to Ryan's life and mine, too.
You are truly an angel. I wish that I could stay around
and watch you go through life, but unfortunately, I cannot.
You see, when Ryan died, it left a huge hole in my heart,
one so big that it could never be filled. I have thought
about moving on with my life, but I'm hurting so bad that
I cannot. All I want is to be with my son, and this is the
only way that I can do that. I hope that you understand.
I just could not bear it any longer; I had to do this. Take
care of yourself, sweetheart, and remember, we will meet
again someday.*

Love,

Ms. Jones

"Why, Mom, why did she have to kill herself? I just talked to her at Ryan's funeral and she said that she was doing okay. Why would she have lied to me?" Cally asked in a state of confusion and shock.

"Oh Cally, I wish that I had the answers, but I don't. No one really knows why people do these things," Kate explained, consoling Cally as she took the bloodstained letter out of her hand so that she would not have to look at it anymore.

"Isn't it obvious, she killed herself because her only son died in a horrific car accident the other night?" Kyle replied bitterly, almost as if he had taken offense to Cally's question.

"How did she do it, Mom? How did Ms. Jones kill herself?" Cally asked, totally ignoring Kyle's sarcastic remark.

"She shot herself in the head with a handgun," Kyle answered, rudely interrupting Cally again.

"How do you know that, Kyle? No one said anything about her shooting herself in the head," Kate said curiously, wondering how Kyle would know something like that.

"Well, that is usually the way most people commit suicide, especially if they want to get the job done right," Kyle answered with a slight stutter, looking more nervous than he had ever looked before.

"You need to be a little more careful about how you answer questions, unless you want to spend the rest of your life in prison," Officer Camp replied, giving Kyle a firm, serious look.

"What are you talking about? How can I go to prison just for providing my opinion?" Kyle snapped with anger, as he stepped closer to Officer Camp.

"Well, let's just put it this way. If you didn't have an alibi, we would be taking you in for questioning, just for the simple fact that you knew how she died," Officer Camp said as he also moved closer to Kyle, letting him know that he was not intimidated at all by him.

"Is there anything else we can do for you? Because if there is not, then I would like to have some private time with my family during this difficult time," Bill said, getting up from his chair, sensing the tension between Kyle and the officer.

"No, I think we have everything we need, but if we should need anything else, I'll contact you by phone," Officer Camp advised as he motioned for his partner, letting him know that it was time to go.

"Thank you, officers. We really appreciate everything you've done," Kate said politely as the police officers walked out the door.

After the police officers left, Kate felt as if she was going to explode with anger. She was absolutely furious with Kyle for the way that he had acted. Kate did not know what was wrong with Kyle, and she did not know why he had acted out the way he did. It was as if he had turned into a different person. Kate knew that she had to draw the line somewhere, and this was the perfect spot. She had to put Kyle in his place because he was starting to get a little out of control, and that was something Kate was not going to allow around her daughter, no matter how much Cally liked him.

"Cally, I need for you to go upstairs. As for you, Kyle, I think that you should be heading home, before your mother starts to worry," Kate ordered as she glared at Kyle.

"But, Mom, Kyle and I didn't even get to spend any time together. You called us home before we had a chance to do anything," Cally whined, hoping that her mother would give in to her small tantrum.

"Absolutely not, young lady. You need to get some rest, and Kyle needs to go home, so that his mother doesn't get worried about him. The two of you can do something tomorrow, but as of right now, I think it would be best if Kyle went home," Kate said in a much firmer voice, letting Cally know that she meant business, so that she would not ask again.

"Your mom is right, Cally. It has been a long day for everyone, and I really should be getting home. I'll call you first thing tomorrow," Kyle said, giving Cally a quick kiss on the cheek before walking out the door.

"Thanks a lot, Mom. You always know how to embarrass me in front of people," Cally smarted off as she stormed off to her bedroom and slammed the door behind her.

Kate could not believe how terribly wrong things were going and how different Kyle was acting. Out of all the years Kate had known Kyle, not once had he ever acted out in that way. Kyle had always been the quiet type, never outspoken. Kate hoped that it was just the drama causing him to act out, because if it wasn't, then that meant that there were some serious issues going on with him. And before he could see Cally again, he would have to sort through them. As Kate paced the floor, Bill could not help but feel sadness and regret. He felt as if he could have prevented the whole mess if he had been a more cautious father. Bill deeply regretted the day that he had let his little girl go to the prom with Ryan. It was the biggest mistake of his life, and now they were all paying dearly for it.

"Kate, could you please stop pacing the floor for a second and come sit down so that we can discuss things?" Bill asked, as he stared into Kate's worried face.

"Look, Bill, I don't have time to sit down and discuss things. I have to figure out a way to help our little girl before it is too late. I know that Ryan is still here. I just have that feeling, and I have to stop him before he ends up hurting Cally, or worse, killing her," Kate said, still pacing the floor like a madwoman.

"Kate, please come and sit down. You're starting to make me really nervous, and I don't think I can handle much more of you pacing the floor," Bill begged as he pulled out a chair beside him for Kate.

"Okay, Bill, you have got five minutes to come up with a plan that is going to save our little girl, or I'm going to take matters into my own hands," Kate said in a hostile voice as she sat down in the chair.

"Kate, if you want to help Cally, you need to pull yourself together and keep your head clear. That way you'll be ready for whatever is coming your way. By the looks of things, I would say there are more bad things to come," Bill said, hoping that Kate would keep her guard up this time.

While Bill and Kate were downstairs trying to come up with a plan, Cally was up in her bedroom, dialing Kyle's number. Cally felt as if she needed to talk to Kyle since she did not have a chance to do so before her mother made him leave. Cally did not know why her mother had flipped out all of a sudden and sent Kyle home; it just did not make any sense to her. Although Kyle had acted strange about Ms. Jones's suicide, Cally still felt as if her mother had no reason to lash out at him for something he said. After all, everyone, including Kyle, was entitled to their own opinion, no matter what it might be.

"Hello?" Kyle said, answering the phone after the first ring.

"Hey, Kyle, it's me, Cally. I just wanted to call and talk to you since I didn't get a chance to earlier, but if you're busy, I'll call you back later," Cally whispered, trying not to sound too pushy or desperate.

"Oh no, I'm not busy at all. I'm actually glad that you called me, because I miss you like crazy and I really want to see you," Kyle replied with the words that Cally wanted to hear.

"Well, we could've spent more time together if it hadn't been for my mom. She has been a real pain in my ass lately," Cally said, still feeling angry with her mother for sending Kyle home so early.

"Come on now, Cally, don't give your mother such a hard time. You know that she loves you and she wants to take care of you. That's why she does the things that she does. Trust me when I tell you that your mom loves you very much. She would never do anything to hurt you," Kyle explained, taking up once more for Kate, hoping that Cally would see things the way he did.

"That's bull. Ever since the accident, she acts as if she cannot trust me. She is always questioning me and telling me what to do, and to be honest with you, I'm getting sick and tired of it," Cally fired back, angry that Kyle would take up for her mother.

Cally did not like it when people sided with her parents, especially Kyle. It made her feel as if no one was on her side, and Cally did not want to be the only one in her corner. She wanted someone who was going to take up for her from time to time. Cally knew that sometimes she was in the wrong and she had no problem admitting that, but she wanted her mother to do the same and admit when she was wrong. In Cally's eyes, right was right and wrong was wrong. She only wished that other people would see it that way, too, but that was wishful thinking and she knew it. Cally's mother would always be right, because she was the parent and Cally was the child.

"So, Kyle, what did you mean earlier when you said that you wanted to see me?" Cally asked, quickly changing the subject to something else besides her mother.

"Well, I know that this is asking a lot, but I was hoping that you could slip out and meet me down the street later, after your parents go to sleep? But if you don't want to, or if you're scared, we can just wait until tomorrow. Either way is fine with me," Kyle said, letting Cally know that he would not be mad if she declined his offer.

"Of course I want to, and no, I'm not scared to do it. It will take a whole lot more than that to scare me. I've slipped out of the house plenty of times and not once have I ever been caught," Cally bragged, trying to seem fearless to Kyle, but knowing deep down that she had never slipped out of her house before in her life.

"Okay, it's settled then. Just give me a call when your parents go to sleep and I'll come pick you up," Kyle said, feeling ecstatic about Cally's response.

"Sounds good to me. I'll talk to you soon," Cally said before hanging up the phone.

After hanging up the phone with Kyle, Cally could not believe what she had agreed to. Once again, she had stuck her big foot into her mouth and put herself into a predicament that would be hard to get out of. She had never left the house without her parents' permission. She had always let them know where she was going and what time she would be back. Cally did not want to cause her parents any more grief. She knew that they had enough to deal with already, but she desperately wanted to see Kyle and talk to him. Cally had so many things on her mind, and she knew that Kyle would listen to her while she got some things off her chest. And that was one thing that Cally needed— someone to talk to and get advice from.

"I should definitely do this. What my parents don't know won't hurt them. After all, it is about time to start making my own decisions," Cally said to herself as she pretended to have a good reason for leaving the house without her parents' permission.

Hearing the sounds of footsteps coming up the stairs, Cally quickly jumped into her bed and pulled the covers over the top of her head, so that whoever it was would think that she was sleeping. Cally did not want to give her parents any indication that she was awake, because the sooner her parents went to bed, the sooner she would get to see Kyle.

Kate slowly cracked the door open and stuck her head inside to have a look and make sure Cally was alright. After seeing that things looked okay, Kate quietly shut the door again.

After Kate left Cally's bedroom, she could not help but feel guilty for even thinking about slipping out of the house without telling her mother. Cally knew that her mother loved her very much; she could tell by the way her mother kept checking up on her. The last thing Cally wanted to do was hurt her mother or give her a reason not to trust her, but on the other hand, she did not want to hurt Kyle, either. Cally was head over heels for Kyle, and she could see their relationship lasting for a long time. She did not want to do anything to jeopardize what they had, so to make sure that did not happen, Cally decided to meet Kyle, if only for a few minutes.

"So, how is our little angel doing? Is she still upset with you, or is she over it by now?" Bill asked, as Kate walked into their bedroom.

"I don't know if she is still upset with me or not. She was sound asleep when I went in, and I didn't want to wake her with a bunch of nonsense. I can always talk to her tomorrow. Besides, she really needs to rest now," Kate answered with a yawn, as she got into bed and rolled over to face Bill.

"Well, I'm sure that she has cooled down by now, and I know that Cally could never stay mad at you. She loves you too much to do that," Bill said, comforting Kate so that she could get a good night's sleep.

"I hope that you're right, Bill, because I hate it whenever Cally and I argue. It drives me crazy. Words cannot express the frustration that I'm feeling right now," Kate said, turning her back to Bill so that he could not see her crying.

"Don't worry, Kate. Tomorrow is a new day, and I know that you and Cally will work everything out," Bill said, wrapping his arms around Kate.

15

Cally lay quietly in her bed and tried her best to listen in on her parents' conversation. She could not hear much of it, but from what she did hear, Cally gathered that they were talking about her. Thirty minutes after the conversation had stopped, Cally heard nothing but dead silence. Figuring that her parents were asleep, Cally got up slowly from her bed, trying not to make a sound. The last thing Cally wanted was for her parents to walk in and bust her before she even had the chance to sneak out. Now that she and Kyle were a couple, Cally felt as if she had to look good for him, so she dabbed some perfume on her neck and slid her favorite gloss across her lips.

Cally could feel her heart pounding with excitement as she picked up the phone to dial Kyle's number. Although it had only been a couple of hours since she last talked to him, she could not wait to hear his voice again. Cally knew that she was falling in love with Kyle way too fast, but she could not help it. Kyle was so sweet and caring, and he made her feel so good. That was something she had not felt in a long time. Double-checking on her parents, Cally pressed her ear firmly to the wall to see if she could hear any movement or talking. Not hearing so much as a peep, Cally started to dial Kyle's number.

"Hey, sweetheart. Are you ready for me to come pick you up?" Kyle asked right away before saying anything else.

"Yeah, I'm ready. Where do you want me to meet you?" Cally asked, hoping it would not be too far away. Just the thought of walking in the dark by herself gave her the chills.

"Just look out your window, and you will see me parked across the street," Kyle instructed, cutting his headlights on and off so that Cally could see exactly where he was.

"Wow, you're here already. I thought I would at least have to wait five or ten minutes on you," Cally said, surprised to see him that soon.

"Well, I can always leave and come back in ten minutes, if you want me to," Kyle joked with a laugh.

"Oh, don't be silly. You know what I meant. I'm glad to see that you are here early. It makes me feel as if you really do want to see me," Cally replied, getting butterflies in her stomach again.

"Of course I want to see you. I miss you like crazy, so hurry up and get your butt down here before I die of loneliness," Kyle said.

After hanging up the phone, Cally walked quietly over to her bedroom door and stopped. Trying not to make a sound, Cally slowly opened the door wide enough for her body to fit through. Once in the hallway, Cally tiptoed to the stairway, hoping and praying that her parents would not hear her and get up. Since Cally had never done anything like this before, she found herself constantly looking over her shoulder, making sure that her parents were not behind her. Nervous and worried about getting caught, Cally could feel her adrenaline pumping. It was one of the best rushes she had ever felt before. She still could not believe that she was sneaking out of the house to see Kyle. Although some things felt wrong, most of them felt right. Cally cared so deeply for Kyle and she wanted to prove it to him, even if it meant disobeying her parents.

When Cally finally reached the front door, she took a deep breath and looked back up the stairway, just to make sure that her parents were not up. Cally could not wait to see Kyle and wrap her arms around him. Just thinking about it gave her goose bumps. She felt like a lovesick schoolgirl. To her it was the best feeling in the world, and she never wanted it to end. Finally, after making very little noise, Cally was out the front door and on her way to meet Kyle across the street. However, to Cally's surprise she did not see Kyle's truck anywhere in sight. It was as if he had just up and vanished. The only vehicle she could see was an eerie-looking black Ford Mustang parked in the same spot where Kyle had been just minutes ago.

"This cannot be right. I know that I saw Kyle out here," Cally said to herself as she chewed nervously on her fingernails and scanned the street once more for Kyle's truck.

"Hey, Cally, what are you waiting for? I'm right over here! Now hurry up and come on, before we get caught," Kyle's voice said out of the darkness.

Cally felt so confused. She heard Kyle's voice, but he was nowhere in sight and neither was his truck. Cally did not know why Kyle would want to play games with her. It just did not make any sense, and the more Cally tried to look for him, the more frustrated she became. Trying to find Kyle on the dark street was like trying to find a needle in a haystack, and that was something that Cally was not going to waste her time doing. It was just too risky. The last thing Cally needed was for her parents to walk outside and see her wandering the street, looking for Kyle. Not only would Cally be in trouble, but Kyle would be, too.

"Okay, Kyle, if you are going to play games, then I'm going back inside," Cally said bitterly as she quickly turned to walk back in the house before her parents got up and caught her in the act of sneaking out.

"Whoa, where do you think you're going? Didn't you hear me calling you?" Kyle asked, bumping into Cally out of the darkness and scaring the hell out of her at the same time.

"Where in the hell did you come from and where did you park your truck?" Cally asked, feeling more confused than ever.

"Oh, don't worry about that old truck. I have got something better than that now. Come on, and I'll show you my new ride. I just know that you are going to love it," Kyle said, taking Cally by her hand and walking her straight toward the creepy black Mustang.

"Kyle, stop. Before we go any further, please tell me that this is not your new car," Cally begged as a huge lump came up in her throat.

"Of course it is. After I saw that Mustang earlier today, I completely fell in love with it, and I knew that I had to have one. Lucky for me, my neighbor was selling his, so I jumped at the chance to buy it," Kyle answered in a thrilled voice as he wiped the hood down with his shirtsleeve, trying to clear up a few water spots.

Cally was stunned. She did not know what to say or do. She could not believe that Kyle would buy a car identical to the one she had almost died in; it just didn't make any sense. Cally had never seen Kyle do something so cold and heartless. She thought that he really cared for her, but this made her think otherwise. It was as if Kyle had turned into a completely different person, a person that Cally did not want to know. After finding out that Kyle had bought the car, Cally knew that she could not bear another second with him. It was all just too painful and creepy for her to cope with. Cally knew that she had to come up with a reason to go back inside, a reason that Kyle would not question.

"Well, I really hate to do this, but it's getting late and I think that I should get back inside before my parents wake up," Cally said, throwing out any excuse that she could to get away from Kyle and his strange behavior before things got any weirder.

"What are you talking about, Cally? You just came outside. Why are you trying to get rid of me so soon? Don't you want to spend some time with me before you go back inside?" Kyle asked, taking Cally by her trembling hand as he stared into her baby blue eyes.

"Oh no, please don't think that I'm trying to get rid of you, because I'm not. It is just that I'm really tired and I think a good night's sleep will do me some good," Cally lied out of fear, hoping that Kyle would not get suspicious and start questioning her.

"Okay, I'll make you a deal. Just let me take you up the street in my new car and then, I swear, I'll leave you alone for the rest of the night," Kyle bargained as he stood in front of Cally with his hands on her shoulders.

Something deep down inside of Cally told her that she should just say no and go back inside, but she really cared about Kyle, and she did not really want to end their relationship over something so stupid. After all, he was not being mean toward her, and he did not resemble Ryan in any way, shape, or form. Before Cally jumped to any conclusions, she wanted to give him the benefit of the doubt, just to see how things would go. Maybe Kyle really did like the car and maybe he had been a secret admirer of hot rods all along. Either way, Cally would never know unless she gave him a chance to prove himself.

"Okay, Kyle, but I can't stay long. I do not want to piss my mother off any more than she already is," Cally said, letting Kyle know that their ride had to be a short one.

"Thanks, Cally. You don't know how much this means to me. I'm so glad that I got you back. I swear this time, we'll be together forever," Kyle said, not sounding like himself at all, sending cold chills down Cally's spine as he slammed her door shut.

"Kyle, what are you talking about? What do you mean that you are glad you got me back? How could you possibly say that when you never had me to begin with?" Cally asked curiously, as Kyle got into the car.

"Well, you know what I meant. I was just saying that I felt as if I had lost you before, when you were going out with Ryan. That's all," Kyle said, quickly rewording his comment.

"Okay, my mistake. I'm sorry that I misconstrued what you said. It's just that I'm really tired and I can't comprehend things when I'm tired, you understand, right?" Cally asked, not really buying in to Kyle's explanation.

"That's okay. There's no need to apologize. You've done nothing wrong," Kyle said as he flashed a big smile and his light brown eyes Cally's way.

Cally noticed that there was something different about Kyle; she just could not put her finger on it. She wondered how many more things he would mess up on before the night was through. Cally did not want to say anything else to Kyle. She wanted for him to spin his own web—that way she could see just how many more times he was going to let certain things slip. In Cally's mind, she thought that he was acting the same way Ryan did, and she could not help but wonder if Ryan was possessing Kyle in some way. To Cally, the signs just said too much, and she was not going to be satisfied until she got to the bottom of things, even if it meant having to face Ryan again.

"You know, after all she has been through, she still purrs like a baby kitten," Kyle said, complimenting the black Mustang as he revved it up a little.

"Tell me, Kyle, just out of curiosity, what exactly has she been through?" Cally asked, catching Kyle totally off guard by her question.

"Oh, my neighbor said that he had an accident in her about five months ago that banged her up pretty good," Kyle said, giving Cally a short answer she really was not looking for.

"Did he or anyone else get hurt in the accident?" Cally asked, trying to keep the conversation going for as long as she could, as Kyle started to slowly drive up the street.

"No, I don't think so, but I really didn't ask, either. I try not to pry in other people's business. It makes me look like a nosy person, and that is something I don't want to be known as," Kyle answered, as if he were giving Cally the hint to stop asking him so many questions.

As Cally and Kyle pulled up to the stop sign at the end of the street, everything was quiet—an awkward quiet. It reminded Cally of prom night all over again, when Ryan had smacked her and busted her lip. Cally did not know what was going on with Kyle; she just prayed that Ryan was not trying to possess him. If there was one time in Cally's life when she wanted to be wrong, right now was that time, but her gut feeling told her that something was going on. Kyle was just acting too strange for things to be okay, and Cally knew she would have to spend a little more time with Kyle in order for her to find out for sure.

"Well, we're here. Would you like for me to turn around and take you back home now?" Kyle asked, seeing if Cally still wanted to cut the night short like she had said earlier.

"No, that's okay. We can sit here and talk for a few minutes, if you still want to," Cally replied, with a nervous feeling in the pit of her stomach.

"You should already know the answer to that. You know that I want to spend as much time with you as I can, and to prove that, I want to give you a gift, just to let you know how much I really do care," Kyle said, taking Cally by her trembling hand.

After Kyle took Cally by her left hand, the only thing Cally could think of was an engagement ring, but she did not want to say anything about it, just for the simple fact that it could be something else. Cally was so excited she felt as if her heart was going to beat out of her chest, but just as soon as Cally got excited, she got scared, too. Everything was starting to come together now; it all made sense. Ryan was, in fact, back. He had never gone anywhere. Cally's plan had failed, and the proof was right in front of her face. Ryan was using Kyle's body to get to her. That was why Kyle was acting so strange about everything. Cally was so scared, but she knew that she had to calm down and keep her head straight so that Ryan would not suspect anything.

"Okay, Cally, before I give you this gift, you have to promise me that you will always love me and never leave me, no matter what," Kyle negotiated, giving Cally's hand a slight squeeze.

"Alright, Kyle, but before I make my promise, I want you to turn on the interior light, so that I can see your face. I want to know that you really want this, the same as I do," Cally said, coming up with a plan of her own.

Cally knew that Ryan would not show his face in the light. In order for his evil to work, he had to use Kyle's appearance, and Cally knew that with the light on, she would be making her promise to Kyle and not Ryan. Cally figured that would be her only advantage over Ryan, and it could possibly be the only way of getting rid of him, too. As soon as Kyle turned on the light, Cally started looking him over from head to toe, making sure that he did not resemble Ryan at all. Cally knew that Ryan could be very tricky, and she wanted to be sure that Kyle did not have any of Ryan's features. The last thing Cally wanted to do was screw things up by making such a promise to Ryan. That would be a huge mistake, one that Cally could not afford to make.

"Okay, Cally, are you satisfied, or do you want to see my ID, too?" Kyle joked as he stared at Cally with his light brown eyes, looking nothing like Ryan.

"Yes, I'm satisfied, Kyle, and I promise that I'll always love you and I'll never leave you, no matter what happens. Now give me my gift before the anticipation kills me," Cally agreed, still staring Kyle down, anxious to see what the gift was.

"Well, here goes. I hope that you like it," Kyle said as he slid a heart-shaped ring on Cally's hand, identical to the one that she had hidden in Ryan's casket earlier.

As soon as Cally saw the ring, her heart felt as if it stopped. She was completely speechless, and she knew that the expression on her terrified face would give her away. Although Cally wanted to tuck tail and run, she knew that running would not solve anything, if she was going to beat Ryan, she had to beat him at his own game. Cally knew that she had to keep her cool and pretend that everything was fine, because if Ryan suspected anything out of the ordinary, then that could cause Cally's plan to come crashing down, and that was something that Cally could not deal with. Ryan was playing a dangerous game of cat and mouse, and this time Cally had no intention of being the mouse. She was going to take Ryan out this time, or die trying.

"Wow, Kyle. This ring is really beautiful, and I would love nothing more than to sit up here and talk all night, but unfortunately, I should be getting home now. My parents are very light sleepers, and they could wake up at any time to check on me. If I'm not in my bed, then they are going to send out a search party," Cally said, throwing out any excuse that she could to get back home.

"Okay, crybaby, I'll get you back home to your nosy-ass parents. They are all you care about anyway," Kyle snapped sarcastically before spinning the Mustang around in the road, with no warning, the same way Ryan did before he had tried to kill her.

"Do not ever talk about my parents that way again. They have been nothing but nice to you, and I'll not stand by and listen to you bash them like that. Do you understand what I'm saying?" Cally asked as she glared at Kyle, making sure she got her point across.

"Okay, Cally, you can calm down now. I swear, you are taking everything so damn personal. You have even said yourself that your parents are nosy," Kyle replied with a sly grin, as he tried to cover up his remark by putting some of the blame on Cally.

"Well, I think that you are the one who needs to calm down and quit being such an asshole. How would you feel if I talked about your mother like that?" Cally asked, turning the tables on Kyle, curious to see his reaction.

"Well, thanks to you, I don't have a mother anymore, so you can talk about her all you want to. It won't bother me in the least bit," Kyle replied with tears coming to his eyes, as he gave Cally a cold stare.

"What are you talking about, Kyle? What happened to your mother?" Cally asked, knowing that it was Ryan talking and not Kyle.

"Oh, nothing happened to her. She just doesn't like the idea of me going out with you," Kyle said, making a quick recovery.

"Whatever, Kyle. Just take me home before my parents wake up. We can continue this discussion tomorrow after we have had time to cool down," Cally replied as she looked straight ahead, knowing in her heart that it was not Kyle talking, it was Ryan.

"Well, since you want to be a little bitch about everything, I think that you should walk home. Besides, the night air might do you some good," Kyle suggested hatefully, as he reached over and opened up Cally's car door.

"Okay, Kyle, that's just fine by me. I would rather walk than be around you right now anyway," Cally smarted off as she kicked Kyle's car door shut out of sheer anger.

No sooner than Cally had slammed the door shut, Kyle took off up the street, squealing the tires, causing every dog in the neighborhood to start barking continuously. Knowing for sure that her parents would wake up to all the noise, Cally took off running down the street, trying her best to make it back home before anyone saw her. As Cally was running down the street, she noticed that there were headlights coming up behind her. Assuming it was Kyle, Cally picked up her pace and started running through the neighbors' yards, just in case Ryan had possessed Kyle enough to try to kill her. Just as the headlights started to gain on her, Cally was already in her front yard, heading for the house. Not giving it a second thought, Cally jumped from the bottom of the steps all the way to the porch, causing a loud thud when she landed. Curious to where the headlights were, Cally turned back around to see, but just like magic, they were gone, vanished into the dark night. Scared of what might happen next, Cally quickly turned to open the door and noticed that one of her parents had just turned on the living room light. While standing there, with nowhere else to go, she could hear the front door starting to open.

"Oh great. As if my night was not bad enough, now I'm going to get grounded for the rest of my life," Cally said to herself, standing on the front porch as the outside light came on.

"Cally, what in the hell are you doing out here? Don't you know how dangerous this is?" Bill asked, after seeing that the trespasser was his own daughter.

"Dad, please don't be mad at me. I only stepped out here to get some fresh air and clear my head. I can't help that I forgot my house key," Cally lied with tears in her eyes, in the hopes that her father would believe her and not get upset.

"It's okay, Cally. You just scared me a bit, that's all. I'm sorry that I over-reacted," Bill said, trying to make Cally feel better.

Bill watched in sadness and concern as Cally walked into the house with her head dropped. He knew that she was not being completely honest with him—the look in her eyes told him that. Bill wanted to talk to Cally and help her with her problems, but he really did not know what to say or where to begin. Bill loved Cally with all of his heart and soul. He was just afraid that he would do more harm than good, and he did not want to harm Cally any more than she had already been harmed. The only thing Bill wanted was for his family to get back to the way they used to be, but something told him that they still had a long, rough road ahead.

16

"Cally, would you like for me to fix you a cup of warm milk to help you sleep? It always works for me whenever I'm having trouble sleeping," Bill offered, hoping that it would break the ice and lead to a conversation.

"No thanks, Dad. I just want to go lie down in my bed and try to relax for a little while. I'm sure after a few minutes, I'll fall asleep with no problem," Cally answered, hiding the heart-shaped ring on her finger as she gave her dad a hug good night.

"Okay, sweetheart, but if you change your mind, I'll be down here for at least another twenty minutes, so feel free to come down and join me," Bill offered a second time, hoping that Cally would change her mind and join him so that they could engage in a much-needed conversation.

"Alright, Dad. I'll keep that in mind, and thanks again for everything you've done for me," Cally replied as she quickly started up the stairway to her bedroom, before her mother woke up and decided to ask more questions.

While Cally was walking up the stairway, she kept staring at the heart-shaped ring on her finger. She wanted to destroy the ring so badly, but she was not sure that destroying the ring would get rid of Ryan. Cally could not believe the nightmare she was experiencing. It seemed as if things were never going to get better, no matter how much time she gave it. Cally never dreamed that her life could become so screwed up. Ever since she was a little girl, she always believed that she would find her Prince Charming, get married, and live happily ever after, but sadly, Cally had to face the cold, bitter truth: her life was no fairy tale; it was more like a horror movie that no one would survive.

Not wanting to wake her mother, Cally slowly opened her bedroom door and tiptoed to her bed. While sitting on the edge of her bed, Cally stared in complete horror at the ring. She could not believe that it had found its way back to her again. Cally felt so confused. She questioned whether she should tell her parents about the ring and about the way Kyle was acting. Cally hated to worry her parents with everything, but since Ryan had obviously possessed Kyle's body, Cally knew that she needed all the help and support she could get. With her mind made up to tell her parents, Cally lay back on her bed and decided to wait until the morning to inform them of Ryan's return.

While lying on her bed, Cally got an eerie feeling that someone was in the room with her. The last thing Cally wanted was to see Ryan, or even Kyle, hiding in the darkness. It horrified Cally to think that her life might never be the same; it was the worst feeling in the world to know that her ex-boyfriend had come back from the dead for her. Cally knew that she had to come up with a better plan, and she had to do it quick, because her time was running out. It would only be a matter of time before Ryan carried out his evil plan to kill her.

As Cally's mind became more cluttered with unpleasant thoughts, her eyelids started to get heavy; she could feel herself starting to nod in and out of sleep as the ticking of the clock echoed throughout the room. Cally really didn't want to go to sleep, but she could not fight it anymore. It was as if her eyelids had ten-pound weights on them. Taking a quick glance around the room again, Cally slowly drifted off to sleep without any hesitation.

No sooner than she had gone to sleep, Bill pushed her door open slowly and looked in on her. Seeing that everything was okay, Bill pulled the door shut and walked out of the room.

"Bill, is that you? Where have you been?" Kate asked as Bill crawled back into bed, trying his best not to wake his wife.

"Yes, honey, it's me. I just got up to check on Cally to see how she was doing," Bill answered, leaving out the part about Cally locking herself outside.

"Well, how was she? Is she still sleeping?" Kate asked as she sat up in bed and looked at Bill with concerned eyes.

"She's perfectly fine, sweetheart, so close your eyes and go back to sleep. There's nothing to worry about," Bill said, hoping that Kate would not get up and go into Cally's bedroom.

"Alright then, I'll see you in the morning," Kate said with a yawn, as she slid back down into the bed and cuddled up next to Bill.

Frustrated and concerned with all the problems that his daughter was facing, Bill began to grow more and more restless by the second. He had so much on his mind that it made it virtually impossible for him to sleep. No matter how much he tossed and turned, he just couldn't get comfortable. Bill wished he could snap his fingers and change everything, but he couldn't. It was going to take a miracle to solve all of the problems that he had and that was something that he didn't have. The only thing Bill could really do was pray to God that everything would work out for the best. Just as Bill was about to give up on falling asleep, his tired, heavy eyelids started to close.

"Bill, are you still awake? Because if you are, then we need to talk about the funeral," Kate said, as she sat up in the bed and looked down at Bill.

"Exactly what funeral are you talking about, Kate, and why did you wait until now to bring it up? Can't this conversation wait until morning?" Bill asked, still half-asleep and totally clueless as to what Kate was talking about.

"Please, Bill, don't play dumb with me. You know good and damn well what funeral I'm talking about," Kate snapped as tears rolled down her face.

"Kate, please be a little more specific with your answer, because I'm having a hard time comprehending what you are saying. Are you talking about the funeral for Ms. Jones?" Bill asked, feeling agitated that Kate was expecting him to be a mind-reader.

"No, Bill, it is not the funeral for Ms. Jones. It is the funeral for our little girl, and I can't believe that you are being so insensitive about the whole matter. You know that it is killing me to have to plan a funeral for my only child," Kate said, still sobbing uncontrollably.

"What in the hell are you talking about? I just saw Cally a few minutes ago, and she was just fine. She is in her bed, fast asleep. There is nothing wrong with her, so stop saying that we need to plan her funeral, because you are starting to really upset me," Bill said, as he tried to control his anger and emotions.

"Please calm down, Bill, and stop living in denial. You have to accept the fact that our little girl is gone and she is not coming back," Kate said, trying to make Bill see the truth.

"Damn it, Kate. What do I have to do to prove to you that Cally is alive and well? Would seeing her face make you come to your senses?" Bill asked in an angry voice, as he slung the covers back on Kate.

Upset and a little angry, Bill walked down the hallway toward Cally's room in a fast pace. Bill had no idea what was going on with Kate, but he intended on getting Cally up, so that Kate could see her for herself and stop with all the nonsense. Bill knew that Kate was having a hard time with everything, but going as far as to say that Cally was dead really concerned Bill, and he did not have the time or energy to worry about Kate and her drama. He had one thing and one thing only on his mind, and that was getting Cally through the difficult times that lay ahead of her. Wanting to prove Kate wrong, Bill walked straight into Cally's room without so much as a knock and flipped on her light.

"Cally, it's Dad. Where are you? There is something I need to talk you about," Bill shouted out as he looked around the room for Cally.

After seeing that her bedroom and bathroom was empty, Bill started downstairs to search the rest of the house. Soon, with only the kitchen left to search, Bill's heart started to pound with fear as he pushed the door open, praying to see his little girl at the table, but instead of Cally being there, it was a newspaper instead. Curious as to why there was a newspaper on the table, Bill took a glance down at it and saw the worst thing that any parent could see. There, in front of his face, was Cally's obituary and an article telling how she had died. After reading about his daughter drowning in Lake Swain, Bill fell to the floor in agony. He could not, nor did he want to believe what he had just read. Kate was right all along. His little girl was, in fact, dead, and the proof was in the paper.

"Why, God, why did my little girl have to die? It is not fair! Please just send her back to me," Bill cried as he laid his head on the kitchen floor and sobbed.

"Bill, honey, wake up! You are having a nightmare," Kate said, shaking Bill, trying to wake him up.

"Oh God, Kate, please tell me that Cally is not dead. Please just tell me that she is okay," Bill begged as he wiped the tears away.

"Of course she's okay. I just got back from checking on her. She's sleeping like a baby," Kate said, assuring Bill that everything was alright so that he would calm down and stop crying.

"Please don't be mad, Kate. I just have to see for myself so that I'll know for sure," Bill said, walking out of the bedroom in a hurry.

Upon reaching Cally's bedroom door, Bill stopped and took a deep breath as he braced himself for the worst. Bill was so confused at this point and he was so scared that he could not breathe. He did not know if he was still dreaming, or if he was awake. Bill did not know what he would do without his little girl. Just the thought of losing Cally made him feel as if he was losing his mind. The only thing Bill wanted to see when he opened the door was his little girl, lying there in her bed alive and well. With his heart pounding and his hands shaking, Bill slowly opened Cally's bedroom door and switched on the light. There, right in front of his face, was his little girl, alive and well.

"Cally, are you okay, sweetheart? It's me, Dad. I have come in here to check on you," Bill said, giving Cally a slight shake to wake her up.

"Yeah, Dad, I'm just fine. Why do you ask? Is everything okay?" Cally asked in confusion as she slowly sat up in her bed and rubbed her tired eyes.

"Oh, everything is just fine. I just came in here to check on you before I went back to bed. I'm sorry that I woke you. Just go back to sleep and I'll see you in the morning," Bill apologized in a happy voice as he gave Cally a hug and a kiss on the cheek.

"Bill, is everything alright in here?" Kate asked, walking in and seeing Bill locked on to Cally's neck, hugging her as if he never wanted to let go.

"Yes, everything is fine, and I could not be happier. It was all just a bad dream, Kate, one big bad dream," Bill said, still hugging Cally's neck tightly.

"Would somebody please tell me what is going on, because you guys are really starting to scare me," Cally said, feeling a little confused as to why her dad had woken her up.

"Your father just had a bad dream is all, and he wanted to come in here and check on you," Kate explained, giving Cally a confused look herself.

"It's okay, Dad. There is nothing wrong with me, I promise. I'm right here and I'm not going anywhere," Cally said, trying to make her dad feel better.

"Cally, I need for you to be completely honest with me about this, and please keep in mind that if you are lying to me, I'll know. Is everything alright with you, or are you hiding things from us again?" Bill asked, hoping that Cally would be straight-up and honest with them.

Cally was stunned. She had expected a question like that from her mother, but she never dreamed that her dad would ask something like that. Cally could not believe that she was about to confess to sneaking out and meeting Kyle. She knew that telling her parents the truth would only land her in trouble, but she knew that it had to be done. Cally knew that it was time to come clean about everything. She had to tell her parents the truth. It was the only way to solve her problems, and it really did not matter if her parents got mad or not. Cally could not keep it a secret any longer. She had to tell them everything, and whatever happened, would just have to happen. Cally was ready to face whatever punishment her parents gave her.

"Well, Cally, would you answer your father? Because your silence has me a little concerned, too," Kate said after seeing a look of guilt cross Cally's face.

"Okay, I'll tell you, but please do not get too upset with me, because I did it for a good reason," Cally explained before her parents jumped to any conclusions.

"Young lady, you had better start explaining yourself before I get upset and ground you for the rest of your life," Kate ordered as she tapped her foot impatiently and waited for Cally to fill them in.

"I'm with your mother on this one. You need to start explaining yourself, so that we are not left in the dark on things. As your parents, we have a right to know everything that is going on with you, especially if it is something bad," Bill said, agreeing with Kate as his eyes filled with tears again.

"Okay, I slipped out earlier and met Kyle so we could go for a ride and spend some time together," Cally blurted out quickly, trying to get her confession over with.

"You did what? You know that you are not supposed to leave the house without our permission, especially to meet Kyle. What in the hell were you thinking? Don't you realize that anything could have happened to you and we would have had no clue as to where you were?" Kate yelled, feeling hurt and disappointed that Cally would go behind their backs and do something that was so dangerous and selfish.

"Well, just out of curiosity, what was your good reason for sneaking out? Not that it is going to make a difference or help you any," Bill asked, wanting to know what reason would be important enough for her to disobey them and put her life in jeopardy for yet another time.

"My reasons were based on suspicions, and my suspicions were right on the money," Cally explained, showing her parents the heart-shaped ring that Kyle had given her—the same heart-shaped ring she and her mother had put into Ryan's casket.

"Oh my God, Cally, where did you get that ring and why is it on your finger?" Kate asked with a gasp as she started to panic.

"Kyle gave it to me tonight, and I have it on my finger so that I'll not lose it," Cally answered, knowing that her parents would probably flip out and go looking for Kyle themselves so that they could get answers from him.

"I don't understand, Cally. Why would Kyle give you a ring that we buried with Ryan? It is just not possible, and it doesn't make any sense. There is no way that he could have got his hands on it, and even if he could, why in the world would he give it to you?" Bill asked, as his mind filled with confusion and chaos.

"Oh, I know how he got the ring, and I know why he gave it to you. Kyle is possessed by Ryan, isn't he, and do not lie to me, Cally, or I'll know," Kate said as she chewed on her nails nervously.

"Yes, Mom, you are right. Ryan has possessed Kyle, and tonight, he tried to run me down with his car after he made me get out and walk home from the top of the road," Cally replied in a fearful voice as she stared down at the floor in shame.

"Wait a minute, Cally. Kyle doesn't even have a car, so how could he run you down in something that he doesn't have?" Bill asked, thinking that he had caught Cally in a lie or some sort of cover-up.

"Well, that is what I thought, too, but when he came to pick me up, he was in a black Mustang, just like the one Ryan used to have, and when I asked him where he got it, he told me that he had bought it from his neighbor," Cally explained, hoping that her parents would believe her after all the other lies she had told.

"Okay, Cally, I believe you, because I don't see why you would lie about something like this," Kate said, giving Cally one of her motherly looks, letting her know that she had better be telling the truth.

"Yeah, I believe you, too. That is why I'm going to have a little chat with Kyle and ask him why he tried to kill you tonight," Bill said, as his whole body filled with anger and his face got blood-red, indicating that he was mad enough to hunt Kyle down and kill him.

"No, Dad, please don't go. This is not going to solve anything. The only thing you are going to do is mess up my plan, and then we will never be able to send Ryan back to hell," Cally begged, jumping in front of her father, trying to stop him from leaving.

"She is right about one thing, Bill. If you go out looking for Kyle, it will only cause more problems for everyone, including Kyle's mother, who is clueless as to what is going on," Kate said, grabbing Bill by his arm, trying to reason with him before he did something crazy that he would end up regretting the rest of his life.

"Okay, you can let go of my arm now. I'm not going anywhere right this second, but I promise you that this is far from over. Now let's hear about this other plan you have come up with," Bill said, pulling his arm away from Kate's grip.

"Well, before Kyle gave me the ring, he made me make a promise to him, and after seeing how strange he was acting, I made him turn on the interior light before I made the promise, just so I could make sure that he did not resemble Ryan in any way. And just like that Ryan walked right into my trap," Cally explained with a giggle, feeling overjoyed with her accomplishment.

"Cally, you need to be a little more specific because I'm not sure that I'm following you," Kate said with confusion and concern.

"Don't you get it, Mom? I made the promise to Kyle, not to Ryan. You see, that is what I was doing when I told him to turn on the interior light. I was making sure that my promise was being made to Kyle and not Ryan," Cally explained, hoping that her parents would see things the way she did.

"Okay, Cally, I understand that part of the plan, but I still do not understand how it is going to get rid of Ryan," Kate said, still feeling a little bit stumped by Cally's explanation.

"It is simple, Mom. Ryan could only get me if I made the promise to *him*, but I didn't. I made it to Kyle, and when I face Ryan tomorrow, he will know that he walked right into my trap. Then he will have no other choice but to leave and never come back," Cally explained with a smile on her face, knowing for sure that her plan would not fail.

"Absolutely not, young lady. You are never to see Kyle again—at least until we can figure out a way to solve this problem with Ryan. Furthermore, you are grounded until I tell you otherwise for sneaking out of the house to go meet Kyle," Bill ordered, feeling fed up with Cally and her silly plans.

"That is not fair, Dad. If you don't let me take care of this while I have the chance, I'll never be able to get rid of Ryan. He will end up haunting me forever, and that is something that I cannot live with," Cally cried out in anger, upset that her father was being so difficult.

"Okay, I think that everyone needs to calm down so that we can discuss this like mature adults," Kate said, basically calling Bill and Cally both children.

"There is nothing more to discuss. I have put my foot down and that is final. I'm the parent and she is the child, so stop trying to change my mind about things because it is not going to work," Bill snapped at Kate, as he became more and more frustrated with the whole situation.

Cally was absolutely furious with her father, and it showed all over her face. She could not believe that he was going to stand in the way of her plan. Nothing made sense to Cally anymore. First Bill was sobbing over her, and then he was yelling at her. Cally knew that Bill loved her, but she could not understand why he did not want her to follow through with her plan to get rid of Ryan. It was almost as if Ryan had possessed him, too. Cally knew what she had to do; she had to disobey her parents one last time. It was the only way for her to finish what she had started and send Ryan back to the grave where he belonged.

"Cally, sweetheart, I think you should go back to bed and try to get some sleep before it gets any later," Kate suggested, after sensing the tension between Bill and Cally.

"Whatever. Just sit down here and share your little secrets with each other. Who cares if my life is going to hell? Maybe if you two are lucky, Ryan will kill me in my sleep and then you will not have to put up with me anymore," Cally smarted off, trying to get her parents to feel sorry for her as she walked out of the room with tears in her eyes.

"Bill, honey, don't you think that you were a little hard on her? After all, she did tell us the truth about things. That should count for something, don't you think?" Kate asked softly, so that Cally would not hear their disagreement.

"No, Kate, I do not think that I was hard on her. If anything, I wasn't hard enough. She should have never left the house without our permission. She knows better than that, and you should know better than to take her side. If you do not start enforcing some rules and punishments around here, then she is going to walk all over you," Bill said raising his voice, treating Kate as if she was hard of hearing.

"Well, if I remember correctly, you were the one who told me to start giving Cally her freedom and trust her more. Now you are telling me not to do that. Damn, Bill, make up your mind because you are starting to confuse the hell out of me," Kate yelled right back, reminding him that it was his idea to treat Cally in a more grown-up way.

17

Cally sat upstairs in her bedroom and tried not to listen to her parents fighting, but it was difficult to avoid with all of the yelling. Cally felt she was the one to blame for everything; she knew her actions and poor judgment had started the whole conflict, and she just wanted it all to end so that her parents would start getting along again. Cally knew what she had to do, but getting out of the house to do it was the problem. Cally knew her parents would never agree to let her see Kyle again, and in order for her plan to work, she had to see him one last time. With that in mind, Cally pulled out a notebook and pen and started to write a letter to her parents, informing them that she had to put an end to Ryan once and for all.

Dear Mom and Dad,

If something were to happen to me, I just want you both to know how much I loved and cared about you, despite our disagreements. I never meant for this to turn out the way it has, but it did and the only way to make things better is to take matters into my own hands. I hope that you both understand why I'm doing this. It is not to hurt you, only to help you. Please don't be mad at me and do not try to find me, for this will only make matters worse. This is something that has to be done, and it has to be done now. If and when everything turns out for the best, I'll contact you, but if things go wrong, just remember that I love you both very much, and don't forget, one day we will be together again.

Love Always and Forever,

Cally

After writing her letter, Cally ripped the page out quietly so that her parents would not hear anything, and placed it on her pillow. Cally hated to put her parents through any more pain and frustration, but this had to be done. She could not just sit back and do nothing while Ryan tried to kill her yet again. Cally had to stop Ryan dead in his tracks, no matter the consequences. Feeling rushed and in a hurry to get out of the house before her parents came up to check on her, Cally grabbed her cell phone off the nightstand and put it in her pocket as she started toward the door. Looking out to make sure the coast was clear, Cally tiptoed down the stairs slowly and quietly. Upon reaching the front door, Cally stopped and listened to her parents who were still arguing in the kitchen. Taking a deep breath and one more last look around the living room, Cally slowly opened the door and walked out.

While Cally was walking through the front yard, she could still hear her parents fighting and bickering. It broke her heart to think that she was the cause of everything, and she was not going to rest, or even return, until she was sure she had sent Ryan back to the grave. Although Cally knew what her plan was, she still did not know exactly how to carry it out; she was so afraid that she might end up hurting or killing Kyle in the process. Cally knew that she had to carefully think things through and get everything right, because if by some means her plan failed, Cally had already made her mind up to take her own life so that her parents could live the rest of their lives in peace, without the worry of Ryan's evil spirit.

As Cally walked down the pitch-black, lonely street, she could not help but wonder if her parents had found her letter yet. It broke Cally's heart to think about her parents finding her bed empty with just a letter on the pillow-case, but Cally could not let her sadness stop her from carrying out her plan. Cally knew that she was taking a huge risk, but she felt that her plan would work; she had to go with her gut feeling and trust her instincts. Although Cally was scared, she put on a brave face and kept walking until she saw the old Branford barn, a safe place where she could hide out until everything was taken care of.

While Cally was trying to find something soft to sleep on in the barn, her parents were still involved in their screaming match. It seemed as if Bill and Kate had forgotten the only thing that really mattered—and that was Cally. Both Bill and Kate were so busy trying to put the blame on one another that they forgot all about the grave danger their daughter was in. Finally seeing how truly childish they were acting, they decided to put their differences aside and pull themselves together for the sake of their little girl and their marriage.

"Stop, Bill, I can't do this anymore. I have more important things to worry about than this, so let's just save the drama for another day and focus on helping our little girl before it is too late," Kate said, stopping the argument before it escalated into another altercation.

"You're right, Kate. I'm sorry I let this get out of hand. It's just that I'm really worried about Cally and I want to protect her, but I can't, and that is what's driving me crazy. I have never felt so helpless in my entire life," Bill said as he broke down in tears.

"Don't worry, Bill. I promise you we will get through this somehow. All we have to do is be strong, supportive, and work together as a team," Kate said as she tried to put a plan together of her own, hoping to save Cally's life before Ryan took it.

"Okay, Kate, you have my word, I'll not start another argument again. I just want to help Cally before something bad happens to her. Right now, I think we should go up and check on her," Bill suggested as he started to walk out of the kitchen.

Upon entering Cally's bedroom, Kate got an eerie feeling that something was wrong. She prayed that it was a false feeling, but after walking in and seeing her bed empty, Kate knew that her feeling was far from false. She had absolutely no idea where Cally could be, and that scared the hell out of her; it was as if her worst nightmare had come true. With her heart racing, Kate flung the covers back, causing Cally's letter to fall into the floor, right at Bill's feet. As soon as Bill's eyes met with the letter, his heart felt as if it had come up into his throat. Before even reading the letter, Bill already had a pretty good idea as to what it said.

"Okay, Bill, while I'm getting my purse and the car keys, you can be calling the police, because I know that we are going to need all the help we can get," Kate said, after reading Cally's chilling and heartfelt letter.

"Well, it looks as if we are on our own because the police cannot do anything unless she has been missing for two days," Bill said in a disappointed voice, after hanging up the phone.

"That is okay. The police probably wouldn't believe our story anyways. Besides, if we hurry, we might be able to catch her before she gets too far," Kate replied, pulling her car keys out of her purse.

While driving slowly up the street, both Bill and Kate were looking out of their windows, calling Cally's name out, praying to God that they would hear her answer. They knew Cally could not have gotten too far by walking; they just hoped that Kyle hadn't picked her up already and taken her somewhere to carry out Ryan's evil plan. After not seeing or hearing Cally, Bill and Kate begin to truly panic. They knew what they were up against, and that was enough to scare them both to death. Just the thought of Cally being all alone frustrated them to their breaking point. All they wanted to do was find Cally and get her back home where she would be safe.

"Oh great, wouldn't you know it? Just when you think things couldn't possibly get any worse, then it starts pouring down rain," Kate said in a hostile voice as she turned on her windshield wipers.

"Don't worry about the rain. It is the least of our problems. We'll just take our time searching for Cally. Besides, she couldn't have got too far. She has to be around here somewhere," Bill said, looking straight ahead at the old Branford barn as the headlights shone on the half-open door.

"What are you thinking, Bill? Do you think Cally could be in the old Branford barn?" Kate asked after seeing how Bill was looking at the barn door.

"Well, there is no harm in checking it out. Who knows? Maybe we'll get lucky and find her hiding in there," Bill answered with his eyes still focused on the open door.

"You stay here, and I'll go inside and look for her. I'll be right back," Bill said, pulling his hood over the top of his head.

"No, I'm going to look, too. Four eyes are better than two, and right now, we don't need to waste any more valuable time, so let's go," Kate said, putting the car into PARK as the heavy rain continued to pour down, making it difficult to see.

"Cally, sweetheart, it's Mom and Dad. Are you in here? Please just answer us. We're worried sick about you," Kate called out, hoping that Cally would hear her desperate pleas.

"Okay, Kate, you take that side of the barn, and I'll take this one. Remember to check in the stalls, too, because she could be anywhere," Bill ordered, looking through every stall he came to.

"It is no use, Bill. We have searched this whole barn and found nothing. We really should be going, so that we can cover more ground," Kate called out as she waited for Bill at the barn door.

As Bill and Kate backed away from the barn, Cally watched their head-lights start to fade away from the loft, the one and only place they did not check. Cally had heard her parents calling for her, but she knew not to answer them because they would only make her go back home, and that was some-thing Cally could not do. Cally knew this would be her one and only chance to get rid of Ryan, and she had to take it, no matter how much it broke her heart to see her parents search for her and then leave. Cally had to be strong and hang in there. She had come too far to turn back now. She just prayed that the plan would work and not be a failure like the one before had.

"Damn, this is like trying to find a needle in a haystack. She could be anywhere, including Kyle's house," Bill cursed as he grew more and more agitated at the thought of his daughter being out by herself in the middle of the night.

"I really don't see her going to Kyle's house tonight. Maybe we should head back home, just in case she comes back on her own," Kate suggested as she pulled into a driveway and turned around.

"Maybe you're right. It is at least worth going back there to check it out," Bill agreed, hoping that his little girl would be back home safe and sound.

No sooner than Kate had pulled into their own driveway, Bill had already jumped out of the car while it was still moving and ran toward the front door with his key in hand. Kate watched as Bill walked through the house in a frantic pace, calling out Cally's name. Kate could see the despair in Bill's eyes. It was nothing like she had ever seen before. It was almost as if Bill was losing his mind completely. Although Kate was hurting, too, she knew that she had to keep her head on straight and stay focused for Cally's sake. There had to be at least one calm parent who could make the right decisions, and Kate knew that she had to be that one at this time. Before making any decisions at all, though, Kate knew she had to calm Bill down before he drove himself crazy.

"Bill, would you please just stop before you drive yourself insane? Cally is not here, or she would have answered you by now," Kate said, wanting Bill to get ahold of himself and calm down.

"Tell me, Kate, what am I supposed to do? Sit around here on my ass and pretend that everything is okay, while my daughter is out there all alone?" Bill asked hatefully as he glared toward Kate, looking at her as if she were stupid.

"Look, Bill, I want to find Cally just as badly as you do, but there is no way that we are going to find her out there tonight. Besides, what if she comes back later and we are not here? Do you know how frightened she would be? I think we should stay put for a little while, at least until the sun comes up, and then we can go back out and look for her," Kate explained rationally, trying to comfort Bill before he had a nervous breakdown.

"I just want my little girl back. I miss her so much, and I'm so afraid that she will get hurt out there all by herself," Bill said, laying his tired head on Kate's shoulder.

"Cally is going to be just fine, I promise you that. She is a very smart girl, and I know in my heart that she is okay. Besides, we only have about two more hours before the sun comes up, so let's get everything ready to go and the time will pass by before we know it," Kate said, hoping to lift Bill's spirits a bit.

While Bill and Kate were back home, getting ready to go out and search again, Cally was still at the Branford barn, wishing she had someone to talk to. Cally could not wait until the sun came up. The first thing she planned on doing was calling Kyle, so that they could meet somewhere. Wanting to meet him somewhere that was secluded, Cally had the perfect place in mind, and that was Swain Lake. Cally knew that there would be no interruptions on the lake, and that was what she needed in order to carry her plan out fully. With her mind cluttered and her body worn out, Cally could not fight it any longer. The sound of the heavy rain beating down on the old barn's tin roof was like an inviting lullaby. She could feel her eyes starting to close slowly, to the beat of the pouring rain. Finally, without any further hesitation, Cally shut her eyes and fell asleep, holding the one and only thing that she had brought with her from home—her cell phone.

Asleep for what seemed like only minutes, Cally was awakened by the alarm on her cell phone, which she had set hours before, so that she could get up and get an early start. The first thing Cally wanted to do was call Kyle before he had a chance to make any other plans. With her hands trembling, Cally opened her cell phone and dialed Kyle's number, waiting patiently as she counted the rings.

"Hello, Cally," Kyle answered in a sarcastic tone, letting her know that Ryan still had a hold on him.

"Hey, Kyle, I was just wondering if you wanted to go somewhere and talk, that is, if you are not too busy," Cally said, trying to pretend that she had no idea that Ryan was possessing Kyle's body.

"It is a bit early for talking, don't you think? Besides, what are your parents going to say about me coming to pick you up? I'm sure that your mom will have to nose in before we leave," Kyle said in a bitter voice, putting Cally's parents down once again, as if they did not matter.

"Well, you do not have to worry about them knowing anything, because I ran away last night. I could not take them trying to run my life anymore. I think that it is about time for me to start living my life the way I want to," Cally lied, hoping that Kyle was buying in to her story so that he would come and pick her up before her parents came back out looking for her. That was the last thing that Cally needed.

"Well, what do you know? Little Miss Perfect finally stood up for herself and did something right for a change. It is about time you stopped trying to impress everybody," Kyle said, cutting Cally down in any way that he could.

"So, are you coming to pick me up or not? Because if you're not, then I need to find somewhere else to go before my parents try to find me," Cally said, trying to rush Kyle into a decision before it got any later.

"Alright, tell me where you are, and I'll be there as soon as I can," Kyle said, almost sounding like his old self again.

"I'm hiding out at the old Branford barn. When I see you pull in, I'll come straight out, and then we can go somewhere else to talk," Cally said, hanging up the phone, not really wanting to give Kyle a chance to object or say anything else.

As Cally was sitting at the old barn, waiting on Kyle, her parents were home, trying to figure out where they should search first. Bill was packing anything and everything that he could think of into a backpack, because he had no intention of returning until they found Cally. Bill and Kate both knew that they had to make that whole day count, and they were not going to leave one stone unturned. They planned on searching every inch of the whole town, while putting out the word about their daughter to anyone and every-one who would listen. Both Bill and Kate prayed to God that they would find their little girl safe, before it was too late.

"It's about time," Cally said to herself as Kyle pulled up to the old barn in his black Mustang.

"You know, I thought you were lying about running away. I figured this whole thing would be one big setup, but I stand corrected," Kyle said in amazement as Cally walked out of the old barn, wearing the same clothes she had on the night before.

"No, it is not a lie or a setup. I'm just ready to get away from my nagging parents before I go crazy. Now let's get out of here before we get caught," Cally said, rushing Kyle as she put on her seat belt.

"So, where are you wanting to go, or do you even know that much?" Kyle asked sarcastically, as he slowly pulled out onto the highway.

"Well, I thought that we could go to Swain Lake today, since no one is ever there. That way we can have a little bit of privacy. What do you think about that?" Cally asked, hoping and praying that Kyle would agree.

"Sounds good to me. As long as we are not stuck hanging around your nosy-ass parents, I'm fine with going anywhere," Kyle replied, stepping on the gas pedal.

"Yeah, my parents can get a little nerve-racking. That is why I had to leave last night. I knew that I was going to lose it if I didn't," Cally agreed as she glanced down at the speed odometer.

"Hey, you are not mad about me losing my temper and making you walk home last night, are you?" Kyle asked, ignoring the part about trying to run her down with his car.

"Don't be silly. I think we both lost our cool last night. Trust me, there are no hard feelings. Besides, that walk did me some good. It really gave me a chance to think about things," Cally said, reassuring Kyle that things were okay between them.

"Good, because after I got home last night, I realized how wrong it was of me to do that to you," Kyle said as he turned on the dirt road that led to Swain Lake.

18

While Cally and Kyle were well on their way to Swain Lake, Bill and Kate were just getting into their car. Although they were getting a slow start, they were so glad to see that the rain had stopped; it made both of them feel a little more positive about their search. They knew that with the rain gone and the sun out, they could spot Cally a whole lot faster and better. Although Bill and Kate did need some help with their search, they had no intention of involving the police until they just had to. They both knew that the police would not do anything until Cally had been missing for forty-eight hours, and Bill and Kate knew that they could not waste another second. Their daughter's life was at stake, and they were not about to gamble with that.

"I pray we have better luck today than we did last night, because I do not know how much more disappointment I can take," Kate said, as tears came to her eyes.

"Well, I have already made my mind up. I'm not going back home until I find my little girl, and that is a promise," Bill said with determination, as he kept his eyes glued to the road.

"Oh my God, Bill, I just thought of something and I don't know why I did not think of it sooner," Kate blurted out, slamming on the brakes so hard that Bill's head flew forward.

"What in the hell are you talking about, and why are you slamming on the brakes so hard?" Bill asked, looking at Kate as if she were a crazy person.

"Her cell phone. We have not even tried to call it," Kate said, feeling a

199

little excited about her revelation as she dug through her purse, looking for her own cell phone.

"Well, is it ringing? Come on now, don't leave me in the dark. Tell me something, anything," Bill said anxiously as he continuously tapped Kate on the arm.

"Nothing is happening. It is going straight to her voice mail. Maybe she has the phone cut off, or maybe the battery is dead. Yeah, that's probably it," Kate said, trying to think of any excuse that would make her feel better.

"It's alright, Kate, we will find her, but we need to get a move on and stop wasting time," Bill said, trying to comfort Kate.

Bill and Kate drove around the whole town for what seemed like hours, asking everyone they saw about their daughter, but everyone's answer was devastating to them: no one had seen their little girl. It was as if Cally had disappeared off the face of the earth, and Bill and Kate had never been more frightened in their lives. It was the worst feeling any parent could ever have or dream of having. Bill and Kate both felt as if their hands were tied. They had done everything and anything they could to find Cally and still they turned up emptyhanded. Knowing that they had done everything in their power, they decided to take things up a notch before it got any later.

"We have done everything that we can do now, and I think that it is time to call the police, or at least round up a search party," Kate said, feeling as if she was at the end of her rope.

"Yeah, that is probably a good idea. God knows we need to do something different before it gets any later," Bill agreed, looking around the streets and sidewalks one last time, hoping that by some chance, he would catch a glimpse of Cally.

"Okay, I'll call the police and explain to them what is going on, and hopefully they will send someone out here to meet us," Kate said, opening her cell phone up.

"Whoa, hang on just one minute before you call the police. I have one more place that I want to check before calling them, and I have a feeling that Cally just may be there," Bill said, suddenlty remembering his nightmare about Cally drowning in Swain Lake.

"What other place are you talking about? We have searched everywhere, and we have not found her yet, and I honestly don't think that we will unless we get some help," Kate said, disagreeing with Bill's decision.

"There is one last place that we did not look. Remember the nightmare I had the other night about Cally dying? Well, I did not tell you how or where she died," Bill said, suddenly feeling positive that his dream would lead them straight to Cally.

"Well, come on now, don't keep me waiting. Where and how did she die in your dream?" Kate asked as her heart pounded with fear.

"In my dream, Cally died by drowning in Swain Lake, and I'm willing to bet my life that my dream was a sign," Bill said as tears rolled down his face at the very thought of his dream becoming reality.

"Okay, Bill, we will go and check Swain Lake, but if she is not there, then we have to call the police and that is final," Kate said, taking some charge of the situation, hoping and praying that Bill's dream would not come true.

"Well, come on. What are you waiting for? Let's go get our daughter so that we can get her back home where she belongs," Bill said, praying that they would make it to Cally in time before something bad happened to her.

As Bill and Kate were on their way to Swain Lake, Cally and Kyle were already there. Cally had her whole plan mapped out, and she prayed that it would work. Cally knew that she could not go on living her life this way. Something had to be done, and she had to be the one to do it, no matter the consequences. Cally was ready to put this nightmare behind her, even if it meant losing her own life to do it. At least then Cally could rest in peace, knowing that her parents were safe from Ryan's evil designs. Just thinking about sending Ryan back to hell gave Cally such a satisfying feeling—she could not wait to see the expression on his ugly face when he found out that she knew it was him all along.

"Alright, Cally, now that you have dragged me all the way out here, I think that it is time for you to start talking and let me know what this is all about," Kyle ordered sarcastically, staring at Cally as if she owed him the whole world and then some.

"Oh, I think you already know what I'm going to say to you—don't you, *Ryan*?" Cally asked as she stared at Kyle's color-changing eyes, letting him know that he didn't have her fooled for a second.

"Very good, Cally. You are not as dumb as you look. And here I have been hiding my face behind this piece of shit," Ryan said bitterly as his evil spirit suddenly came out of Kyle's lifeless body.

"Tell me one thing, Ryan. Why are you doing this to me? Didn't you treat me badly enough when you were alive? I mean, come on, why can't you just accept the fact that I don't love you anymore, and I sure as hell don't want to be with you? I would rather eat shit and die than be around you at all," Cally screamed out in anger, letting him know that she was not afraid of him anymore.

"You should watch your mouth, bitch, before you piss me off even more, and trust me, you don't want to do that," Ryan said, putting his burned, maggot-infested face in Cally's, as if he were trying to intimidate her and back her down like a scared pup.

Cally stared into Ryan's neon-green eyes, trying not to show any kind of fear. Although she was worried about Kyle's lifeless body lying on the ground in front of her, she could not let Ryan sense any fear. Cally knew that she had to stay strong and focused in order for her plan to work. She had Ryan right where she wanted him this time, and she was not going to do anything to mess that up. Still, feeling a little nervous about the whole ordeal, Cally took a few deep breaths and continued to stare Ryan down, showing no feelings or remorse whatsoever toward him. She wanted Ryan to know that she was not going to back down from him this time. This time, she was going to fight him until the bitter end.

"So, what do you plan on doing with me this time, Ryan, or did you even plan that far ahead?" Cally asked, moving a little closer to Ryan's disgusting-looking face, showing him that she could stand her own ground.

"Well, since you are so eager to find out, please allow me to explain. First, I'm going to kill Kyle slowly and painfully while you watch. And as for you, I don't have to do anything because you took care of that all by yourself," Ryan said with a devilish laugh, as pieces of burned flesh and maggots fell off his face, making Cally sick to her stomach.

"Why would you want to kill Kyle? He has never done anything to you. Besides, I'm the one you want, not him, so why can't you spare his life?" Cally asked, praying that Ryan would change his mind about Kyle.

Without saying a word, Ryan just stood there in front of Cally with an evil grin on his face, showing her that he was enjoying himself at her expense. Ryan knew that Cally cared for Kyle and she always had. He knew that it would absolutely kill her to watch Kyle die, and just knowing that made Ryan feel as if he had all the power in the world. He knew he had Cally right where he wanted her. No matter how calm she tried to act, she wasn't pulling anything over on him. He had already grown too wise to her games and he was not about to back down from her, no matter how big and tough she tried to act. Nothing was going to stand in his way this time—or so he thought.

"Keep smiling, Ryan, because I'm not worried one bit about you or your threats. After all, you couldn't accomplish anything the first time you tried to kill me, so what makes you think that you can do any better this time?" Cally asked, giving Ryan a sarcastic smile so that he would focus more on her and less on Kyle.

"Oh Cally, I think you are going to enjoy this a whole lot," Ryan said, totally ignoring Cally's attempt to save Kyle.

"No, Ryan, please just stop and leave him alone. Don't do anything to hurt him. Please, I'm begging you, just leave him out of this," Cally screamed as she tried to pull Kyle away from Ryan's strong grasp.

"Oh, this is so sweet. A little whore trying to save her precious boyfriend. Please stop, you are breaking my heart," Ryan said with a laugh as he started to choke Kyle with his powerful hand.

"Please just stop and let him go before you kill him. I promise I'll do whatever you want," Cally begged, still trying to reason with Ryan as he dropped Kyle's lifeless body onto the ground.

"Oh my god, Kyle, can you hear me? Are you alright? Please answer me. I need to hear your voice," Cally screamed, shaking Kyle's lifeless body, hoping he would respond to her cries.

"I hope you enjoyed seeing that, Cally, because you are the one who drove me to do it," Ryan said, walking toward Cally as if he was ready to kill her, too.

"No, Ryan, you only did that because you knew I loved him and not you. I hate you, and I wish you would go back to hell where you belong," Cally screamed at the top of her lungs, taking her focus off of Kyle and putting it on Ryan.

"Well, I hope you are ready to join me, because I came back to get you and I'm not leaving without you. So let's go. I have wasted enough time on you," Ryan ordered as he grabbed a hold of Cally's arm.

"I'm not going anywhere with you, and there is no way that you can make me, so go back to hell by yourself. I'm staying right here where I belong," Cally said in a strong and angry voice as she got right up in Ryan's face.

"You have to go with me, Cally. You promised, remember? When I put the ring on your finger last night. You see, I could not take you back with me unless you promised to love and be with me forever, and since you walked right into my trap, that means that you are mine and you have to do as I say. There is no other way, so take my hand and join me in the depths of hell," Ryan demanded, feeling as if he had Cally right where he wanted her.

"Aren't you forgetting something, Ryan, the one most important thing that changes everything?" Cally asked with a sly grin on her face, as she stared down at the heart-shaped ring.

"Okay, Cally, to save some time, why don't you just tell me what I'm forgetting," Ryan said as he grew more and more impatient with Cally and her games.

"Do you see this ring on my finger, Ryan? Take a good look at it, because I accepted the ring from *Kyle*, not you. When I made the promise, the interior light was on and I was looking into Kyle's face, not yours. So like I said before, go back to hell by yourself, because I'm not going anywhere with you. I'm staying right here with my one and only true love, and that is Kyle," Cally said as she watched a disappointed Ryan slowly disappear into thin air.

With Ryan gone, Cally knelt down beside Kyle and grabbed his hand, praying to God that he would be alright. Doing what she had been taught in school, Cally looked Kyle over to see if he was still breathing. To her surprise, Kyle was still alive. His breathing was shallow, but he was, in fact, alive. Cally had never been so happy in her whole life. Finally, after being put through hell and back, the nightmare was over. It had finally ended. Ryan was in hell where he belonged, and Cally had done it all on her own. She was so glad that her plan did not fail. It had succeeded, and so had she. Now she could get on with her new life, a life with the boy she loved, Kyle.

"Hey, Cally, did you really mean what you said about loving me forever?" Kyle asked in a whisper, as Cally rubbed his dark brown hair back from his face.

"Oh my god, Kyle, are you okay? Do I need to call you an ambulance?" Cally asked, shocked but happy to hear Kyle's sweet voice.

"No, I don't need an ambulance. You should know by now that I'm made of steel," Kyle said with a laugh, trying to make Cally feel better.

As Cally and Kyle sat on the lakeside holding hands, they heard a car coming down the road. Cally prayed that it would be her parents, and to her surprise, it was. Cally could not believe how well things were turning out: first, Ryan and his ugly Mustang had disappeared, then she found out Kyle was alive. It was like a dream come true. Finally things were going Cally's way, and she could not be happier. Now the only thing left to do was explain herself to her parents and face the harsh punishment that followed, because Cally knew that her parents would most definitely not take it easy on her. But that did not matter to Cally. The only thing that mattered was right in front of her.

"Mom, Dad, we're over here!" Cally shouted out after seeing her parents.

"Oh Cally, are you alright? We were worried sick about you!" Kate cried, wrapping her arms around Cally's neck.

"Yes, Mom. We're alright now. Ryan is gone, and he's not coming back. My plan worked and now we don't ever have to worry about him again," Cally said, as tears of joy streamed down her face.

"Okay, you two, let's get you home where you belong," Bill said with a smile, as he helped Cally and Kyle up off the ground.

"Not so fast, Dad. There is one thing that I have to do before we go," Cally said, as she took the heart-shaped ring off her finger and threw it into Swain Lake.

"Okay, now I'm ready," Cally said with a smile, as she hugged her father and walked away.

Three months have passed since that bone-chilling day. Cally and Kyle are still going strong in their relationship, and the best part is, neither of them has seen Ryan's evil spirit or the heart-shaped ring. Cally still drives by Swain Lake from time to time and looks across the waters, wondering where the heart-shaped ring ended up. Cally hopes that the ring is buried so deep in the mud that no one will ever find it, but something inside of her tells her that is wishful thinking. Cally just prays that she will not know the unlucky person who finds it. For the first time in Cally's life, she can rest easy. She finally feels as if her life has the fairy-tale ending she was searching for.

about the author

Cora Hudson lives in Rutherfordton, North Carolina. Her hobbies include writing and spending time with her five beautiful children. She would love nothing more than to dedicate this book to her family, giving a special thanks to her parents for telling her all those ghost stories when she was little. They are the ones who gave Cora her vivid imagination, and for that, she is thankful.

www.ingramcontent.com/pod-product-compliance
Lightning Source LLC
Chambersburg PA
CBHW031423250626
47155CB00004B/1599